I0679632

AUCASSIN AND
NICOLETTE

AUCASSIN AND NICOLETTE

TRANSLATED BY
EUGENE MASON

WILDSIDE PRESS

AUCASSIN AND NICOLETTE

Published by Wildside Press LLC.
www.wildsidebooks.com

AUCASSIN AND NICOLETTE

INTRODUCTION

THE little tales brought together in this volume are drawn from the literature of the Middle Ages, and in many cases were written in France of the thirteenth century. I hope that they may be found interesting in themselves, but to appreciate them fully they should be considered in their relations to a definite historical background. Their conceptions of society, of religion, of politics, of humour—that precious gift which always dies so young—are not common to all of us to-day. They are of the thirteenth century, and we of the twentieth. We may not be better than our forefathers, but a great chasm of seven hundred years yawns between us and them. To enjoy their work without reserve it is necessary for a time to breathe the same air that was breathed—roughly speaking—by the subjects of St. Louis of France.

It is possible to love the period known as the Middle Ages, or it is possible to detest it. But you cannot ignore it, nor find it flavourless on the palate, because that period possesses character, "character, that personal quality, that idiosyncrasy which, no doubt, you are the richer for possessing, be it morally bad or good—for it is surely better to have a bad character than none, and if you are a church, better to be like the Badia than the City Temple." Indeed, it is evident that the personal equation must largely determine what any writer's conception of the Middle Ages is. A great modern poet, for instance, loved the Middle Ages because economic conditions pressed less hardly on the poor ; because London was small and white and clean ; because chivalry afforded opportunity for that decorative treatment of knightly episodes which makes his poetry so attractive. Yet across the Channel, much at the same time, an equally distinguished poet treated of the same period in a book of poems which it is instructive to consider side by side with the work of William Morris, and the Frenchman's verse is

lurid with fire and bigotry, and the tale of man's inhumanity
to man.   And the strange point is that both writers could
give chapter and verse for the very different type of story
they selected.   Again, the religious temperament is apt to
look back fondly to the Middle Ages as the "Age of Faith."
To such minds mediævalism is a period of easy acquiescence
in spiritual authority, a state of health before the world
grew sick with our modern disease of doubt.   Certainly these
centuries produced saints whose arresting examples and
haunting words must always be the glory of Christianity,
and it is equally certain that the offices and doctrines of the
Church entered far more intimately into the lives of the
common folk than they do to-day.   But side by side with
faith there was a "spirit of rebellion and revolt against the
moral and religious ideas of the time."   It may be found in
many strangely different shapes : in the life of Abelard; in
the extraordinary spread of witchcraft; and—in its supreme
literary expression, perhaps—in a famous passage of
"Aucassin and Nicolette."   And, to take a third illustration
of the same difficulty, were the Middle Ages years of sheer
lyric beauty, or rather years of inexpressible ugliness and
filth?   "If you love the very words 'Middle Age'; if they
conjure up to your mind glowing old folios of black letter
with gilt and florid initials; crimson and green and blue
pages in which slim ladies with spiked head-dresses walk
amid sparse flowers and trees like bouquets, or where men-
at-arms attack walled cities no bigger than themselves, or
long-legged youths with tight waists and frizzed hair kiss
girls under apple-trees; or a king is on a daïs with gold
lilies for his background, minstrels on their knees before
him, lovers in the gallery "—well, if you accept all this
dainty circumstance, you get sheer lyric beauty, and nothing
else.   Only there is another side, a side not very pleasant
to dwell upon, and it may perhaps be hinted at by saying
that such a necessary of the toilet as a pocket-handkerchief
was not generally known in this Age of Beauty.   Perhaps
it would be truer to hold that the Middle Ages comprised
all these things—the knight-errant and the tormentor; the
altar and the witch's Sabbath; a dream of loveliness having
its roots in slime and squalor.   These centuries were both
"enormous and delicate."   They were great enough to
include opposites, and to square the circle.   You may love

them, or you may hate them; but they cannot be given the
go-by.

The philosophy of the Middle Ages—that is to say, the
idea which governed their political and theological conceptions—was both simple and profound. The Emperor or
King was considered to be the guardian of the temporal
order of things, just as the Pope was held to be the supreme
authority in matters of eternal and spiritual concern. It was
an idea fascinating in its simplicity, but life is a tangled
and complex matter, and in practice, planets, which in theory
moved strictly in their own orbits, were continually striking
across each other's path. Even St. Louis, the King, who
carried saintliness to the extreme limit permitted to man,
was involved in frequent political quarrels with the supreme
head of his Church, and by one of the little ironies of fate
came within measurable distance of excommunication. The
King—again in theory—was the owner of all his realm.
This was necessary to abolish Heptarchies. But for the
support of the Crown he parcelled out his realm amongst
great lords, and thus established Heptarchies again. The
great barons, in their turn, divided their estates amongst
knights, bound to assist them in their quarrels, and to
furnish a certain number of soldiers to their service.
Amongst these knights sprang up one of the supreme
institutions of the Middle Ages—the institution of chivalry.
"It took its birth in the interior of the feudal mansions,
without any set purpose beyond that of declaring, first, the
admission of the young man to the rank and occupation of
the warrior; secondly, the tie which bound him to his feudal
superior—his lord, who conferred upon him the arms of
knighthood. But when once the feudal society had acquired
some degree of stability and confidence, the usages, the
feelings, the circumstances of every kind which attended
the young man's admission among the vassal warriors, came
under two influences, which soon gave them a fresh direction,
and impressed them with a novel character. Religion and
imagination, poetry and the Church, laid hold on chivalry,
and used it as a powerful means of attaining the objects
they had in view, of meeting the moral wants which it was
their business to provide for." Throughout a long apprenticeship, in a castle which contained practically but one
woman, the wife of his lord and she removed how infinitely

from him in distance and in station, the young squire was trained to feel towards all women something of the dreamy devotion with which art and religion taught him to regard Our Lady herself. And the apprenticeship culminated in the ceremony of knighthood, with all the mystical significance of the symbolism preserved for us in the little story of Sir Hugh of Tabarie and the Sultan Saladin, carefully calculated to impress the recipient in the highest degree. Devotion to God, to his king, and to his lady—these were the ideals of knighthood, not always, unfortunately, its realities. But ideals are difficult of realization in so faulty a world as ours. The Black Prince was the very pattern of chivalry in his youth, yet Froissart remarks in his account of the battle of Poitiers that "the Prince of Wales, who was as courageous and cruel as a lion, took great pleasure this day in fighting and chasing his enemies." The conduct of that perfect gentle knight, Sir Graelent, towards the lady he discovered bathing in the fountain, was far from chivalrous, according to modern notions, and yet I can assure the reader that I have walked delicately as Agag, and gone to the verge of weakness, in recounting the incident. Finally, here is a passage from a letter written by a knight of the fourteenth century to the Tyrant of Mantua, relating to a French girl, Jeannette, which is sufficiently explicit. "Let her be detained at my suit, for if you should have a thousand golden florins spent for her, I will pay them without delay, for if I should have to follow her to Avignon I will obtain this woman. Now, my lord, should I be asking a trifle contrary to law, yet ought you not to cross me in this, for some day I shall do more for you than a thousand united women could effect; and if there be need of me in a matter of greater import, you shall have for the asking a thousand spears at my back." Ah, well, ideals that are realized cease to be ideals.

Just as this worship of woman was the great social note of the Middle Ages, so the devotion to the Blessed Virgin was the distinguishing religious feature of those times. In honour of Our Lady were erected the magnificent Gothic cathedrals—those masterpieces of moral elevation—which stud the fair land of France like painted capitals upon a written page. In these buildings the genius of the Middle Ages found its supreme expression. Above the crowded market-place and narrow mediæval street rose those incomparable churches, "like Gothic queens at prayer, alone, silent and adorned." In her honour, too, they were made beautiful with glass and statuary, so that never before nor since were churches filled with such an entrancing congregation, never had buildings such wonderful eyes. And at a time when masons built to her honour and theologians defined her position, the story-tellers were not slack in her praise. The three legends relating to the Virgin, which I have included in this book of translations, are but specimens of an immense literature devoted to her service. "Our Lady's Tumbler" is, to the modern taste, one of the most appealing of all these legends, but there are others nearly, if not quite, so beautiful. Once upon a time there was a monk who was so ignorant that he was exposed to the rebuke of his brethren. But in his devotion to Our Lady he took for his meditation five psalms, each commencing with a letter of her name. And when it pleased God that his end should come, there happened a very beauteous miracle, for from his mouth came forth five fresh roses, sweet, crimson and leafy, in honour of the five letters of the name of Maria. Again, how exquisite is the story of the nun who by frailty of heart fled from her cloister to give herself over to sin. After many long years she returned to the nunnery, having lost her innocence, but not her faith, for during all her wanderings she had never omitted her habit of prayer to Our Lady. But, to her surprise, always she was addressed by her sisters as if she had never gone from amongst them. For the Blessed Virgin, having clothed herself with the vesture and seeming of the truant who loved her, even in sin, took also upon her the duties of a sacristan from which she had fled, so that no single person had noticed the absence from her cloister of the faithless nun.

Yet, after all, the Middle Ages delighted to honour Our Lady as the tender Mother rather than as the Queen of Heaven. In numberless miniatures, and on the portals of the cathedrals raised to her glory, she stands presenting her Child to the adoration of men. It is as the instrument of the Incarnation that her ultimate dignity consists. Indeed, the religion of the Middle Ages can only be appreciated by regarding it in the light of the doctrine of the Incarnation. Christ is God. The Mass—the popular service instituted by Himself—is an extension of His Incarnation. The Blessed

Virgin is to be held in peculiar veneration as the Mother
of God. The two threads can easily be seen twined together
in that story of how Our Lady tourneyed whilst the knight
was at Mass. But belief in the Incarnation is the keystone
of mediæval theology, and the only explanation of the lives
of those saints who poured out their years like water in the
service of God and man.

The authors of the stories brought together in this book
from various sources are, in some cases, identified, but in
others are unknown. They may, perhaps, be regarded as
representative of the three classes who are responsible for
this kind of fiction—the monk, the trouvère and the pro-
fessional minstrel. The monk, for his part, wrote in French
seldom enough. He was a scholar, and when he had something to say, preferred to deliver himself in Latin, the
language common to all educated men. But, for once, in
the thirteenth century, a monk of Soissons, named Gautier
de Coinci, translated into French verse a great collection of
the miracles of Our Lady. From this garner I have selected
the legend "Of a Jew who took as Surety the Image of
Our Lady." Gautier de Coinci may not have been a supreme
poet—that saving grace comes seldom enough—but his
industry was certainly abnormal. His labour of love must
have been the occupation of a lifetime, and it is pleasant to
recall the old monk, in silent scriptorium and shady cloister,
turning the Latin legends into fluent and pious verse.

The trouvère was drawn from the same class as the
troubadour, and the circumstances of their lives were in
essentials much the same. He lived very probably in some
nobleman's castle, where he composed his stories as a sort
of amateur, and recited the verses to an audience more or
less select. His pride forbade him to appear personally
before the populace, but it permitted him to provide wandering minstrels with copies of these poems, and so entertain
the common folk by deputy. In the lord's castle it was, of
course, another matter. On summer afternoons he would
recite before the baron's household, where they were seated
on the steps of the garden terrace, each in his order and
degree. You can feel the hush and heat of the Provençal
evening, whilst the sombre cypresses spire into the sky, and
the olives whisper, and, far below, the broad stretches of the
Rhone are suffused with the lovely light and colour of

southern France. Or, in winter, after supper, when the
tables were cleared, the trouvère would recite in hall. At
the feet of the ladies sat their knights on silken cushions,
fettered with silver chains, each to his friend. It was an
audience rich and idle, familiar with the fantastic lives of the
troubadours, and with the wanton judgments of the Courts
of Love. For such a company no flower of sentiment could
be too highly scented, and no tale come amiss, save only
that it spoke of love.

If the trouvères were "the aristocracy of this literature,"
the minstrel was its "democracy." Sometimes he rose
almost to the status of the trouvère, composing his own
stories, and reciting them even in kings' houses. Generally,
however, the minstrel was but a strolling player, speaking
other men's thoughts, and wandering over the length and
breadth of the land. Occasionally he went alone with his
viol. At other times he was accompanied by bears, or a
little troupe of singing boys or dancing girls. The minstrel
might have the good fortune to give his entertainment
before some knight or count. At any rate, the common folk
heard him gladly, before the church or on the village green.
If he was lucky, the homeless minstrel got free lodgings for
the night at some hospitable monastery, but occasionally he
was turned from the door, with hard words, because of St.
Bernard's saying that "the tricks of the jongleurs can never
please God." Once upon a time such a minstrel as this
knocked at a monastery door, and asked for hospitality.
He was received without indecent joy, and the guest-master,
forgetting that a grace conferred unwillingly is no favour
at all, provided the guest with black bread, salted vegetables,
cold water, and a hard and dirty pallet. The abbot obviously
felt no passion for strolling vagabonds, and had appointed a
guest-master after his own heart. On the morrow, when
the minstrel was leaving the monastery, he met the abbot
returning from a short journey. To revenge himself, at any
rate, on one of the two, the minstrel accosted him effusively.
"My lord," said he, "I thank you and all the community
from the bottom of my heart, for Brother such-an-one has
welcomed me like Christ Himself last night. He lighted a
fire in my chamber, and served me with choice wines,
excellent fish, and more dishes than I am able to recall.
And this morning when he bade me farewell he gave me

shoes, and these leathern laces, and a knife." When the abbot heard this he was filled with anger, and, parting shortly from the minstrel, he hastened to the monastery, and promptly relieved the guest-master of his office, before the latter could offer a word of explanation. Thus was the minstrel revenged on this grudging heart.

If, however, any reader would like to see closer the actual life of a minstrel of the thirteenth century, I would suggest that he obtain the excellent little book on Rutebeuf, one of the most famous of them all, published in the Grands Écrivains Français series. There he may read of the poet's bare cupboard, and the unfurnished lodging, where he lived with his ugly and dowerless old wife, who brought him but fifty years with her soup. He coughs with cold and gapes with hunger. He has no mattress, but only straw, and a bed of straw is not a bed. He fears to face his wife without money for food and rent. If he cannot dig, emphatically, to beg he is not ashamed. All his goods are in pawn, and his time is wasted in the tavern, playing dice, which are his curse and his downfall. Well, Rutebeuf is not the first nor the last to be ruined by dice. How the Devil must smile! Do you remember the legend of the making of these little figures? A merchant who sold himself to the Devil was bidden by him to make a six-sided piece of bone, and to mark each side with a number. One point was to insult the only true God. Two points were to insult God and the Blessed Virgin. Three points to insult the Holy Trinity. Four points to insult the four Evangelists. Five points to insult the Sacred Wounds; and six points to insult the Days of Creation. From that hour the little figures spread rapidly through the world, to man's confusion. Such is the picture Rutebeuf paints of his life—a life curiously anticipative of that of many a Bohemian poet since. It is not a very attractive picture, and though for artistic and other reasons the shadows may be unduly darkened, yet in the main it is doubtless substantially correct.

The stories written by such men as these are racy of their soil, and give the very form and pressure of their times. I have tried to make my little selection representative, and have included in this book not only romances of love and chivalry, but legends of devotion and moralities. Greatly daring, I have translated a specimen of their humour even

—not too characteristic, I hope, of the robust merriment of the feudal period. These stories will be found illustrative of some of the ideas with which the mind of the Middle Ages was concerned. The devotion to the Blessed Sacrament and to Our Lady; the languid and overwrought sentiment of love; the mystical ceremonies of knighthood; all these things are illuminated by the tales which follow this Introduction. Bound up with them are customs and ideas which to the modern mind are, perhaps, less happy. It seems odd, for instance, that the feudal knight should see nothing repugnant in accepting money and clothing from the lady who had given him already the supreme favour of her love. It is possible to entertain a high ideal of friendship without being prepared to cut the throats of your children for the sake of your friend. Yet this is what Amile did for Amis in the great epic of friendship of the Middle Ages. In its stark adherence to a superhuman standard, it puts one in mind of the animal-like patience of Griselda—which story (not included here) may perhaps be regarded as the modest ideal of the mediæval husband. It is strange, too, to find in stories so concerned with the knightly exercises of the tourney and the joust, no hint of the singular disfavour in which these games (or, perhaps, pursuits) were held by the Church. Popes prohibited them; St. Louis forbade them. Those slain therein were refused burial in consecrated ground. The Church testified, "Of those who fell in tournament there is no question but that they go down to hell, unless they are aided by the great benefit of absolution." At Cologne sixty knights and squires were killed, and the cries were heard all about of demons carrying off their souls to perdition. Apparently all this tremendous machinery failed utterly in its purpose. The most pious knights strove in tournaments equally with the most reckless, and—according to Miss Knox, to whose admirable *Court of a Saint* I am indebted—a son of St. Louis himself was thrown at a tourney, and was afterwards weak in intellect as a consequence.

Nor is it only with the lives of the rich that the mediæval minstrel was concerned. He dealt, too, with the lives and aspirations of that yet more numerous class, the poor. Such a story as "The Three Thieves" is indeed a picture of the home of the hind. We see the mean mud and timber hovel, into which the thieves broke so easily, with its cauldron upon the fire of fagots, its big bedstead, and the little lean-to byre. The peasant's tools stood around the wall, whilst outside was the garden, in which a wise ordinance of St. Louis required that pot-herbs should be planted. And if the tale of "The Three Thieves" shows us the home of the peasant, his soul is stripped for us to the quick, in—of all places in the world of literature—"Aucassin and Nicolette." Amongst the full-blown flowers of sentiment in that incomparable love-story is placed an episode which, in its violence and harsh realism, has been likened to a spot of blood and mud on a silver ground. Possibly it was inserted merely to show the hero's good heart, or is simply an instance of that artistic use of contrast so noticeable throughout the book. Any way, there are few things in feudal literature more striking than the meeting of the "dansellon" with the tattered, hideous ploughman, the one weeping in delicate grief, the other telling, dry-eyed, the sordid story of the abject poor. It is very far from being the happiest incident in the romance, but it is certainly one of the most memorable. One wonders how it was taken by an audience that concerned itself so little with the interests of the serf, and whose literature never mentioned that class, except in scorn. Was the author possibly of the ploughman's kindred, like Chaucer's parish priest in *The Canterbury Tales?* Had the stinging whips of captivity taught him sympathy with unpoetical sorrows; or is this an early hint of the coming storm! "They are clothed in velvet, and warm in their furs and their ermines, while we are covered with rags. They have wine and spices and fair bread; and we, oat-cake and straw, and water to drink. They have leisure and fine houses; we have pain and labour, the rain and the wind in the fields." We cannot tell; but comparing this dainty make-believe with that tragic misery, we feel the significance of the peasant's cry, "Woe to those who shall sorrow at the tears of such as these."

I hope I have not dwelt unduly on these stories considered as pictures of the customs and philosophy of their times. Perhaps, after all, these matters are of interest to the archæologist and the ecclesiologist rather than to the general reader. Not being a scholar myself, I have no pretension to write for scholars. My object is more modest. I have tried to bring together a little garland for the pleasure of the amateurs of beautiful tales. To me these mediæval stories are beautiful, and I have striven to decant them from one language into another with as little loss as may be. To this end I have refined a phrase, or, perhaps, softened an incident here and there. I do not pretend that they are perfect works of art. "All poets are unequal, except the bad, and they are uniformly bad." Sometimes a story drags, or there are wearisome repetitions. The psychology occasionally strikes a modern reader as remarkably summary. When Amis, for example, became a leper, we are gravely told that his wife held him in bitter hatred, and many a time strove to strangle him. Here is an author who, obviously, is astonished at nothing. But in reading these narratives you will remember how they have delighted, and been used by, writers in some cases greater than their own authors. Is it possible, for instance, to peruse "The Lay of the Little Bird" without recalling Shelley's "Sensitive Plant"? The tale of "The Divided Horsecloth" is told, in another version, both by Montaigne and Browning. The principal incident of "King Florus and the Fair Jehane" is used by Shakespeare in "Cymbeline." "Our Lady's Tumbler" and "A Jew who took as Surety the Image of Our Lady" have been re-written by Monsieur Anatole France with such perfection of art and artistry as to be the admiration and despair of all who come after him.

It should not be forgotten that the majority of these stories were intended to be recited, and not read. Repetition, therefore, is the more easily excused. This also accounts for the dramatic use of dialogue, so noticeable in "The Palfrey" and in "Aucassin and Nicolette." But it is evident that this Introduction, already over-long, will not permit me to go *seriatim* through these tales, "Item, a grey eye or so. Item, two lips, indifferent red." Let me therefore content myself with appreciating the most lovely of them all, "Aucassin and Nicolette."

A single copy of "Aucassin and Nicolette," transcribed in the thirteenth century, and preserved as by miracle, has retained for us not only a charming tale, but also an unique specimen of the minstrel's craft. Without it we could not have gathered that so elaborate a blending of prose and verse was possible to a strolling player of mediæval France.

The cante-fable was designed for recitation, with illustrative gesture, to the accompaniment of viol and pipes. In this, and not only in this, it seems to suggest an Eastern origin, and to-day, in any Moorish coffee-house, the tales of the *Arabian Nights* are delivered in a manner very similar to that witnessed in Provence seven hundred years ago. The peculiar quality of pleasure afforded by "Aucassin and Nicolette" is not to be found in the story itself. That, indeed, is very simple, and, perhaps, a trifle hackneyed. Aucassin, the only son of the Count of Beaucaire, is passionately in love with Nicolette, a beautiful girl of unknown parentage, bought of the Saracens, whom his father will not permit him to marry. The story turns on the adventures of these fond lovers, until at the end their common fidelity is rewarded. Portions have faded sadly, like old tapestry, and the laughter sounds especially hollow, for of all precious things fun dies soonest. But in "Aucassin" the part is emphatically greater than the whole, and its charm must rather be sought in its graceful turns of speech—jewels, five words long—and in the pictorial quality which makes it more a series of pictures than a narrative. Who can forget the still night of May on which Nicolette escapes from her prison, and hurries through the garden, kilting her skirt against the dew; or the ruined tower in whose kindly shadow she remains hidden, whilst the watch march along the moonlit street, their swords beneath their mantles; or that bower of branches, built by her own white hands, through the trellis-work of which her lover looks upon the stars! In such felicitous picture-making the dainty little classic is equalled by no work of its period.

May I express the pious wish that every reader may find it all as delightful to read as I have found it to transcribe?

EUGENE MASON.

NOTE.—The originals of these narratives are to be found in Romania; in the *Fabliaux et Contes des Poètes François*, edited by Barbazan et Méon; in two volumes of the *Nouvelles Françoises en prose*, edited by Moland and D'Héricault; and in *Les Miracles de la Sainte Vierge*, by Gautier de Coinci.

CONTENTS

MEDIÆVAL ROMANCE

'TIS OF AUCASSIN AND OF NICOLETTE

Who will deign to hear the song
Solace of a captive's wrong,
Telling how two children met,
Aucassin and Nicolette;
How by grievous pains distraught,
Noble deeds the varlet wrought
For his love, and her bright face!
Sweet my rhyme, and full of grace,
Fair my tale, and debonair.
He who lists—though full of care,
Sore astonied, much amazed,
All cast down, by men mispraised,
Sick in body, sick in soul,
Hearing shall be glad and whole,
  So sweet the tale.

Now they say and tell and relate:

How the Count Bougars of Valence made war on
Count Garin of Beaucaire, war so great, so wonderful, and so mortal, that never dawned the day but
that he was at the gates and walls and barriers of the
town, with a hundred knights and ten thousand
men-at-arms, on foot and on horse. So he burned
the Count's land, and spoiled his heritage, and
dealt death to his men. The Count Garin of Beaucaire was full of years, and frail; he had long outworn his day. He had no heir, neither son nor
daughter, save one only varlet, and he was such
as I will tell you. Aucassin was the name of the
lad. Fair he was, and pleasant to look upon, tall

B

and shapely of body in every whit of him. His hair was golden, and curled in little rings about his head; he had grey and dancing eyes, a clear, oval face, a nose high and comely, and he was so gracious in all good graces that nought in him was found to blame, but good alone. But Love, that high prince, so utterly had cast him down, that he cared not to become knight, neither to bear arms, nor to tilt at tourneys, nor yet to do aught that it became his name to do.

His father and his mother spake him thus—

"Son, don now thy mail, mount thy horse, keep thy land, and render aid to thy men. Should they see thee amongst them the better will the men-at-arms defend their bodies and their substance, thy fief and mine."

"Father," said Aucassin, "why speakest thou in such fashion to me? May God give me nothing of my desire if I become knight, or mount to horse, or thrust into the press to strike other or be smitten down, save only that thou give me Nicolette, my sweet friend, whom I love so well."

"Son," answered the father, "this may not be. Put Nicolette from mind. For Nicolette is but a captive maid, come hither from a far country, and the Viscount of this town bought her with money from the Saracens, and set her in this place. He hath nourished and baptized her, and held her at the font. On a near day he will give her to some young bachelor, who will gain her bread in all honour. With this what hast thou to do? Ask for a wife, and I will find thee the daughter of a king, or a count. Were he the richest man in France his daughter shalt thou have, if so thou wilt."

"Faith, my father," said Aucassin, "what honour of all this world would not Nicolette, my very sweet friend, most richly become! Were she Empress of Byzantium or of Allemaigne, or Queen of France

or England, low enough would be her degree, so
noble is she, so courteous and debonair, and
gracious in all good graces."

Now is sung:

> Aucassin was of Beaucaire,
> Of the mighty castle there,
> But his heart was ever set
> On his fair friend, Nicolette.
> Small he heeds his father's blame,
> Or the harsh words of his dame.
> "Fool, to weep the livelong day,
> Nicolette trips light and gay.
> Scouring she from far Carthàge,
> Bought of Paynims for a wage.
> Since a wife beseems thee good
> Take a wife of wholesome blood."
> "Mother, naught for this I care,
> Nicolette is debonair;
> Slim the body, fair the face,
> Make my heart a lighted place;
> Love has set her as my peer,
>   Too sweet, my dear."

Now they say and tell and relate:
When the Count Garin of Beaucaire found that
in nowise could he withdraw Aucassin his son from
the love of Nicolette, he sought out the Viscount
of the town, who was his man, and spake him
thus—

"Sir Count, send Nicolette your god-child
straightly from this place. Cursed be the land
wherefrom she was carried to this realm; for because
of her I lose Aucassin, who will not become knight,
nor do aught that it becometh knight to do. Know
well that were she once within my power I would
hurry her to the fire; and look well to yourself,
for you stand in utmost peril and fear."

"Sire," answered the Viscount, "this lies heavy

upon me, that ever Aucassin goes and he comes seeking speech with my ward. I have bought her with my money, and nourished and baptized her, and held her at the font. Moreover, I am fain to give her to some young bachelor, who will gain her bread in all honour. With this Aucassin your son had nought to do. But since this is your will and your pleasure, I will send her to so far a country that nevermore shall he see her with his eyes."

"Walk warily," replied the Count Garin, "for great evil easily may fall to you of this."

So they went their ways.

Now the Viscount was a very rich man, and had a rich palace standing within a garden. In a certain chamber of an upper floor he set Nicolette in ward, with an old woman to bear her company, and to watch; and he put there bread and meat and wine and all things for their need. Then he placed a seal upon the door, so that none might enter in, nor issue forth, save only that there was a window looking on the garden, strict and close, whereby they breathed a little fresh air.

Now is sung:

> Nicolette is prisoned fast,
> In a vaulted chamber cast,
> Shaped and carven wondrous well,
> Painted as by miracle.
> At the marble casement stayed
> On her elbow leaned the maid;
> Golden showed her golden hair,
> Softly curved her eyebrows rare,
> Fair her face, and brightly flushed,
> Sweeter maiden never blushed.
> In the garden from her room
> She might watch the roses bloom,
> Hear the birds make tender moan;
> Then she knew herself alone.

" 'Lack, great pity 'tis to place
Maid in such an evil case.
Aucassin, my liege, my squire,
Friend, and dear, and heart's desire,
Since thou dost not hate me quite
Men have done me foul despite,
Sealed me in this vaulted room,
Thrust me to this bitter doom.
But by God, Our Lady's Son,
Soon will I from here begone,
　　　So it be won."

Now they say and tell and relate:
Nicolette was prisoned in the chamber, as you
have heard and known. The cry and the haro
went through all the land that Nicolette was stolen
away. Some said that she had fled the country,
and some that the Count Garin of Beaucaire had
done her to death. Whatever man may have
rejoiced, Aucassin had no joy therein, so he
sought out the Viscount of the town and spake him
thus—

"Sir Viscount, what have you done with Nicolette, my very sweet friend, the thing that most I
love in all the world? Have you borne her off, or
hidden her from my sight? Be sure that should I
die hereof, my blood will be required of you, as is
most just, for I am slain of your two hands, since
you steal from me the thing that most I love in all
the world."

"Fair sire," answered the Viscount, "put this
from mind. Nicolette is a captive maid whom
I brought here from a far country. For her price I
trafficked with the Saracens, and I have bred and
baptized her, and held her at the font. I have
nourished her duly, and on a day will give her to
some young bachelor who will gain her bread in
honourable fashion. With this you have nought to
do; but only to wed the daughter of some count

or king. Beyond this, what profit would you have, had you become her lover, and taken her to your bed? Little enough would be your gain therefrom, for your soul would lie tormented in Hell all the days of all time, so that to Paradise never should you win."

"In Paradise what have I to do? I care not to enter, but only to have Nicolette, my very sweet friend, whom I love so dearly well. For into Paradise go none but such people as I will tell you of. There go those agèd priests, and those old cripples, and the maimed, who all day long and all night cough before the altars, and in the crypts beneath the churches; those who go in worn old mantles and old tattered habits; who are naked, and barefoot, and full of sores; who are dying of hunger and of thirst, of cold and of wretchedness. Such as these enter in Paradise, and with them have I nought to do. But in Hell will I go. For to Hell go the fair clerks and the fair knights who are slain in the tourney and the great wars, and the stout archer and the loyal man. With them will I go. And there go the fair and courteous ladies, who have friends, two or three, together with their wedded lords. And there pass the gold and the silver, the ermine and all rich furs, harpers and minstrels, and the happy of the world. With these will I go, so only that I have Nicolette, my very sweet friend, by my side."

"Truly," cried the Viscount, "you talk idly, for never shall you see her more; yea, and if perchance you spoke together, and your father heard thereof, he would burn both me and her in one fire, and yourself might well have every fear."

"This lies heavy upon me," answered Aucassin.

Thus he parted from the Viscount making great sorrow.

Now is sung:

Aucassin departed thus
Sad at heart and dolorous;
Gone is she his fairest friend,
None may comfort give or mend,
None by counsel make good end.
To the palace turned he home,
Climbed the stair, and sought his room.
In the chamber all alone
Bitterly he made his moan,
Presently began to weep
For the love he might not keep.
"Nicolette, so gent, so sweet,
Fair the faring of thy feet,
Fair thy laughter, sweet thy speech,
Fair our playing each with each,
Fair thy clasping, fair thy kiss,
Yet it endeth all in this.
Since from me my love is ta'en
I misdoubt that I am slain;
        Sister, sweet friend."

Now they say and tell and relate:
Whilst Aucassin was in the chamber lamenting
Nicolette, his friend, the Count Bougars of Valence,
wishful to end the war, pressed on his quarrel, and
setting his pikemen and horsemen in array, drew
near the castle to take it by storm. Then the cry
arose, and the tumult; and the knights and the men-
at-arms took their weapons, and hastened to the
gates and the walls to defend the castle, and the
burgesses climbed to the battlements, flinging
quarrels and sharpened darts upon the foe. Whilst
the siege was so loud and perilous the Count Garin
of Beaucaire sought the chamber where Aucassin
lay mourning, assotted upon Nicolette, his very
sweet friend, whom he loved so well.

"Ha, son," cried he, "craven art thou and
shamed, that seest thy best and fairest castle so
hardly beset. Know well that if thou lose it thou

art a naked man. Son, arm thyself lightly, mount
to horse, keep thy land, aid thy men, hurtle into
the press. Thou needest not to strike another,
neither to be smitten down, but if they see thee
amongst them, the better will they defend their
goods and their bodies, thy land and mine. And
thou art so stout and strong that very easily thou
canst do this thing, as is but right."

"Father," answered Aucassin, "what sayest thou
now? May God give me nought that I require of
Him if I become knight, or mount to horse, or
thrust into the press to strike knight or be smitten
down, save only thou givest me Nicolette, my sweet
friend, whom I love so well."

"Son," replied the father, "this can never be.
Rather will I suffer to lose my heritage, and go bare
of all, than that thou shouldest have her, either as
woman or as dame."

So he turned without farewell. But when
Aucassin saw him part he stayed him, saying—

"Father, come now, I will make a true bargain
with thee."

"What bargain, fair son?"

"I will arm me, and thrust into the press on
such bargain as this, that if God bring me again
safe and sound, thou wilt let me look on Nicolette,
my sweet friend, so long that I may have with her
two words or three, and kiss her one only time."

"I pledge my word to this," said the father.

Of this covenant had Aucassin much joy.

Now is sung:

> Aucassin the more was fain
> Of the kiss he sought to gain,
> Rather than his coffers hold
> A hundred thousand marks of gold.
> At the call his squire drew near,
> Armed him fast in battle gear;

Shirt and hauberk donned the lad,
Laced the helmet on his head,
Girt his golden-hilted sword,
Came the war-horse at his word,
Gripped the buckler and the lance,
At the stirrups cast a glance;
Then most brave from plume to heel
Pricked the charger with the steel,
Called to mind his absent dear,
Passed the gateway without fear
Straight to the fight.

Now they say and tell and relate:
Aucassin was armed and horsed as you have
heard. God! how bravely showed the shield about
his neck, the helmet on his head, and the fringes
of the baldric upon his left thigh. The lad was
tall and strong, slender and comely to look upon,
and the steed he bestrode was great and speedy, and
fiercely had he charged clear of the gate. Now
think not that he sought spoil of oxen and cattle,
nor to smite others and himself escape. Nay, but
of all this he took no heed. Another was with him,
and he thought so dearly upon Nicolette, his fair
friend, that the reins fell from his hand, and he
struck never a blow. Then the charger, yet smart-
ing from the spur, bore him into the battle, amidst
the thickest of the foe, so that hands were laid upon
him from every side, and he was made prisoner.
Thus they spoiled him of shield and lance, and
forthwith led him from the field a captive, question-
ing amongst themselves by what death he should
be slain. When Aucassin marked their words,

"Ha, God," cried he, "sweet Creature, these are
my mortal foes who lead me captive, and who soon
will strike off my head; and when my head is
smitten, never again may I have fair speech with
Nicolette, my sweet friend, whom I hold so dear.
Yet have I a good sword, and my horse is yet

unblown. Now if I defend me not for her sake,
may God keep her never, should she love me still."

The varlet was hardy and stout, and the charger
he bestrode was right fierce. He plucked forth his
sword, and smote suddenly on the right hand and
on the left, cutting sheer through nasal and headpiece, gauntlet and arm, making such ruin around
him as the wild boar deals when brought to bay by
hounds in the wood; until he had struck down ten
knights, and hurt seven more, and won clear of
the *mêlée,* and rode back at utmost speed, sword in
his hand.

The Count Bougars of Valence heard tell that
his men were about to hang Aucassin, his foe, in
shameful wise, so he hastened to the sight, and
Aucassin passed him not by. His sword was yet in
hand, and he struck the Count so fiercely upon the
helm, that the headpiece was cleft and shattered
upon the head. So bewildered was he by the stroke
that he tumbled to the ground, and Aucassin
stretched forth his hand, and took him, and led him
captive by the nasal of the helmet, and delivered
him to his father.

"Father," said Aucassin, "behold the foe who
wrought such war and mischief upon you! Twenty
years hath this war endured, and none was there to
bring it to an end."

"Fair son," replied his father, "better are such
deeds as these than foolish dreams."

"Father," returned Aucassin, "preach me no
preachings; but carry out our bargain."

"Ha, what bargain, fair son?"

"How now, father, hast thou returned from the
market? By my head, I will remember, whosoever may forget; so close is it to my heart. Didst
thou not bargain with me when I armed me and
fared into the press, that if God brought me again
safe and sound, thou wouldst grant me sight of

Nicolette, my sweet friend, so long that I might have with her two words or three, and kiss her once? Such was the bargain, so be thou honest dealer."

"I," cried the father, "God aid me never should I keep such terms. Were she here I would set her in the flames, and thou thyself might well have every fear."

"Is this the very end?" said Aucassin.

"So help me God," said his father; "yea."

"Certes," said Aucassin, "grey hairs go ill with a lying tongue."

"Count of Valence," said Aucassin, "thou art my prisoner?"

"Sire," answered the Count, "it is verily and truly so."

"Give me thy hand," said Aucassin.

"Sire, as you wish."

So each took the other's hand.

"Plight me thy faith," said Aucassin, "that so long as thou drawest breath, never shall pass a day but thou shalt deal with my father in shameful fashion, either in goods or person, if so thou canst!"

"Sire, for God's love make me not a jest, but name me a price for my ransom. Whether you ask gold or silver, steed or palfrey, pelt or fur, hawk or hound, it shall be paid."

"What!" said Aucassin; "art thou not my prisoner?"

"Truly, sire," said the Count Bougars.

"God aid me never," quoth Aucassin, "but I send thy head flying, save thou plight me such faith as I said."

"In God's name," cried he, "I plight such affiance as seems most meet to thee."

He pledged his troth, so Aucassin set him upon a horse, and brought him into a place of surety, himself riding by his side.

Now is sung:

When Count Garin knew his son
Aucassin still loved but one,
That his heart was ever set
Fondly on fond Nicolette;
Straight a prison he hath found,
Paved with marble, walled around,
Where in vault beneath the earth
Aucassin made little mirth,
But with wailing filled his cell
In such wise as now I tell.
"Nicolette, white lily-flow'r,
Sweetest lady found in bow'r;
Sweet as grape that brimmeth up
Sweetness in the spicèd cup.
On a day this chanced to you;
Out of Limousin there drew
One, a pilgrim, sore adread,
Lay in pain upon his bed,
Tossed, and took with fear his breath,
Very dolent, near to death.
Then you entered, pure and white,
Softly to the sick man's sight,
Raised the train that swept adown,
Raised the ermine-bordered gown,
Raised the smock, and bared to him
Daintily each lovely limb.
Then a wondrous thing befell,
Straight he rose up sound and well,
Left his bed, took cross in hand,
Sought again his own dear land.
Lily-flow'r, so white, so sweet,
Fair the faring of thy feet,
Fair thy laughter, fair thy speech,
Fair our playing each with each.
Sweet thy kisses, soft thy touch,
All must love thee over much.
'Tis for thee that I am thrown
In this vaulted cell alone;

'Tis for thee that I attend
Death, that comes to make an end,
For thee, sweet friend."

Now they say and tell and relate :

Aucassin was set in prison as you have heard
tell, and Nicolette for her part was shut in the
chamber. It was in the time of summer heat, in
the month of May, when the days are warm, long
and clear, and the nights coy and serene. Nicolette
lay one night sleepless on her bed, and watched
the moon shine brightly through the casement, and
listened to the nightingale plain in the garden.
Then she bethought her of Aucassin, her friend,
whom she loved so well. She called also to mind
the Count Garin of Beaucaire, her mortal foe, and
feared greatly to remain lest her hiding-place
should be told to him, and she be put to death in
some shameful fashion. She made certain that the
old woman who held her in ward was sound asleep.
So she rose, and wrapped herself in a very fair
silk mantle, the best she had, and taking the sheets
from her bed and the towels of her bath, knotted
them together to make so long a rope as she was
able, tied it about a pillar of the window, and
slipped down into the garden. Then she took her
skirt in both hands, the one before, and the other
behind, and kilted her lightly against the dew
which lay thickly upon the grass, and so passed
through the garden. Her hair was golden, with
little love-locks; her eyes blue and laughing; her
face most dainty to see, with lips more vermeil
than ever was rose or cherry in the time of summer
heat; her teeth white and small; her breasts so
firm that they showed beneath her vesture like two
rounded nuts; so frail was she about the girdle
that your two hands could have spanned her, and
the daisies that she brake with her feet in passing,

showed altogether black against her instep and
her flesh, so white was the fair young maiden.

She came to the postern, and unbarring the gate,
issued forth upon the streets of Beaucaire, taking
heed to keep within the shadows, for the moon
shone very bright, and thus she fared until she
chanced upon the tower where her lover was
prisoned. The tower was buttressed with pieces
of wood in many places, and Nicolette hid herself
amongst the pillars, wrapped close in her mantle.
She set her face to a crevice of the tower, which
was old and ruinous, and there she heard Aucassin weeping within, making great sorrow for the
sweet friend whom he held so dear; and when she
had hearkened awhile she began to speak.

Now is sung :

> Nicolette, so bright of face,
> Leaned within this buttressed place,
> Heard her lover weep within,
> Marked the woe of Aucassin.
> Then in words her thought she told,
> "Aucassin, fond heart and bold,
> What avails thine heart should ache
> For a Paynim maiden's sake.
> Ne'er may she become thy mate,
> Since we prove thy father's hate,
> Since thy kinsfolk hate me too;
> What for me is left to do?
> Nothing, but to seek the strand,
> Pass o'er sea to some far land."
> Shore she then one golden tress,
> Thrust it in her love's duress;
> Aucassin hath seen the gold
> Shining bright in that dark hold,
> Took the lock at her behest,
> Kissed and placed it in his breast,
> Then once more his eyes were wet
> 　　For Nicolette.

Now they say and tell and relate :

When Aucassin heard Nicolette say that she would fare into another country, he was filled with anger.

"Fair sweet friend," said he, "this be far from thee, for then wouldst thou have slain me. And the first man who saw thee, if so he might, would take thee forthwith and carry thee to his bed, and make thee his leman. Be sure that if thou wert found in any man's bed, save it be mine, I should not need a dagger to pierce my heart and slay me. Certes, no; wait would I not for a knife; but on the first wall or the nearest stone would I cast myself, and beat out my brains altogether. Better to die so foul a death as this, than know thee to be in any man's bed, save mine."

"Aucassin," said she, "I doubt that thou lovest me less than thy words; and that my love is fonder than thine."

"Alack," cried Aucassin, "fair sweet friend, how can it be that thy love should be so great? Woman cannot love man, as man loves woman; for woman's love is in the glance of her eye, and the blossom of her breast, and the tip of the toe of her foot; but the love of man is set deep in the hold of his heart, from whence it cannot be torn away."

Whilst Aucassin and Nicolette were thus at odds together, the town watch entered the street, bearing naked swords beneath their mantles, for Count Garin had charged them strictly, once she were taken, to put her to death. The warder from his post upon the tower marked their approach, and as they drew near heard them speaking of Nicolette, menacing her with death.

"God," said he, "it is great pity that so fair a damsel should be slain, and a rich alms should I give if I could warn her privily, and so she escape the snare; for of her death Aucassin, my liege, were dead already, and truly this were a piteous case."

Now is sung:

> Brave the warder, full of guile,
> Straight he sought some cunning wile;
> Sought and found a song betime,
> Raised this sweet and pleasant rhyme.
> "Lady of the loyal mind,
> Slender, gracious, very kind,
> Gleaming head and golden hair,
> Laughing lips and eyes of vair!
> Easy, Lady, 'tis to tell
> Two have speech who love full well.
> Yet in peril are they met,
> Set the snare, and spread the net.
> Lo, the hunters draw this way,
> Cloaked, with privy knives, to slay.
> Ere the huntsmen spie the chace
> Let the quarry haste apace
>   And keep her well."

Now they say and tell and relate.

"Ah," said Nicolette, "may the soul of thy father and of thy mother find sweetest rest, since in so fair and courteous a manner hast thou warned me. So God please, I will indeed keep myself close, and may He keep me too."

She drew the folds of her cloak about her, and crouched in the darkness of the pillars till the watch had passed beyond; then she bade farewell to Aucassin, and bent her steps to the castle wall. The wall was very ruinous, and mended with timber, so she climbed the fence, and went her way till she found herself between wall and moat. Gazing below, she saw that the fosse was very deep and perilous, and the maid had great fear.

"Ah, God," cried she, "sweet Creature, should I fall, my neck must be broken; and if I stay, to-morrow shall I be taken, and men will burn my body in a fire. Yet were it better to die, now, in this place, than to be made a show to-morrow in the market."

She crossed her brow, and let herself slide down into the moat, and when she reached the bottom, her fair feet and pretty hands, which had never learned that they could be hurt, were so bruised and wounded that the blood came from them in places a many; yet knew she neither ill nor dolour because of the mightiness of her fear. But if with pain she had entered in, still more it cost her to issue forth. She called to mind that it were death to tarry, and by chance found there a stake of sharpened wood, which those within the keep had flung forth in their defence of the tower. With this she cut herself a foothold, one step above the other, till with extreme labour she climbed forth from the moat. Now the forest lay but the distance of two bolts from a crossbow, and ran some thirty leagues in length and breadth; moreover, within were many wild beasts and serpents. She feared these greatly, lest they should do her a mischief; but presently she remembered that should men lay hands upon her, they would lead her back to the city to burn her at the fire.

Now is sung:

> Nicolette the fair, the fond,
> Climbed the fosse and won beyond;
> There she kneeled her, and implored
> Very help of Christ the Lord.
> "Father, King of majesty,
> Where to turn I know not, I.
> So, within the woodland gloom
> Wolf and boar and lion roam,
> Fearful things, with rav'ning maw,
> Rending tusk and tooth and claw.
> Yet, if all adread I stay,
> Men will come at break of day,

c

Treat me to their heart's desire,
Burn my body in the fire.
But by God's dear majesty
Such a death I will not die;
Since I die, ah, better then
Trust the boar than trust to men.
Since all's evil, men and beast,
    Choose I the least."

Now they say and tell and relate:

Nicolette made great sorrow in such manner as you have heard. She commended herself to God's keeping, and fared on until she entered the forest. She kept upon the fringes of the woodland, for dread of the wild beasts and reptiles; and hiding herself within some thick bush, sleep overtook her, and she slept fast until six hours of the morn, when shepherds and herdsmen come from the city to lead their flocks to pasture between the wood and the river. The shepherds sat by a clear, sweet spring, which bubbled forth on the outskirts of the greenwood, and spreading a cloak upon the grass, set bread thereon. Whilst they ate together, Nicolette awoke at the song of the birds and the laughter, and hastened to the well.

"Fair children," said she, "God have you in His keeping."

"God bless you also," answered one who was more fluent of tongue than his companions.

"Fair child," said she, "do you know Aucassin, the son of Count Garin of this realm?"

"Yes, we know him well."

"So God keep you, pretty boy," said she, "as you tell him that within this wood there is a fair quarry for his hunting; and if he may take her he would not part with one of her members for a hundred golden marks, nor for five hundred, nay, nor for aught that man can give."

Then looking upon her steadfastly, their hearts were troubled, the maid was so beautiful.

"Will I tell him?" cried he who was readier of word than his companions. "Woe to him who speaks of it ever, or tells Aucassin what you say. You speak not truth but faery, for in all this forest there is no beast—neither stag, nor lion, nor boar —one of whose legs would be worth two pence, or three at the very best, and you talk of five hundred marks of gold. Woe betide him who believes your story, or shall spread it abroad. You are a fay, and no fit company for such as us, so pass upon your road."

"Ah, fair child," answered she, "yet you will do as I pray. For this beast is the only medicine that may heal Aucassin of his hurt. And I have here five sous in my purse, take them, and give him my message. For within three days must he hunt this chace, and if within three days he find not the quarry, never may he cure him of his wound."

"By my faith," said he, "we will take the money, and if he comes this way we will give him your message, but certainly we will not go and look for him."

"As God pleases," answered she.

So she bade farewell to the shepherds, and went her way.

Now is sung:

> Nicolette as you heard tell
> Bade the shepherd lads farewell,
> Through deep woodlands warily
> Fared she 'neath the leafy tree;
> Till the grass-grown way she trod
> Brought her to a forest road,
> Whence, like fingers on a hand,
> Forked sev'n paths throughout the land.

There she called to heart her love,
There bethought her she would prove
Whether true her lover's vows.
Plucked she then young sapling boughs,
Grasses, leaves that branches yield,
Oak shoots, lilies of the field;
Built a lodge with frond and flow'r,
Fairest mason, fairest bow'r!
Swore then by the truth of God
Should her lover come that road,
Nor for love of her who made
Dream a little in its shade,
'Spite his oath no true love, he,
     Nor fond heart, she.

Now they say and tell and relate:
Nicolette builded the lodge, as you have heard;
very pretty it was and very dainty, and well furnished, both outside and in, with a tapestry of
flowers and of leaves. Then she withdrew herself
a little way from the bower, and hid within a
thicket to spy what Aucassin would do. And the
cry and the haro went through all the realm that
Nicolette was lost. Some had it that she had stolen
away, and others that Count Garin had done her to
death. Whoever had joy thereof, Aucassin had
little pleasure. His father, Count Garin, brought
him out of his prison, and sent letters to the lords
and ladies of those parts bidding them to a very
rich feast, so that Aucassin, his son, might cease
to dote. When the feast was at its merriest,
Aucassin leaned against the musicians' gallery, sad
and all discomforted. No laugh had he for any jest,
since she, whom most he loved, was not amongst
the ladies set in hall. A certain knight marked
his grief, and coming presently to him, said—

"Aucassin, of such fever as yours I, too, have
been sick. I can give you good counsel, if you
are willing to listen."

"Sir knight," said Aucassin, "great thanks; good counsel, above all things, I would hear."

"Get to horse," said he; "take your pleasure in the woodland, amongst flowers and bracken and the songs of the birds. Perchance, who knows? you may hear some word of which you will be glad."

"Sir knight," answered Aucassin, "great thanks; this I will do."

He left the hall privily, and went down-stairs to the stable where was his horse. He caused the charger to be saddled and bridled, then put foot in stirrup, mounted, and left the castle, riding till he entered the forest, and so by adventure came upon the well whereby the shepherd lads were sitting, and it was then about three hours after noon. They had spread a cloak upon the grass, and were eating their bread, with great mirth and jollity.

Now is sung:

> Round about the well were set
> Martin, Robin, Esmeret;
> Jolly shepherds, gaily met,
> Frulin, Jack and Aubriet.
> Laughed the one, "God keep in ward
> Aucassin, our brave young lord.
> Keep besides the damsel fair,
> Blue of eye and gold of hair,
> Gave us wherewithal to buy
> Cate and sheath knife presently,
> Horn and quarter staff and fruit,
> Shepherd's pipe and country flute;
> God make him well."

Now they say and tell and relate:

When Aucassin marked the song of the herd-boys he called to heart Nicolette, his very sweet friend, whom he held so dear. He thought she must have passed that way, so he struck his horse with the spurs and came quickly to the shepherds.

"Fair children, God keep you."

"God bless you," replied he who was readier of tongue than his fellows.

"Fair children," said he, "tell over again the song that you told but now."

"We will not tell it," answered he who was more fluent of speech than the others; "sorrow be his who sings it to you, fair sir."

"Fair children," returned Aucassin, "do you not know me?"

"Oh yes, we know well that you are Aucassin, our young lord; but we are not your men; we belong to the Count."

"Fair children, sing me the song once more, I pray you!"

"By the Wounded Heart, what fine words! Why should I sing for you, if I have no wish to do so? Why, the richest man in all the land—saving the presence of Count Garin—would not dare to drive my sheep and oxen and cows from out his wheat-field or his pasture, for fear of losing his eyes. Wherefore, then, should I sing for you, if I have no wish to do so?"

"God keep you, fair children; yet you will do this thing for me. Take these ten sous that I have here in my purse."

"Sire, we will take the money; but I will not sing for you, since I have sworn not to do so; but I will tell it in plain prose, if such be your pleasure."

"As God pleases," answered Aucassin; "better the tale in prose than no story at all."

"Sire, we were in this glade between six and nine of the morn, and were breaking our bread by the well, just as we are doing now, when a girl came by, the loveliest thing in all the world, so

fair that we doubted her a fay, and she brimmed
our wood with light.   She gave us money, and
made a bargain with us that if you came here we
would tell you that you must hunt in this forest,
for in it is such a quarry that if you may take her
you would not part with one of her members for
five hundred silver marks, nor for aught that man
can give.   For in the quest is so sweet a salve that
if you take her you shall be cured of your wound;
and within three days must the chace be taken, for
if she be not found by then, never will you see her
more.   Now go to your hunting if you will, and
if you will not, let it go, for truly have I carried
out my bargain with her."

"Fair children," cried Aucassin, "enough have
you spoken, and may God set me on her track."

Now is sung:

> Aucassin's fond heart was moved
> When this hidden word he proved
> Sent him by the maid he loved.
> Straight his charger he bestrode,
> Bade farewell, and swiftly rode
> Deep within the forest dim,
> Saying o'er and o'er to him;
> "Nicolette, so sweet, so good,
> 'Tis for you I search this wood;
> Antlered stag nor boar I chase,
> Hot I follow on your trace.
> Slender shape and deep, blue eyes,
> Dainty laughter, low replies,
> Fledge the arrow in my heart.
> Ah, to find you, ne'er to part!
> Pray God give so fair an end,
> > Sister, sweet friend.

Now they say and tell and relate:

Aucassin rode through the wood in search of
Nicolette, and the charger went right speedily.   Do

not think that the spines and thorns were pitiful to
him.   Truly it was not so; for his raiment was so
torn that the least tattered of his garments could
scarcely hold to his body, and the blood ran from
his arms and legs and flanks in forty places, or at
least in thirty, so that you could have followed
after him by the blood which he left upon the
grass.   But he thought so fondly of Nicolette, his
sweet friend, that he felt neither ill nor dolour.
Thus all day long he searched the forest in this
fashion, but might learn no news of her, and when
it drew towards dusk he commenced to weep because he had heard nothing.   He rode at adventure down an old grass-grown road, and looking
before him saw a young man standing, such as
I will tell you.   Tall he was, and marvellously
ugly and hideous.   His head was big and
blacker than smoked meat; the palm of your hand
could easily have gone between his two eyes;
he had very large cheeks and a monstrous flat
nose with great nostrils; lips redder than
uncooked flesh; teeth yellow and foul; he was shod
with shoes and gaiters of bull's hide, bound about
the leg with ropes to well above the knee; upon
his back was a rough cloak; and he stood leaning
on a huge club.   Aucassin urged his steed towards
him, but was all afeared when he saw him as he
was.

"Fair brother, God keep you."

"God bless you too," said he.

"As God keeps you, what do you here?"

"What is that to you?" said he.

"Truly, naught," answered Aucassin.   "I asked
with no wish to do you wrong."

"And you, for what cause do you weep?" asked
the other, "and make such heavy sorrow? Certainly, were I so rich a man as you are, not the
whole world should make me shed a tear."

"Do you know me, then?" said Aucassin.

"Yes, well I know you to be Aucassin, the son of the Count, and if you will tell me why you weep, well, then I will tell you what I do here."

"Certes," said Aucassin, "I will tell you with all my heart. I came this morning to hunt in the forest, and with me a white greyhound, the swiftest in the whole world. I have lost him, and that is why I weep."

"Hear him," cried he, "by the Sacred Heart, and you make all this lamentation for a filthy dog! Sorrow be his who shall esteem you more. Why, there is not a man of substance in these parts who would not give you ten or fifteen or twenty hounds —if so your father wished—and be right glad to make you the gift. But for my part I have full reason to weep and cry aloud."

"And what is your grief, brother?"

"Sire, I will tell you. I was hired by a rich farmer to drive his plough, with a yoke of four oxen. Now three days ago, by great mischance, I lost the best of my bullocks, Roget, the very best ox in the plough. I have been looking for him ever since, and have neither eaten nor drunk for three days, since I dare not go back to the town, because men would put me into prison, as I have no money to pay for my loss. Of all the riches of the world I have nought but the rags upon my back. My poor old mother, too, who had nothing but one worn-out mattress, why, they have taken that from under her, and left her lying on the naked straw. That hurts me more than my own trouble. For money comes and money goes; if I have lost to-day, why, I may win to-morrow; and I will pay for my ox when pay I can. Not for this will I wring my hands. And you—you weep aloud for a filthy cur. Sorrow take him who shall esteem you more."

"Certes, thou art a true comforter, fair brother, and blessed may you be. What is the worth of your bullock?"

"Sire, the villein demands twenty sous for his ox. I cannot beat the price down by a single farthing."

"Hold out your hand," said Aucassin; "take these twenty sous which I have in my purse, and pay for your ox."

"Sire," answered the hind, "many thanks, and God grant you find that for which you seek."

So they parted from each other, and Aucassin rode upon his way. The night was beautiful and still, and so he fared along the forest path until he came to the seven cross-roads where Nicolette had builded her bower. Very pretty it was, and very dainty, and well furnished both outside and in, ceiling and floor, with arras and carpet of freshly plucked flowers; no sweeter habitation could man desire to see. When Aucassin came upon it he reined back his horse sharply, and the moonbeams fell within the lodge.

"Dear God," cried Aucassin, "here was Nicolette, my sweet friend, and this has she builded with her fair white hands. For the sweetness of the house and for love of her, now will I dismount, and here will I refresh me this night."

He withdrew his foot from the stirrup, and the charger was tall and high. He dreamed so deeply on Nicolette, his very sweet friend, that he fell heavily upon a great stone, and his shoulder came from its socket. He knew himself to be grievously wounded, but he forced him to do all that he was able, and fastened his horse with the other hand to a thorn. Then he turned on his side, and crawled as best he might into the lodge. Looking through a crevice of the bower he saw the stars shining in the sky, and one brighter than all the others, so he began to repeat—

Now is sung:

> Little Star I gaze upon
> Sweetly drawing to the moon,
> In such golden haunt is set
> Love, and bright-haired Nicolette.
> God hath taken from our war
> Beauty, like a shining star.
> Ah, to reach her, though I fell
> From her Heaven to my Hell.
> Who were worthy such a thing,
> Were he emperor or king?
> Still you shine, oh, perfect Star,
>   Beyond, afar.

Now they say and tell and relate:

When Nicolette heard Aucassin speak these words she hastened to him from where she was hidden near by. She entered in the bower, and clasping her arms about his neck, kissed and embraced him straitly.

"Fair sweet friend, very glad am I to find you."

"And you, fair sweet friend, glad am I to meet."

So they kissed, and held each other fast, and their joy was lovely to see.

"Ah, sweet friend," cried Aucassin, "it was but now that I was in grievous pain with my shoulder, but since I hold you close I feel neither sorrow nor wound."

Nicolette searched his hurt, and perceived that the shoulder was out of joint. She handled it so deftly with her white hands, and used such skilful surgery, that by the grace of God (who loveth all true lovers) the shoulder came back to its place. Then she plucked flowers, and fresh grass and green leafage, and bound them tightly about the setting with the hem torn from her shift, and he was altogether healed.

"Aucassin," said she, "fair sweet friend, let us

take thought together as to what must be done. If
your father beats the wood to-morrow, and men
take me, whatever may chance to you, certainly I
shall be slain."

"Certes, fair sweet friend, the sorer grief would
be mine. But so I may help, never shall you come
to his hands."

So he mounted to horse, and setting his love
before him, held her fast in his arms, kissing her as
he rode, and thus they came forth to the open fields.

Now is sung:

> Aucassin, that loving squire,
> Dainty fair to heart's desire,
> Rode from out the forest dim
> Clasping her he loved to him.
> 'Laced upon the saddle bow
> There he kissed her, chin and brow,
> There embraced her, mouth and eyes.
> But she spake him, sweetly wise;
> "Love, a term to dalliance,
> Since for us no home in France
> Seek we Rome or far Byzance?"
> "Sweet my love, all's one to me,
> Dale or woodland, earth or sea;
> Nothing care I where we ride
> So I hold you at my side."
> So, enlaced, the lovers went,
> Skirting town and battlement,
> Rocky scaur, and quiet lawn;
> Till one morning, with the dawn,
> Broke the cliffs down to the shore,
> Loud they heard the surges roar,
>   Stood by the sea.

Now they say and tell and relate:
Aucassin dismounted upon the sand, he and
Nicolette together, as you have heard tell. He took
his horse by the bridle, and his damsel by the
hand, and walked along the beach. Soon they

perceived a ship, belonging to merchants of those
parts, sailing close by, so Aucassin made signs to
the sailors, and presently they came to him. For
a certain price they agreed to take them upon the
ship, but when they had reached the open sea a
great and marvellous storm broke upon the vessel,
and drove them from land to land until they drew
to a far-off country, and cast anchor in the port of
the castle of Torelore. Then they asked to what
realm they had fared, and men told them that it
was the fief of the King of Torelore. Then inquired
Aucassin what manner of man was this king, and
whether there was any war, and men answered—

"Yes, a mighty war."

So Aucassin bade farewell to the merchants, and
they commended him to God. He belted his sword
about him, climbed to horse, taking his love before
him on the saddle bow, and went his way till he
came to the castle. He asked where the King
might be found, and was told that he was in child-
bed.

"Where, then, is his wife?"

And they answered that she was with the host,
and had carried with her all the armed men of those
parts. When Aucassin heard these things he
marvelled very greatly. He came to the palace
door and there dismounted, bidding Nicolette to
hold the bridle. Then, making his sword ready,
he climbed the palace stair, and searched until he
came to the chamber where the King lay.

Now is sung :

> Hot from searching, Aucassin
> Found the room and entered in;
> There before the couch he stayed
> Where the King, alone, was laid,
> Marked the King, and marked the bed,
> Marked this lying-in, then said,
> "Fool, why doest thou this thing?"

> "I'm a mother," quoth the King:
> "When my month is gone at length,
> And I come to health and strength,
> Then shall I hear Mass once more
> As my fathers did before,
> Arm me lightly, take my lance,
> Set my foe a right fair dance,
> Where horses prance."

Now they say and tell and relate:

When Aucassin heard the King speak thus he took the linen from the bed, and flung it about the chamber. He saw a staff in the corner, so he seized it, returned to the bed, and beat the King so rudely therewith, that he was near to die.

"Ha, fair sire," cried the King, "what do you require of me? Are you mad that you treat me thus in my own house?"

"By the Sacred Heart," said Aucassin, "bad son of a shameless mother, I will strike with the sword if you do not swear to me that man shall never lie in child-bed in your realm again."

He plighted troth, and when he was thus pledged, "Sire," required Aucassin, "bring me now where your wife is with the host."

"Sire, willingly," said the King.

He got to horse, and Aucassin mounted his, leaving Nicolette at peace in the Queen's chamber. The King and Aucassin rode at adventure until they came to where the Queen was set, and they found that the battle was joined with roasted crab-apples and eggs and fresh cheeses. So Aucassin gazed upon the sight and marvelled greatly.

Now is sung:

> Aucassin hath drawn his rein,
> From the saddle stared amain,
> Marked the set and stricken field,
> Cheered the hearts that would not yield.

They had carried to the fight
Mushrooms, apples baked aright,
And for arrows, if you please,
Pelted each with good fresh cheese.
He who muddied most the ford
Bore the prize in that award.
Aucassin, the brave, the true,
Watched these deeds of derring do,
    Laughed loudly too.

Now they say and tell and relate:
When Aucassin saw this strange sight he went
to the King and asked of him—
"Sire, are these your foes?"
"Yea, sire," answered the King.
"And would you that I should avenge you on
them?"
"Yea," answered he, "right willingly."
So Aucassin took sword in hand, and throwing
himself in the *mêlée,* struck fiercely on the right
and on the left, and slew many. When the King
saw the death that Aucassin dealt he snatched at
his bridle and cried—
"Hold, fair sire, deal not with them so cruelly."
"What," said Aucassin, "was it not your wish
that I should avenge you on your enemies?"
"Sire," replied the King, "too ready is such payment as yours. It is not our custom, nor theirs,
to fight a quarrel to the death."
Thereon the foemen fled the field.
The King and Aucassin returned in triumph to
the castle of Torelore, and the men of the country
persuaded the King that he should cast Aucassin
forth from the realm, and give Nicolette to his son,
for she seemed a fair woman of high lineage.
When Nicolette heard thereof she had little comfort, so began to say—
Now is sung:

Simple folk, and simple King,
Deeming maid so slight a thing.
When my lover finds me sweet,
Sweetly shapen, brow to feet,
Then know I such dalliance,
No delight of harp, or dance,
Sweetest tune, or fairest mirth,
All the play of all the earth
    Seems aught of worth.

Now they say and tell and relate:
Aucassin abode in the castle of Torelore in ease
and great delight, having with him Nicolette his
sweet friend, whom he loved so well. Whilst his
days passed in so easy and delightful a manner a
great company of Saracens came in galleys oversea
and beset the castle, and presently took it by storm.
They gathered together the spoil, and bore off the
townsfolk, both men and women, into captivity.
Amongst these were seized Nicolette and Aucassin,
and having bound Aucassin, both hands and feet,
they flung him into one vessel, and bestowed Nicolette upon another. Thereafter a great tempest
arose at sea, and drove these galleys apart. The
ship whereon Aucassin lay bound, drifted idly, here
and there, on wind and tide, till by chance she
went ashore near by the castle of Beaucaire, and
the men of that part hurrying to the wreck, found
Aucassin, and knew him again. When the men
of Beaucaire saw their lord they had much joy, for
Aucassin had lived at the castle of Torelore in all
ease for three full years, and his father and his
mother were dead. They brought him to the castle
of Beaucaire, and knelt before him; so held he his
realm in peace.
    Now is sung:

Aucassin hath gained Beaucaire,
Men have done him homage there;

Holds he now in peace his fief,
Castellan and count and chief.
Yet with heaviness and grief
Goeth he in that fair place,
Lacking love and one sweet face;
Grieving more for one bright head
Than he mourneth for his dead.
"Dearest love, and lady kind,
Treasure I may never find,
God hath never made that strand
Far o'er sea or long by land,
Where I would not seek such prize
    And merchandize."

Now they say and tell and relate:
Now leave we Aucassin and let us tell of Nicolette. The ship which carried Nicolette belonged
to the King of Carthage, and he was her father,
and she had twelve brothers, all princes or kings
in the land. When they saw the beauty of the
girl, they made much of her, and bore her in great
reverence, and questioned her straitly as to her
degree, for certainly she seemed to them a very
gracious lady and of high lineage. But she could
not tell them aught thereof, for she was but a little
child when men sold her into captivity. So the
oarsmen rowed until the galley cast anchor beneath
the city of Carthage, and when Nicolette gazed on
the battlements and the country round about, she
called to mind that there had she been cherished,
and from thence borne away when but an unripe
maid; yet she was not snatched away so young but
that she could clearly remember that she was the
daughter of the King of Carthage, and once was
nourished in the city.

Now is sung:

Nicolette, that maid demure,
Set her foot on alien shore;

D

Marked the city fenced with walls,
Gazed on palaces and halls.
Then she sighed, "Ah, little worth
All the pomp of all the earth,
Since the daughter of a king,
Come of Sultan's blood, they bring
Stripped to market, as a slave.
Aucassin, true heart and brave,
Sweet thy love upon me steals,
Urges, clamours, pleads, appeals;
Would to God that peril past
In my arms I held you fast;
Would to God that in this place
We were stayed in one embrace,
Fell your kisses on my face,
    My dear, my fere."

Now they say and tell and relate:
When the King of Carthage heard Nicolette
speak in this wise he put his arms about her neck.

"Fair sweet friend," said he, "tell me truly who
you are, and be not esmayed of me."

"Sire," answered she, "truly am I daughter to
the King of Carthage, and was stolen away when
but a little child, full fifteen years ago."

When they heard her say this thing they were
assured that her words were true, so they rejoiced
greatly, and brought her to the palace in such
pomp as became the daughter of a king. They
sought to give her some king of those parts as
husband and baron, but she had no care to marry.
She stayed in the palace three or four days, and
considered in her mind by what means she might
flee and seek Aucassin. So she obtained a viol,
and learned to play thereon; and when on a certain
day they would have given her in marriage to a
rich king among the Paynim, she rose at night and
stole away secretly, wandering until she came to
the seaport, where she lodged with some poor

woman in a house near the shore. There, by means
of a herb, she stained her head and face, so that
her fairness was all dark and discoloured; and
having made herself coat and mantle, shirt and
hose, she equipped her in the guise of a minstrel.
Then, taking her viol, she sought out a sailor, and
persuaded him sweetly to grant her a passage in
his ship. They hoisted sail, and voyaged over the
rough seas until they came to the land of Provence;
and Nicolette set foot on shore, carrying her viol,
and fared playing through the country, until she
came to the castle of Beaucaire, in the very place
where Aucassin was.

Now is sung:

> 'Neath the keep of strong Beaucaire
> On a day of summer fair,
> At his pleasure, Aucassin
> Sat with baron, friend and kin.
> Then upon the scent of flow'rs,
> Song of birds, and golden hours,
> Full of beauty, love, regret,
> Stole the dream of Nicolette,
> Came the tenderness of years;
> So he drew apart in tears.
> Then there entered to his eyes
> Nicolette, in minstrel guise,
> Touched the viol with the bow,
> Sang as I will let you know.
> "Lords and ladies, list to me,
> High and low, of what degree;
> Now I sing, for your delight,
> Aucassin, that loyal knight,
> And his fond friend, Nicolette.
> Such the love betwixt them set
> When his kinsfolk sought her head
> Fast he followed where she fled.
> From their refuge in the keep
> Paynims bore them o'er the deep.
> Nought of him I know to end.

But for Nicolette, his friend,
Dear she is, desirable,
For her father loves her well;
Famous Carthage owns him king,
Where she has sweet cherishing.
Now, as lord he seeks for her,
Sultan, Caliph, proud Emir.
But the maid of these will none,
For she loves a dansellon,
Aucassin, who plighted troth.
Sworn has she some pretty oath
Ne'er shall she be wife or bride,
Never lie at baron's side
      Be he denied."

Now they say and tell and relate:
When Aucassin heard Nicolette sing in this
fashion he was glad at heart, so he drew her aside,
and asked—

"Fair sweet friend," said Aucassin, "know you
naught of this Nicolette, whose ballad you have
sung?"

"Sire, truly, yes; well I know her for the most
loyal of creatures, and as the most winning and
modest of maidens born. She is daughter to the
King of Carthage, who took her when Aucassin
also was taken, and brought her to the city of
Carthage, till he knew for certain that she was his
child, whereat he rejoiced greatly. Any day he
would give her for husband one of the highest
kings in all Spain; but rather would she be hanged
or burned than take him, however rich he be."

"Ah, fair sweet friend," cried the Count
Aucassin, "if you would return to that country
and persuade her to have speech with me here, I
would give you of my riches more than you would
dare to ask of me or to take. Know that for love
of her I choose not to have a wife, however proud
her race, but I stand and wait: for never will there

be wife of mine if it be not her, and if I knew
where to find her I should not need to grope
blindly for her thus."

"Sire," answered she, "if you will do these
things I will go and seek her for your sake, and
for hers too; because to me she is very dear."

He pledged his word, and caused her to be
given twenty pounds. So she bade him farewell,
and he was weeping for the sweetness of Nicolette.
And when she saw his tears—

"Sire," said she, "take it not so much to heart;
in so short a space will I bring her to this town,
and you shall see her with your eyes."

When Aucassin knew this he rejoiced greatly.
So she parted from him, and fared in the town to
the house of the Viscountess, for the Viscount,
her god-father, was dead. There she lodged, and
opened her mind fully to the lady on all the business; and the Viscountess recalled the past, and
knew well that it was Nicolette whom she had
cherished. So she caused the bath to be heated,
and made her take her ease for fully eight days.
Then Nicolette sought a herb that was called celan-
dine, and washed herself therewith, and became so
fair as she had never been before. She arrayed
her in a rich silken gown from the lady's goodly
store; and seated herself in the chamber on a rich
stuff of broidered sendal; then she whispered the
dame, and begged her to fetch Aucassin, her
friend. This she did. When she reached the
palace, lo, Aucassin in tears, making great sorrow
for the long tarrying of Nicolette, his friend; and
the lady called to him, and said—

"Aucassin, behave not so wildly; but come with
me, and I will show you that thing you love best
in all the world; for Nicolette, your sweet friend,
is here from a far country to seek her love."

So Aucassin was glad at heart.

Now is sung:

> When he learned that in Beaucaire
> Lodged his lady, sweet and fair,
> Aucassin arose, and came
> To her hostel, with the dame:
> Entered in, and passed straightway
> To the chamber where she lay.
> When she saw him, Nicolette
> Had such joy as never yet;
> Sprang she lightly to her feet
> Swiftly came with welcome meet.
> When he saw her, Aucassin
> Oped both arms, and drew her in,
> Clasped her close in fond embrace,
> Kissed her eyes and kissed her face.
> In such greeting sped the night,
> Till, at dawning of the light,
> Aucassin, with pomp most rare,
> Crowned her Countess of Beaucaire.
> Such delight these lovers met,
> Aucassin and Nicolette.
> Length of days and joy did win,
> Nicolette and Aucassin,
> Endeth song and tale I tell
>   With marriage bell.

THE STORY OF KING CONSTANT, THE EMPEROR

Now telleth the tale that once upon a time there lived an Emperor of Byzantium, the which town is now called Constantinople, but in ancient days it was called Byzantium. In days long since there reigned in this city an Emperor; a Paynim he was, and was held to be a great clerk in the laws of his religion. He was learned in a science called astronomy, and knew the courses of the stars, the planets and the moon; moreover, in the stars he read many marvels; he had knowledge of many things which the Paynims study deeply, and had faith in divinations, and in the answers of the Evil One—that is to say, the Adversary. He knew, besides, much of enchantments and sorceries, as many a Paynim doth to this very day.

Now it chanced that the Emperor Muselin fared forth one night, he and a certain lord of his together, and went their ways about this city of Constantinople, and the moon shone very clear. They heard a Christian woman, travailing of child, cry aloud as they passed before her house; but the husband of this dame was set in the terrace upon his roof, and now he prayed God to deliver her from her peril, and again he prayed that she might not be delivered. When the Emperor had listened to his words for a long time, he said to the knight—

"Have you heard this caitif who prays now that his wife may not be delivered of her child, and again that she may be delivered? Surely he is viler than any thief, for every man should show pity to woman, and the greater pity to her in pain with child. But may Mahound and Termagaunt aid me never if I hang him not by the neck, so he give me not fair reason for this deed. Let us now go to him."

So they went, and the Emperor spake him thus, "Caitif, tell me truly why thou prayest thy God in this fashion, now that He should deliver thy wife in her labour, and again that she should not be delivered; this must I know!"

"Sire," answered he, "I will tell you readily. Truly I am a clerk, and know much of a science that men call astrology. I have learned, too, the courses of the stars and the planets, and thus I knew well that were my wife delivered in that hour when I prayed God to close her womb, then the child must be for ever lost, and certainly would he be hanged, or drowned, or set within the fire. But when I saw the hour was good, and the case fair, then I prayed God that she might be delivered; and I cried to Him, so that of His mercy He heard my prayer, and now the boy is born to a goodly heritage; blessed be God and praisèd be His Name."

"Now tell me," said the King, "to what fair heritage is this child born?"

"Sire," said he, "with all my heart. Know, sire, of a truth that the child born in this place shall have to wife the daughter of the Emperor of this town, she who was born but eight days since, and shall become Emperor and lord of this city, and of the whole world."

"Caitif," cried the Emperor, "never can it come to pass as thou sayest."

"Sire," answered he, "so shall it be seen, and thus behoveth it to be."

"Certes," said the Emperor, "great faith hath he who receives it."

Then they went from the house, but the Emperor commanded his knight that he should bear away the child in so privy a manner, if he were able, that none should see the deed. The knight came again to the house, and found two women in the chamber, diligently tending the mother in her bed, but the child was wrapt in linen clothes, and was laid upon a stool. Thereupon the knight entered the room, and set hands upon the child, and placed him on a certain table used for chess, and carried him to the Emperor, in so secret a fashion that neither nurse nor mother saw aught thereof. Then the Emperor struck the child with a knife, wounding him from the stomach to the navel, protesting to the knight that never should son of such a miscreant have his daughter to wife, nor come to sit upon his throne. He would even have plucked the heart from out the breast, but the knight dissuaded him, saying—

"Ah, sire, for the love of God, what is this thing that you would do! Such a deed becomes you naught, and if men heard thereof, great reproach would be yours. Enough have you done, for he is more than dead already. But if it be your pleasure to take further trouble in the matter, give him to me, and I will cast him in the sea."

"Yea," cried the Emperor, "throw him in the water, for I hate him too much."

The knight took the child, wrapped him in a piece of broidered silk, and went with him towards the water. But on his way, pity came into his heart, and he thought within himself that never should new-born babe be drowned by him; so he set him, swathed in the silken cloth, on a warm muck-heap, before the gate of a certain abbey of monks, who at that hour were chanting matins. When the monks kept silence from their singing, they heard the crying of the child, and carried him

to the Lord Abbot, who commanded that so fair
a boy should be cherished of them. So they un-
swathed him from the piece of stuff, and saw the
grisly wound upon his body. As soon, therefore,
as it was day the Abbot sent for physicians, and
inquired of them at what cost they would cure the
child of his hurt; and they asked of him one
hundred pieces of gold. But he answered that
such a sum was beyond his means, and that the
saving of the child would prove too costly. Then
he made a bargain with the surgeons to heal the
child of his wound for eighty golden pieces; and
afterwards he brought him to the font, and caused
him to be named COUSTANT, because of his costing
the abbey so great a sum to be made whole.

Whilst the doctors were about this business, the
Abbot sought out a healthy nurse, in whose breast
the infant lay till he was healed of his hurt, for his
flesh was soft and tender, and the knife wound
grew together quickly, but ever after on his body
showed the gash. The child grew in stature, and
to great beauty. When he was seven years old the
Abbot put him to school, where he proved so fair
a scholar that he passed all his class-mates in apt-
ness and knowledge. When he was twelve years
of age the boy had come to marvellous beauty; no
fairer could you find in all the land; and when the
Abbot saw how comely was the lad and how
gracious, he caused him to ride in his train when
he went abroad.

Now it chanced that the Abbot wished to complain to the Emperor of a certain wrong that his
servants had done to the abbey. So the Abbot
made ready a rich present, for the abbey and
monastery were his vassals, although this Emperor
was but a Saracen. When the Abbot had proffered
his goodly gift, the Emperor appointed a time,
three days thence, to inquire into the matter, when

he would lie at a castle of his, some three miles out
from the city of Byzantium. On the day fixed by
the Emperor, the Abbot got to horse, with his chaplain, his squire, and his train; and amongst them
rode Constant, so goodly in every whit that all
men praised his exceeding beauty, and said
amongst themselves that certainly he came of high
peerage, and would rise to rank and wealth. Thus
rode the Abbot towards the castle where the
Emperor lay, and when they met, he greeted him
and did him homage, and the Emperor bade him
to enter within the castle, where he would speak
with him of his wrong. The Abbot bowed before
him and answered—

"Sire, as God wills."

The Abbot called Constant to him, for the lad
carried the prelate's hat of felt, whilst he talked
with the Emperor, and the Emperor gazed on the
varlet, and saw him so comely and winning, that
never before had he seen so fair a person. Then
he asked who the boy was; and the Abbot answered
that he knew little, save that he was his man, and
that the abbey had nourished him from his birth—
"and truly were this business of ours finished, I
could relate fine marvels concerning him."

"Is this so?" said the Emperor; "come now with
me to the castle, and there you shall tell me the
truth."

The Emperor returned to the castle, and the
Abbot was ever at his side, as one who had a heavy
business, and he made the best bargain that he
might, for the Emperor was his lord and suzerain.
But the matter did not put from the Emperor's
mind the great beauty of the lad, and he commanded the Abbot to bring the varlet before him.
So the boy was sent for, and came with speed.
When Constant stood in the presence, the Emperor praised his beauty, and said to the Abbot

that it was a great pity that so fair a child should
be a Christian. The Abbot replied that it was
rather a great happiness, for one day he would
render to God an unspotted soul. When the
Emperor heard this thing he laughed at his folly,
saying the laws of Christ were of nothing worth,
and that hell was the portion of such as put faith
in them. Sorely grieved was the Abbot when he
heard the Paynim jest in this fashion, but he dared
not to answer as he wished, and spake soft words to
him right humbly.

"Sire, so it pleases the Almighty, such souls are
not lost, for, with all sinners, they go to the mercy
of the Merciful."

The Emperor inquired when the boy came to
his hands, and the Abbot replied that fifteen years
before he was found by night on the muck-heap
before the abbey door.

"Our monks heard the wail of a tiny child as
they came from chanting matins, so they searched
for him, and carried him to me. I looked on the
child, and he was very fair, so that I bade them to
take him to the font and to cherish him duly. He
was swathed in a rich stuff of scarlet silk, and
when he was unwrapped I saw on his stomach a
grievous wound; so I sent for doctors and surgeons,
and bargained with them to cure him of his hurt
for eighty pieces of gold. Afterwards we baptized
him, and gave him the name of COUSTANT, because
of his costing so great a sum to be made whole.
Yet, though he be healed of his wound, never will
his body lose the mark of that grisly gash."

When the Emperor heard this story he knew well
that it was the child whom he had sought to slay
in so felon a fashion; so he prayed the Abbot to
give the lad to his charge. Then replied the Abbot
that he would put the matter before his Chapter,
but that for his own part the boy should be given

to the King very willingly. Never a word, for good
or evil, spake the King; so the Abbot took leave,
and returned to the monastery, and calling a
Chapter of his monks, told them that the Emperor
demanded Constant from their hands.

"But I answered that I must speak to you to
know your pleasure therein. Now answer if I
have done aright."

"What, sire, done rightly!" cried the gravest
and wisest of all the monks; "evilly and foolishly
have you done in not giving him just what he asked
at once. If you will hear our counsel, send Constant to him now as he requires, lest he be angry
with us, for quickly can he do us much mischief."

Since it seemed to all the Chapter good that Constant should be sent to the Emperor, the Abbot
bade the prior to go upon this errand, and he
obeyed, saying, "As God pleases."

He got to horse, and Constant with him, and
riding to the Emperor, greeted him in the name of
the Abbot and the abbey; then taking Constant by
the hand, gave him to the Emperor formally, in
such names and in their stead. The Paynim received him as one angered that a nameless man
and vagabond must have a king's daughter to wife,
and well he thought in his heart to serve him some
evil turn.

When the Emperor held Constant in his power,
he pondered deeply how he might slay him, and
no man speak a word. It chanced at this time
that the Emperor had business which called him
to the frontier of his realm, a very long way off,
a full twelve days' journey. He set forth, carrying
Constant in his train, yet brooding how to do him
to death; and presently he caused letters to be
written in this wise to the castellan of Byzantium.

"I, the Emperor of Byzantium, and lord of

Greece, make him, the governor of my city, to
know that as soon as he shall read this letter he
shall slay, or cause to be slain, the bearer of this
letter, forthwith upon the delivery thereof. As
your proper body to you is dear, so fail not this
command."

Such was the letter Constant carried, and little
he knew that it was his death he held in hand.
He took the warrant, which was closely sealed, and
set out upon his way, riding in such manner that in
less than fifteen days he reached Byzantium, the
town we now call Constantinople. When the
varlet rode through the gate it was the dinner-hour,
so (by the will of God) he thought he would not
carry his letter to table, but would wait till men
had dined. He came with his horse to the palace
garden, and the weather was very hot, for it was
near to Midsummer day. The pleasaunce was deep
and beautiful, and the lad unbitted his horse,
loosened the saddle, and let him graze; then he
threw himself down beneath the shelter of a tree,
and in that sweet and peaceful place presently fell
sound asleep.

Now it happened that when the fair daughter of
the Emperor had dined, she entered the garden,
and with her four of her maidens, and soon they
began to run one after the other, in such play as
is the wont of damsels when alone. Playing thus,
the fair daughter of the Emperor found herself
beneath the tree where Constant lay sleeping, and
he was flushed as any rose. When the Princess
saw him, she would not willingly withdraw her
eyes, saying to her own heart that never in her life
had she beheld so comely a person. Then she
called to her that one of her companions who was
her closest friend, and made excuses to send the
others forth from the garden. The fair maiden

took her playfellow by the hand, and brought her towards the slumbering youth, saying—

"Sweet friend, here is rich and hidden treasure. Certes, never in all my days have I seen so gracious a person. He is the bearer of letters, and right willingly would I learn his news."

The two damsels came near the sleeping lad, and softly withdrew the letter. When the Princess read the warrant she began to weep very bitterly, and said to her companion, "Certainly this is a heavy matter."

"Ah, madame," said her fellow, "tell me all the case."

"Truly," answered the Princess, "could I but trust you fully, such heaviness should soon be turned to joy."

"Lady," replied she, "surely you may trust me; never will I make known that which you desire to be hid."

So that maiden, the daughter of the Emperor, caused her fellow to pledge faith by all that she held most dear, and then she revealed what the letter held; and the girl answered her—

"Lady, what would you do herein?"

"I will tell you readily," said the Princess. "I will put within his girdle another letter from my father in place of this, bidding the castellan to give me as wife to this comely youth, and to call all the people of this realm to the wedding banquet; for be sure that the youth is loyal and true, and a man of peerage."

When the maiden heard this she said within herself that such a turn were good to play.

"But, Lady, how may you get the seal of your father to the letter?"

"Very easily," answered the Princess; "ere my father left for the marches he gave me eight sheets of parchment, sealed at the foot with his seal, but

with nothing written thereon, and there will I set
all that I have told you."

"Lady," said she, "right wisely have you
spoken; but lose no time, and hasten lest he
awake."

"I will go now," said the Princess.

The fair maiden, the daughter of the Emperor,
went straight to her wedding chest, and drew
therefrom one of the sealed parchments left her
by her father, so that she might borrow moneys in
his name should occasion arise. For, always was
this king and his people at war with felon and
mighty princes whose frontiers were upon his
borders. Thereon she wrote her letter in such
manner as this—

"I, King Muselin, Emperor of Greece and of
Byzantium the great city, to my Castellan of
Byzantium greeting. I command you to give the
bearer of this letter to my fair daughter in marriage, according to our holy law; for I have heard,
and am well persuaded, that he is of noble descent
and right worthy the daughter of a king. And,
moreover, at such time grant holiday and proclaim
high festival to all burgesses of the city, and
throughout my realm."

In such fashion wrote and witnessed the letter
of that fair maiden the daughter of the Emperor.
So when her letter was finished she hastened to
the garden, she and her playmate together, and
finding Constant yet asleep, placed privily the
letter beneath his girdle. Then the two girls began
to sing and to make such stir as must needs arouse
him. The lad awoke from his slumber, and was
all amazed at the beauty of the lady and her companion. They drew near, and the Princess gave
him gracious greeting, whereupon Constant got to

his feet and returned her salutation right courteously. She inquired of him as to his name and
his business, and he answered that he was the
bearer of letters from the Emperor to the governor
of the city. The girl replied that she would bring
him at once to the presence of the castellan; so
she took him by the hand and led him within the
palace; and all within the hall rose at the girl's
approach, and did reverence to their Lady.

The demoiselle sought after the castellan, who
was in his chamber, and there she brought the
varlet, who held forth his letter, and added thereto
the Emperor's greeting. The seneschal made
much of the lad, kissing his hand; but the maid
for her part kissed both letter and seal, as one
moved with delight, for it was long since she had
learned her father's news. Afterwards she said to
the governor that it were well to read the dispatch
in counsel together, and this she said innocently
as one who knew nothing of what was therein.
To this the castellan agreed, so he and the maiden
passed to the council chamber alone. Thereupon
the girl unfolded the letter, and made it known to
the governor, and she seemed altogether amazed
and distraught as she read. But the castellan took
her to task.

"Lady, certainly the will of my lord your father
must be done; otherwise will his blame come upon
us with a heavy hand."

But the girl made answer to this—

"How, then, should I be married, and my lord
and father far away? A strange thing this would
be; and certainly will I not be wed."

"Ah, lady," cried the castellan, "what words are
these? Your father's letter biddeth you to marry,
so give not nay for yea."

"Sire," said the demoiselle, to whom time went
heavy till all was done—"speak you to the lords

E

and dignitaries of this realm, and take counsel together. So they deem that thus it must be, who am I to gainsay them?"

The castellan approved such modest and becoming words, so he took counsel with the barons, and showed them his letter, and all agreed that the letter must be obeyed, and the commandment of the Emperor done. Thus was wedded according to Paynim ritual Constant, that comely lad, to the fair daughter of the Emperor. The marriage feast lasted fifteen days, and all Byzantium kept holiday and high festival; no business was thought of in the city, save that of eating and drinking and making merry. This was all the work men did.

The Emperor tarried a long time in the borders of his land, but when his task was ended he returned towards Byzantium. Whilst he was about two days' journey from the city, there met him a messenger with letters of moment. The King inquired of him as to the news of the capital, and the messenger made answer that there men thought of nought else but drinking and eating and taking their ease, and had so done for a whole fortnight.

"Why is this?" asked the Emperor.

"Why, sire, do you not remember?"

"Truly, no," said the Emperor; "so tell me the reason."

"Sire," replied the varlet, "you sent to your castellan a certain comely lad, and he bore with him letters from you commanding that he should be wed to your daughter, the fair Princess, since after your death he would be Emperor in your stead, for he was a man of lineage, and well worthy so high a bride. But your daughter refused to marry such an one, till the castellan had spoken with the lords; so he showed the council your letter, and they all advised him to carry out your will. When your daughter knew that they were all of one mind, she dared no longer to withstand you, and consented to your purpose. In just such manner as this was your daughter wedded, and a merrier city than yours could no man wish to see."

When the Emperor heard this thing from the messenger, he marvelled beyond measure, and turned it over in his thoughts; so presently he inquired of the varlet how long it was since Constant had wedded his daughter, and whether he had bedded with her.

"Yea, sire," answered the varlet, "and since it is more than three weeks that they were married, perchance one day will she be mother as well as wife."

"Truly it were a happy hazard," said the Emperor, "and since the thing has fallen thus, let me endure it with a smiling face, for nothing else is left to do."

The Emperor went on his way until he reached Byzantium, and all the city gave him loyal greeting. Amongst those who came to meet him was the fair Princess with her husband, Constant, so gracious in person that no man was ever goodlier. The Emperor, who was a wise prince, made much of both of them, and laid his two hands on their two heads, and held them so for long, for such is the fashion of blessing amongst the Paynim. That night the Emperor considered this strange adventure, and how it must have chanced, and so deeply did he think upon it that well he knew that the game had been played him by his daughter. He did not reproach her, but bade them bring the letter he sent to the governor, and when it was shown him he read the writing therein, and saw that it was sealed with his very seal. So, seeing the way in which the thing had come to pass, he said within himself that he had striven against those things which were written in the stars.

After this the Emperor made Constant, his newly wedded son, a belted knight, and gave and delivered to him his whole realm in heritage after his death. Constant bore himself wisely and well, as became a good knight, bold and chivalrous, and defended the land right well against all its foes. In no long while his lord the Emperor died, and was laid in the grave, according to Paynim ritual, with great pomp and ceremony. The Emperor Constant reigned in his stead, and greatly he loved and honoured the Abbot who had cherished him, and he made him Chancellor of his kingdom. Then, by the advice of the Abbot, and according to the will of God, the All Powerful, the Emperor Constant brought his wife to the font, and caused all men of that realm to be converted to the law of Jesus Christ. He begot on his wife an heir, whom he christened Constantine, and who became true Christian and a very perfect knight. In his day was the city first called Constantinople, because of Constant his father, who cost the abbey so great a sum, but before then was the city known as Byzantium.

So endeth in this place the story of King Constant the Emperor.

OUR LADY'S TUMBLER

AMONGST the lives of the ancient Fathers, wherein may be found much profitable matter, this story is told for a true ensample. I do not say that you may not often have heard a fairer story, but at least this is not to be despised, and is well worth the telling. Now therefore will I say and narrate what chanced to this minstrel.

He erred up and down, to and fro, so often and in so many places, that he took the whole world in despite, and sought rest in a certain Holy Order. Horses and raiment and money, yea, all that he had, he straightway put from him, and seeking shelter from the world, was firmly set never to put foot within it more. For this cause he took refuge in this Holy Order, amongst the monks of Clairvaux. Now, though this dancer was comely of face and shapely of person, yet when he had once entered the monastery he found that he was master of no craft practised therein. In the world he had gained his bread by tumbling and dancing and feats of address. To leap, to spring, such matters he knew well, but of greater things he knew nothing, for he had never spelled from book—nor Paternoster, nor canticle, nor creed, nor Hail Mary, nor aught concerning his soul's salvation.

When the minstrel had joined himself to the Order he marked how the tonsured monks spoke amongst themselves by signs, no words coming from their lips, so he thought within himself that they were dumb. But when he learned that truly it was by way of penance that speech was forbidden

to their mouths, and that for holy obedience were
they silent, then considered he that silence became
him also; and he refrained his tongue from words,
so discreetly and for so long a space, that day in,
day out, he spake never, save by commandment;
so that the cloister often rang with the brothers'
mirth. The tumbler moved amongst his fellows
like a man ashamed, for he had neither part nor lot
in all the business of the monastery, and for this
he was right sad and sorrowful. He saw the
monks and the penitents about him, each serving
God, in this place and that, according to his office
and degree. He marked the priests at their ritual
before the altars; the deacons at the gospels; the
sub-deacons at the epistles; and the ministers about
the vigils. This one repeats the introit; this other
the lesson; cantors chant from the psalter; penitents spell out the Miserere—for thus are all things
sweetly ordered—yea, and the most ignorant
amongst them yet can pray his Paternoster.
Wherever he went, here or there, in office or cloister, in every quiet corner and nook, there he found
five, or three, or two, or at least one. He gazes
earnestly, if so he is able, upon each. Such an one
laments; this other is in tears; yet another grieves
and sighs. He marvels at their sorrow. Then he
said, "Holy Mary, what bitter grief have all these
men that they smite the breast so grievously!
Too sad of heart, meseems, are they who make such
bitter dole together. Ah, St. Mary, alas, what
words are these I say! These men are calling on
the mercy of God, but I—what do I here! Here
there is none so mean or vile but who serves God
in his office and degree, save only me, for I work
not, neither can I preach. Caitif and shamed was
I when I thrust myself herein, seeing that I can
do nothing well, either in labour or in prayer. I
see my brothers upon their errands, one behind

the other; but I do naught but fill my belly with
the meat that they provide. If they perceive this
thing, certainly shall I be in an evil case, for they
will cast me out amongst the dogs, and none will
take pity on the glutton and the idle man. Truly
am I a caitif, set in a high place for a sign."
Then he wept for very woe, and would that he was
quiet in the grave. "Mary, Mother," quoth he,
"pray now your Heavenly Father that He keep
me in His pleasure, and give me such good counsel
that I may truly serve both Him and you; yea, and
may deserve that meat which now is bitter in my
mouth."

Driven mad with thoughts such as these, he
wandered about the abbey until he found himself
within the crypt, and took sanctuary by the altar,
crouching close as he was able. Above the altar
was carved the statue of Madame St. Mary.
Truly his steps had not erred when he sought that
refuge; nay, but rather, God who knows His own
had led him thither by the hand. When he heard
the bells ring for Mass he sprang to his feet all
dismayed. "Ha!" said he; "now am I betrayed.
Each adds his mite to the great offering, save only
me. Like a tethered ox, naught I do but chew
the cud, and waste good victuals on a useless man.
Shall I speak my thought? Shall I work my will?
By the Mother of God, thus am I set to do. None
is here to blame. I will do that which I can, and
honour with my craft the Mother of God in her
monastery. Since others honour her with chant,
then I will serve with tumbling."

He takes off his cowl, and removes his garments,
placing them near the altar, but so that his body
be not naked he dons a tunic, very thin and fine,
of scarce more substance than a shirt. So, light
and comely of body, with gown girt closely about
his loins, he comes before the Image right humbly.

Then raising his eyes, "Lady," said he, "to your fair charge I give my body and my soul. Sweet Queen, sweet Lady, scorn not the thing I know, for with the help of God I will essay to serve you in good faith, even as I may. I cannot read your Hours nor chant your praise, but at the least I can set before you what art I have. Now will I be as the lamb that plays and skips before his mother. Oh, Lady, who art nowise bitter to those who serve you with a good intent, that which thy servant is, that he is for you."

Then commenced he his merry play, leaping low and small, tall and high, over and under. Then once more he knelt upon his knees before the statue, and meekly bowed his head. "Ha!" said he, "most gracious Queen, of your pity and your charity scorn not this my service." Again he leaped and played, and for holiday and festival, made the somersault of .Metz. Again he bowed before the Image, did reverence, and paid it all the honour that he might. Afterwards he did the French vault, then the vault of Champagne, then the Spanish vault, then the vaults they love in Brittany, then the vault of Lorraine, and all these feats he did as best he was able. Afterwards he did the Roman vault, and then, with hands before his brow, danced daintily before the altar, gazing with a humble heart at the statue of God's Mother. "Lady," said he, "I set before you a fair play. This travail I do for you alone; so help me God, for you, Lady, and your Son. Think not I tumble for my own delight; but I serve you, and look for no other guerdon on my carpet. My brothers serve you, yea, and so do I. Lady, scorn not your villein, for he toils for your good pleasure; and, Lady, you are my delight and the sweetness of the world." Then he walked on his two hands, with his feet in the air, and his head near the

ground. He twirled with his feet, and wept with
his eyes. "Lady," said he, "I worship you with
heart, with body, feet and hands, for this I can
neither add to nor take away. Now am I your very
minstrel. Others may chant your praises in the
church, but here in the crypt will I tumble for your
delight. Lady, lead me truly in your way, and
for the love of God hold me not in utter despite."
Then he smote upon his breast, he sighed and wept
most tenderly, since he knew no better prayer than
tears. Then he turned him about, and leaped once
again. "Lady," said he, "as God is my Saviour,
never have I turned this somersault before. Never
has tumbler done such a feat, and, certes, it is not
bad. Lady, what delight is his who may harbour
with you in your glorious manor. For God's love,
Lady, grant me such fair hostelry, since I am
yours, and am nothing of my own." Once again
he did the vault of Metz; again he danced and
tumbled. Then when the chants rose louder from
the choir, he, too, forced the note, and put forward
all his skill. So long as the priest was about that
Mass, so long his flesh endured to dance, and leap
and spring, till at the last, nigh fainting, he could
stand no longer upon his feet, but fell for weariness
on the ground. From head to heel sweat stood
upon him, drop by drop, as blood falls from meat
turning upon the hearth. "Lady," said he, "I can
no more, but truly will I seek you again." Fire
consumed him utterly. He took his habit once
more, and when he was wrapped close therein,
he rose to his feet, and bending low before the
statue, went his way. "Farewell," said he, "gentlest
Friend. For God's love take it not to heart, for
so I may I will soon return. Not one Hour shall
pass but that I will serve you with right good will,
so I may come, and so my service is pleasing in
your sight." Thus he went from the crypt, yet

gazing on his Lady. "Lady," said he, "my heart
is sore that I cannot read your Hours. How would
I love them for love of you, most gentle Lady!
Into your care I commend my soul and my body."

In this fashion passed many days, for at every
Hour he sought the crypt to do service, and pay
homage before the Image. His service was so
much to his mind that never once was he too weary
to set out his most cunning feats to distract the
Mother of God, nor did he ever wish for other play
than this. Now, doubtless, the monks knew well
enough that day by day he sought the crypt, but
not a man on earth—save God alone—was aware
of aught that passed there; neither would he, for
all the wealth of the world, have let his goings in
be seen, save by the Lord his God alone. For
truly he believed that were his secret once espied
he would be hunted from the cloister, and flung
once more into the foul, sinful world, and for his
part he was more fain to fall on death than to
suffer any taint of sin. But God considering his
simplicity, his sorrow for all he had wrought amiss,
and the love which moved him to this deed, would
that this toil should be known; and the Lord willed
that the work of His friend should be made plain
to men, for the glory of the Mother whom he worshipped, and so that all men should know and
hear, and receive that God refuses none who seeks
His face in love, however low his degree, save only
he love God and strive to do His will.

Now think you that the Lord would have
accepted this service, had it not been done for love
of Him? Verily and truly, no, however much this
juggler tumbled; but God called him friend,
because he loved Him much. Toil and labour,
keep fast and vigil, sigh and weep, watch and pray,
ply the sharp scourge, be diligent at Matins and at
Mass, owe no man anything, give alms of all you

have—and yet, if you love not God with all your heart, all these good deeds are so much loss—mark well my words—and profit you naught for the saving of your soul. Without charity and love, works avail a man nothing. God asks not gold, neither for silver, but only for love unfeigned in His people's hearts, and since the tumbler loved Him beyond measure, for this reason God was willing to accept his service.

Thus things went well with this good man for a great space. For more years than I know the count of, he lived greatly at his ease, but the time came when the good man was sorely vexed, for a certain monk thought upon him, and blamed him in his heart that he was never set in choir for Matins. The monk marvelled much at his absence, and said within himself that he would never rest till it was clear what manner of man this was, and how he spent the Hours, and for what service the convent gave him bread. So he spied and pried and followed, till he marked him plainly, sweating at his craft in just such fashion as you have heard. "By my faith," said he, "this is a merry jest, and a fairer festival than we observe altogether. Whilst others are at prayers, and about the business of the House, this tumbler dances daintily, as though one had given him a hundred silver marks. He prides himself on being so nimble of foot, and thus he repays us what he owes. Truly it is this for that; we chant for him, and he tumbles for us. We throw him largesse: he doles us alms. We weep his sins, and he dries our eyes. Would that the monastery could see him, as I do, with their very eyes; willingly therefore would I fast till Vespers. Not one could refrain from mirth at the sight of this simple fool doing himself to death with his tumbling, for on himself he has no pity. Since his folly is free from malice, may God grant

it to him as penance. Certainly I will not impute
it to him as sin, for in all simplicity and good
faith, I firmly believe, he does this thing, so that
he may deserve his bread." So the monk saw with
his very eyes how the tumbler did service at all
the Hours, without pause or rest, and he laughed
with pure mirth and delight, for in his heart was
joy and pity.

The monk went straight to the Abbot and told
him the thing from beginning to end, just as you
have heard. The Abbot got him on his feet, and
said to the monk, "By holy obedience I bid you
hold your peace, and tell not this tale abroad
against your brother. I lay on you my strict command to speak of this matter to none, save me.
Come now, we will go forthwith to see what this
can be, and let us pray the Heavenly King, and
His very sweet, dear Mother, so precious and so
bright, that in her gentleness she will plead with
her Son, her Father, and her Lord, that I may look
on this work—if thus it pleases Him—so that the
good man be not wrongly blamed, and that God
may be the more beloved, yet so that thus is His
good pleasure." Then they secretly sought the
crypt, and found a privy place near the altar,
where they could see, and yet not be seen. From
there the Abbot and his monk marked the business
of the penitent. They saw the vaults he varied so
cunningly, his nimble leaping and his dancing,
his salutations of Our Lady, and his springing and
his bounding, till he was nigh to faint. So weak
was he that he sank on the ground, all outworn,
and the sweat fell from his body upon the pavement
of the crypt. But presently, in this his need, came
she, his refuge, to his aid. Well she knew that
guileless heart.

Whilst the Abbot looked, forthwith there came
down from the vault a Dame so glorious, that cer-

tainly no man had seen one so precious, nor so
richly crowned. She was more beautiful than the
daughters of men, and her vesture was heavy with
gold and gleaming stones. In her train came the
hosts of Heaven, angel and archangel also; and
these pressed close about the minstrel, and solaced
and refreshed him. When their shining ranks
drew near, peace fell upon his heart; for they con-
tended to do him service, and were the servants of
the servitor of that Dame who is the rarest Jewel
of God. Then the sweet and courteous Queen herself took a white napkin in her hand, and with it
gently fanned her minstrel before the altar.
Courteous and debonair, the Lady refreshed his
neck, his body and his brow. Meekly she served
him as a handmaid in his need. But these things
were hidden from the good man, for he neither saw
nor knew that about him stood so fair a company.

The holy angels honour him greatly, but they
can no longer stay, for their Lady turns to go.
She blesses her minstrel with the sign of God, and
the holy angels throng about her, still gazing back
with delight upon their companion, for they await
the hour when God shall release him from the
burden of the world, and they possess his soul.

This marvel the Abbot and his monk saw at least
four times, and thus at each Hour came the
Mother of God with aid and succour for her man.
Never doth she fail her servants in their need.
Great joy had the Abbot that this thing was made
plain to him. But the monk was filled with shame,
since God had shown His pleasure in the service
of His poor fool. His confusion burnt him like
fire. "Dominus," said he to the Abbot, "grant me
grace. Certainly this is a holy man, and since I
have judged him amiss, it is very right that my
body should smart. Give me now fast or vigil or
the scourge, for without question he is a saint.

We are witnesses to the whole matter, nor is it possible that we can be deceived." But the Abbot replied, "You speak truly, for God has made us to know that He has bound him with the cords of love. So I lay my commandment upon you, in virtue of obedience, and under pain of your person, that you tell no word to any man of that you have seen, save to God alone and me." "Lord," said he, "thus I will do." On these words they turned them, and hastened from the crypt; and the good man, having brought his tumbling to an end, presently clothed himself in his habit, and joyously went his way to the monastery.

Thus time went and returned, till it chanced that in a little while the Abbot sent for him who was so filled with virtue. When he heard that he was bidden of the Abbot, his heart was sore with grief, for he could think of nothing profitable to say. "Alas!" said he, "I am undone; not a day of my days but I shall know misery and sorrow and shame, for well I trow that my service is not pleasing to God. Alas! plainly doth He show that it displeases Him, since He causes the truth to be made clear. Could I believe that such work and play as mine could give delight to the mighty God! He had no pleasure therein, and all my toil was thrown away. Ah me, what shall I do? what shall I say? Fair, gentle God, what portion will be mine? Either shall I die in shame, or else shall I be banished from this place, and set up as a mark to the world and all the evil thereof. Sweet Lady, St. Mary, since I am all bewildered, and since there is none to give me counsel, Lady, come thou to my aid. Fair, gentle God, help me in my need. Stay not, neither tarry, but come quickly with Your Mother. For God's love, come not without her, but hasten both to me in my peril, for truly I know not what to plead. Before one word can

pass my lips, surely will they bid me 'Begone.'
Wretched that I am, what reply is he to make
who has no advocate? Yet, why this dole, since
go I must?" He came before the Abbot, with the
tears yet wet upon his cheeks, and he was still
weeping when he knelt upon the ground. "Lord,"
prayed he, "for the love of God deal not harshly
with me. Would you send me from your door?
Tell me what you would have me do, and thus it
shall be done." Then replied the Abbot, "Answer
me truly. Winter and summer have you lived
here for a great space; now, tell me, what service
have you given, and how have you deserved your
bread?" "Alas!" said the tumbler, "well I knew
that quickly I should be put upon the street when
once this business was heard of you, and that you
would keep me no more. Lord," said he, "I take
my leave. Miserable I am, and miserable shall I
ever be. Never yet have I made a penny for all
my juggling." But the Abbot answered, "Not so
said I; but I ask and require of you—nay, more,
by virtue of holy obedience I command you—to
seek within your conscience and tell me truly by
what craft you have furthered the business of our
monastery." "Lord," cried he, "now have you
slain me, for this commandment is a sword." Then
he laid bare before the Abbot the story of his days,
from the first thing to the last, whatsoever pain it
cost him; not a word did he leave out, but he told
it all without a pause, just as I have told you the
tale. He told it with clasped hands, and with
tears, and at the close he kissed the Abbot's feet,
and sighed.

The holy Abbot leaned above him, and, all in
tears, raised him up, kissing both his eyes.
"Brother," said he, "hold now your peace, for I
make with you this true covenant, that you shall
ever be of our monastery. God grant, rather, that

we may be of yours, for all the worship you have brought to ours. I and you will call each other friend. Fair, sweet brother, pray you for me, and I for my part will pray for you. And now I pray you, my sweet friend, and lay this bidding upon you, without pretence, that you continue to do your service, even as you were wont heretofore—yea, and with greater craft yet, if so you may." "Lord," said he, "truly is this so?" "Yea," said the Abbot, "and verily." So he charged him, under peril of discipline, to put all doubts from his mind; for which reason the good man rejoiced so greatly that, as telleth the rhyme, he was all bemused, so that the blood left his cheeks, and his knees failed beneath him. When his courage came back, his very heart thrilled with joy; but so perilous was that quickening that therefrom he shortly died. But theretofore with a good heart he went about his service without rest, and Matins and Vespers, night and day, he missed no Hour till he became too sick to perform his office. So sore was his sickness upon him that he might not rise from his bed. Marvellous was the shame he proved when no more was he able to pay his rent. This was the grief that lay the heaviest upon him, for of his sickness he spake never a word, but he feared greatly lest he should fall from grace since he travailed no longer at his craft. He reckoned himself an idle man, and prayed God to take him to Himself before the sluggard might come to blame. For it was bitter to him to consider that all about him knew his case, so bitter that the burden was heavier than his heart could bear, yet there without remedy he must lie. The holy Abbot does him all honour; he and his monks chant the Hours about his bed, and in these praises of God he felt such delight that not for them would he have taken the province of Poitou, so great was his happiness therein.

Fair and contrite was his confession, but still he was not at peace; yet why say more of this, for the hour had struck, and he must rise and go.

The Abbot was in that cell with all his monks; there, too, was company of many a priest and many a canon. These all humbly watched the dying man, and saw with open eyes this wonder happen. Clear to their very sight, about that lowly bed, stood the Mother of God, with angel and archangel, to wait the passing of his soul. Over against them were set, like wild beasts, devils and the Adversary, so they might snatch his spirit. I speak not to you in parable. But little profit had they for all their coming, their waiting, and their straining on the leash. Never might they have part in such a soul as his. When the soul took leave of his body, it fell not in their hands at all, for the Mother of God gathered it to her bosom, and the holy angels thronging round, quired for joy, as the bright train swept to Heaven with its burthen, according to the will of God. To these things the whole of the monastery was witness, besides such others as were there. So knew they and perceived that God sought no more to hide the love He bore to His poor servant, but rather would that his virtues should be plain to each man in that place; and very wonderful and joyful seemed this deed to them. Then with meet reverence they bore the body on its bier within the abbey church, and with high pomp commended their brother to the care of God; nor was there monk who did not chant or read his portion that day within the choir of the mighty church.

Thus with great honour they laid him to his rest, and kept his holy body amongst them as a relic. At that time spake the Abbot plainly to their ears, telling them the story of this tumbler and of all his life, just as you have heard, and of all that

F

he himself beheld within the crypt. No brother but kept awake during that sermon. "Certes," said they, "easy is it to give credence to such a tale; nor should any doubt your words, seeing that the truth bears testimony to itself, and witness comes with need; yea, without any doubt have we full assurance that his discipline is done." Great joy amongst themselves have all within that place.

Thus endeth the story of the minstrel. Fair was his tumbling, fair was his service, for thereby gained he such high honour as is above all earthly gain. So the holy Fathers narrate that in such fashion these things chanced to this minstrel. Now, therefore, let us pray to God—He Who is above all other—that He may grant us so to do such faithful service that we may win the guerdon of His love.

Here endeth the Tumbler of Our Lady.

THE LAY OF THE LITTLE BIRD

ONCE upon a time, more than a hundred years ago, there lived a rich villein whose name I cannot now tell, who owned meadows and woods and waters, and all things which go to the making of a rich man. His manor was so fair and so delightsome that all the world did not contain its peer. My true story would seem to you but idle fable if I set its beauty before you, for verily I believe that never yet was built so strong a keep and so gracious a tower. A river flowed around this fair domain, and enclosed an orchard planted with all manner of fruitful trees. This sweet fief was builded by a certain knight, whose heir sold it to a villein; for thus pass baronies from hand to hand, and town and manor change their master, always falling from bad to worse. The orchard was fair beyond content. Herbs grew there of every fashion, more than I am able to name. But at least I can tell you that so sweet was the savour of roses and other flowers and simples, that sick persons, borne within that garden in a litter, walked forth sound and well for having passed the night in so lovely a place. Indeed, so smooth and level was the sward, so tall the trees, so various the fruit, that the cunning gardener must surely have been a magician, as appears by certain infallible proofs.

Now in the middle of this great orchard sprang a fountain of clear, pure water. It boiled forth out of the ground, but was always colder than any marble. Tall trees stood about the well, and their leafy branches made a cool shadow there, even

67

during the longest day of summer heat. Not a ray
of the sun fell within that spot, though it were the
month of May, so thick and close was the leafage.
Of all these trees the fairest and the most pleasant
was a pine. To this pine came a singing bird
twice every day for ease of heart. Early in the
morning he came, when monks chant their matins,
and again in the evening, a little after vespers. He
was smaller than a sparrow, but larger than a wren,
and he sang so sweetly that neither lark nor
nightingale nor blackbird, nay, nor siren even,
was so grateful to the ear. He sang lays and
ballads, and the newest refrain of the minstrel and
the spinner at her wheel. Sweeter was his tune
than harp or viol, and gayer than the country
dance. No man had heard so marvellous a thing;
for such was the virtue in his song that the saddest
and the most dolent forgot to grieve whilst he
listened to the tune, love flowered sweetly in his
heart, and for a space he was rich and happy as
any emperor or king, though but a burgess of the
city or a villein of the field. Yea, if that ditty had
lasted a hundred years, yet would he have stayed
the century through to listen to so lovely a song,
for it gave to every man whilst he hearkened, love,
and riches, and his heart's desire.

But all the beauty of the pleasaunce drew its
being from the song of the bird; for from his
chant flowed love which gives its shadow to the
tree, its healing to the simple, and its colour to the
flower. Without that song the fountain would
have ceased to spring, and the green garden
become a little dry dust, for in its sweetness lay all
their virtue.

The villein, who was lord of this domain, walked
every day within his garden to hearken to the bird.
On a certain morning he came to the well to bathe
his face in the cold spring, and the bird, hidden

close within the pine branches, poured out his full
heart in a delightful lay, from which rich profit
might be drawn.

"Listen," chanted the bird in his own tongue,
"listen to my voice, oh, knight, and clerk, and layman, ye who concern yourselves with love, and
suffer with its dolours : listen, also, ye maidens,
fair and coy and gracious, who seek first the gifts
and beauty of the world. I speak truth and do
not lie. Closer should you cleave to God than to
any earthly lover, right willingly should you seek
His altar, more firmly should you hold to His commandment than to any mortal's pleasure. So you
serve God and Love in such fashion, no harm can
come to any, for God and Love are one. God
loves sense and chivalry ; and Love holds them not
in despite. God hates pride and false seeming ;
and Love loveth loyalty. God praiseth honour
and courtesy ; and fair Love disdaineth them not.
God lendeth His ear to prayer ; neither doth Love
refuse it her heart. God granteth largesse to the
generous ; but the grudging man, and the envious,
the felon and the wrathful, doth He abhor. But
courtesy and honour, good sense and loyalty, are
the leal vassals of Love, and so you hold truly to
them, God and the beauty of the world shall be
added to you besides."

Thus told the bird in his song.

But when he saw the villein beneath the pine
hearkening to his words, straight he changed
his note, for well he knew him to be covetous
and disloyal, and so he sang in quite another
fashion.

"Oh, river, cease to flow; crumble, thou manor,
keep and tower; let the grass wither with the rose,
and the tall tree stand bare, for the gentle dames
and knights come no more who once delighted in
my song, and to whom this fountain was dear.

In place of the brave and generous knights, set
upon honour, stands this envious churl, greedy
of naught but money. Those came to hear my
song for solace, and for love of love; he but
to eat and drink the more, and for ease of his
gluttony."

And when the bird had thus spoken he took his
flight.

Now the villein, who had listened to this song,
thought within himself that might he snare so
marvellous a bird, very easily could he sell him
at a great price; or if he might not sell him, at
least he could set him fast in a cage and hearken
his lay at pleasure both early and late. So he
climbed within the tree and sought and searched
and pried until he marked the branch from whence
the bird was wont to sing. There he set a cunning
snare, and waited to see what time should make
clear. At the hour of vespers the bird returned to
the orchard, and lighting upon the branch was
fast taken in the net. Then the villein came forth,
and mounting quickly, joyously seized him in his
hand.

"Small profit will you have of your labour," said
the bird, "for I can pay but a poor ransom."

"At least I shall be paid in songs," answered the
villein. "You were wont to sing for your own
pleasure, now you will carol for mine."

"Think not so," replied the bird. "He who is
used to the freedom of wood and meadow and river
cannot live prisoned in a cage. What solace may
I find there, or joy? Open your hand, fair sweet
friend, for be assured no captive has a heart for
songs."

"By my faith, then, you shall be served at
table."

"Never will you have dined worse, for there is

nothing of me. I pray you to let me go, for it were a sin to slay me."

"By my faith, you talk and talk; the more you plead, the less will I grant."

"Certes," answered the bird, "you are in your right, for such is the law. Many a time have I heard tell that the uncharitable granteth no alms. But there is a proverb that teaches that often man gives in his own interest what cannot be taken from him by force. Now, if you release me from this net I will make you free of three secrets which are little known to men of your lineage, and from which you may draw much profit."

"Tell me these secrets," said the villein, "and I will open my hand."

"Such faith have I in you," answered the bird, "that I will speak only when you free me from the snare."

The villein opened his hand, and the bird flew to a place of surety. His feathers were all ruffled, for he had been grossly handled by a glove not of silk but of wool, so he preened and plumed himself carefully with his beak. But the villein grew impatient, and urged him to pay his ransom. Now the bird was full of guile, so presently he made answer to the churl.

"Hear now the first of my three weighty secrets —Do not believe all that you may hear."

The villein frowned with anger, and answered that he knew it well.

"Fair friend, forget it never," replied the bird.

"Much I fear that I did foolishly in letting you from the snare. This secret was plain to me before; but now tell me the two others."

"They are fair and wise," said the bird. "Listen well to my second weighty secret—Do not regret what you have never lost."

"You mock me," cried the villein, "and do wrong to the faith you plighted with me. You pledged your word to tell me three secrets known but little to men of such lineage as mine, and you give me musty proverbs told over by all the world. Certes, what manner of man is he who weeps over what he has never had ! "

"Shall I tell it once again," replied the bird, "for great fear have I lest it should travel from your mind."

"By my head," answered the villein, "I am a fairer scholar than you think. These two proverbs have naught to teach me; but hold truly to our covenant and bargain, and let the third secret contain a graver matter."

"Listen well to my third secret," said the bird, "for he who receives it shall never be poor."

"Ah, tell me this secret quickly," cried the churl, "for it draws near the hour of meat, and truly, beyond all things, do I desire to grow rich."

Now when the bird heard him—

"This be thy punishment, oh, thou false churl— What you hold in your hand, never throw between your feet."

Then was the villein all wrathful; but when words came to him to speak, he said—

"And are these your three mighty secrets ! Why, these are but children's riddles, which I have known ever since I was born. You have but lied to me, and of all your teaching had I full knowledge long before."

"By my faith," responded the bird, "had you known my third secret never would you have let me from your hand."

"You say well," said the villein, "but at least knew I the two other proverbs."

"Ah," said the bird, with malice, "but this proverb was worth a hundred of the others."

"In what manner?" inquired the villein.

"What, know you not what has chanced to you? Had you slain me when I was in your power that day would have been the happiest of your life. For in my body is a jewel, so precious and so rare, that it weighs at least three ounces. Yea, the virtue of this stone is such that he who owns it has but to wish, and lo, his desire is fulfilled."

When the villein heard this thing he beat upon his breast, he tore his raiment, and disfigured his face with his nails, crying out that he was wretched and undone. The bird from his refuge in the tree rejoiced greatly to observe the churl's miserable plight, and said nothing till his enemy's clothes were torn to rags, and his hands sore wounded in many places. Then he spake—

"Miserable churl, when you held me fast in your rude hand, easy was it to know that I was no larger than a sparrow or a finch, and weighed less than half an ounce. How, then, could a precious stone, three ounces in weight, be hid in my body? Now will I prove to you that of my three secrets you understood not a single one. You asked me what man was fool enough to weep over that which he had never lost, and even now I watch your tears fall for a jewel which was never yours, nor will be ever. You had faith in all that I was pleased to tell you, trusting all you heard; and in your folly you flung the bird you held in hand between your very feet. Fair friend, con over my three secrets, and learn wisdom even from the counsel of a bird."

When he had spoken thus he took his flight, and from that hour the orchard knew him no more. With the ceasing of his song the leaves withered from the pine, the garden became a little dry dust, and the fountain forgot to flow. Thus the rich villein lost his pleasaunce, which once was fair beyond content. And remember well, fair lords and dames, that truly speaks the proverb, "He who covet another's good, oft loses his own," as we may learn from the "Lay of the Little Bird."

THE DIVIDED HORSECLOTH

EACH owes it to his fellows to tell as best he may, or, better still, to write with fair enticing words, such deeds and adventures as are good and profitable for us to know. For as men come and go about their business in the world, many things are told them which it is seemly to keep in remembrance. Therefore, it becomes those who say and relate, diligently and with fair intent to keep such matters in thought and study, even as did our fathers before us. Theirs is the school to which we all should pass, and he who would prove an apt scholar, and live beyond his day, must not be idle at his task. But the world dims our fine gold : the minstrel is slothful, and singers forget to sing, because of the pain and travail which go to the finding of their songs. So without waiting for any to-morrow, I will bring before you a certain adventure which chanced, even as it was told to me.

Some seven years ago it befell that a rich burgess of Abbeville departed from the town, together with his wife, his only son, and all his wealth, his goods and plenishing. This he did like a prudent man, since he found himself at enmity with men who were stronger and of more substance than he. So, fearing lest a worse thing should bechance him, from Abbeville he went up to Paris. There he sought a shop and dwelling, and paying his service, made himself vassal and burgess of the King. The merchant was diligent and courteous, his wife smiling and gracious, and their son was not given over to folly, but went soberly, even as

his parents taught him.   Much were they praised
of their neighbours, and those who lived in the
same street often set foot in their dwelling.   For
very greatly are those loved and esteemed by their
fellows who are courteous in speech and address.
He who has fair words in his mouth receives again
sweet words in his ear, and foul words and foul
deeds bring naught but bitterness and railing.
Thus was it with this prudent merchant.   For more
than seven years he went about his business, buy-
ing and selling, concerning himself with matters
of which he had full knowledge, putting by of his
earnings a little every day, like a wise and worthy
citizen.   So this wealthy merchant lived a happy
blameless life, till, by the will of God, his wife was
taken from him, who had been his companion for
some thirty years.   Now these parents had but one
only child, a son, even as I have told you before.
Very grievously did he mourn the death of her who
had cherished him so softly, and lamented his
mother with many tears, till he came nigh to
swoon.   Then, to put a little comfort in his heart,
his father said to him—

"Fair son, thy mother is dead, and we will pray
to God that He grant her mercy in that day.   But
dry now thine eyes and thy face, for tears can
profit thee nothing.   By that road we all must go,
neither can any man pass Death upon the way,
nor return to bring us any word.   Fair son, for thee
there is goodly comfort.   Thou art a young
bachelor, and it is time to take thee a wife.   I am
full of years, and so I may find thee a fair marriage
in an honourable house I will endow thee with my
substance.   I will now seek a bride for thee of
birth and breeding—one of family and descent,
one come of ancient race, with relations and friends
a gracious company, a wife from honest folk and
from an honest home.   There, where it is good

and profitable to be, I will set thee gladly, nor of wealth and moneys shalt thou find a lack."

Now in that place were three brethren, knights of high lineage, cousins to mighty lords of peerage, bearing rich and honourable blazons on their shields. But these knights had no heritage, since they had pawned all that they owned of woods and houses and lands, the better to take their pleasure at the tourney. Passing heavy and tormented were these brethren because in no wise might they redeem their pledge. The eldest of these brothers had a daughter, but the mother of the maid was dead. Now this damsel owned in Paris a certain fair house, over against the mansion of the wealthy merchant. The house was not of her father's heritage, but came to her from her mother, who had put the maid in ward to guardians, so that the house was free from pledge. She received in rent therefrom the sum of twenty Paris pounds every year, and her dues were paid her right willingly. So the merchant, esteeming her a lady of family and estate, demanded her hand in marriage of her father and of all her friends. The knight inquired in his turn of the means and substance of the merchant, who answered very frankly—

"In merchandise and in moneys I have near upon fifteen hundred pounds. Should I tell you that I had more, I should lie, and speak not the truth. I have besides one hundred Paris pounds, which I have gained in honest dealings. Of all this I will give my son the half."

"Fair sir," made answer the knight, "in no wise can this be agreed to. Had you become a Templar, or a White or a Black monk you would have granted the whole of your wealth either to the Temple or your Abbey. By my faith, we cannot consent to so grudging an offer, certes, sir merchant, no."

"Tell me then what you would have me do."

"Very willingly, fair, dear sir. We would that you grant to your son the sum and total of your substance, so that he be seised of all your wealth, and this in such fashion that neither you, nor any in your name, may claim return of any part thereof. If you consent to this the marriage can be made, but otherwise he shall never wed our child and niece."

The merchant turned this over for a while, now looking upon his son, now deep in thought. But very badly he was served of all his thought and pondering. For at the last he made reply to him and said—

"Lord, it shall even be done according to your will. This is our covenant and bargain, that so your daughter is given to my son I will grant him all that I have of worth. I take this company as witness that here I strip myself of everything I own, so that naught is mine, but all is his, of what I once was seised and possessed."

Thus before the witnesses he divested himself utterly of all his wealth, and became naked as a peeled wand in the eyes of the world, for this merchant now had neither purse nor penny, nor wherewithal to break his fast, save it were given him by his son. So when the words were spoken and the merchant altogether spoiled, then the knight took his daughter by the hand and handfasted her with the bachelor, and she became his wife.

For two years after this marriage the husband and the dame lived a quiet and peaceful life. Then a fair son was born to the bachelor, and the lady cherished and guarded him fondly. With them dwelt the merchant in the same lodging, but very soon he perceived that he had given himself a mortal blow in despoiling himself of his substance to live on the charity of others. But perforce he

remained of their household for more than twelve
years, until the lad had grown up tall, and began
to take notice, and to remember that which often
he heard of the making of his father's marriage.
And well he promised himself that it should never
go from mind.

The merchant was full of years. He leaned upon
his staff, and went bent with age, as one who
searches for his lost youth. His son was weary of
his presence, and would gladly have paid for the
spinning of his shroud. The dame, who was proud
and disdainful, held him in utter despite, for
greatly he was against her heart. Never was she
silent, but always was she saying to her lord—

"Husband, for love of me, send your father upon
his business. I lose all appetite just for the sight
of him about the house."

"Wife," answered he, "this shall be done according to your wish."

So because of his wife's anger and importunity,
he sought out his father straightway, and said—

"Father, father, get you gone from here. I tell
you that you must do the best you can, for we may
no longer concern ourselves with you and your
lodging. For twelve years and more we have
given you food and raiment in our house. Now
all is done, so rise and depart forthwith, and fend
for yourself, as fend you must."

When the father heard these words he wept
bitterly, and often he cursed the day and the hour
in which he found he had lived too long.

"Ah, fair, sweet son, what is this thou sayest
to me! For the love of God turn me not from thy
door. I lie so close that thou canst not want my
room. I require of thee neither seat in the
chimney corner, nor soft bed of feathers, no, nor
carpet on the floor; but only the attic, where I may
bide on a little straw. Throw me not from thy

house because I eat of thy bread, but feed me without grudging for the short while I have to live. In the eyes of God this charity will cover all thy sins better than if thou went in haircloth next the flesh."

"Fair father," replied the bachelor, "preach me no preachings, but get you forth at once, for reason that my wife would have you gone."

"Fair son, where then shall I go, who am esteemed of nothing worth?"

"Get you gone to the town, for amongst ten thousand others very easily you may light on good fortune. Very unlucky you will be if there you cannot find a way to live. Seek your fortune bravely. Perchance some of your friends and acquaintance will receive you into their houses."

"Son, how then shall men take me to their lodging, when you turn me from the house which I have given you? Why should the stranger welcome that guest whom the son chases from his door? Why should I be received gladly by him to whom I have given naught, when I am evilly entreated of the rich man for whose sake I go naked?"

"Father," said he, "right or wrong, I take the blame upon my own head; but go you must because it is according to my will."

Then the father grieved so bitterly that for a little his very heart would have broken. Weak as he was, he raised himself to his feet and went forth from the house, weeping.

"Son," said he, "I commend thee to God; but since thou wilt that I go, for the love of Him give me at least a portion of packing cloth to shelter me against the wind. I am asking no great matter; nothing but a little cloth to wrap about

me, because I am but lightly clad, and fear to die
for reason of the cold."

Then he who shrank from any grace of charity
made reply—

"Father, I have no cloth, so neither can I bestow,
nor have it taken from me."

"Fair, sweet son, my heart trembles within me,
so greatly do I dread the cold. Give me, then, the
cloth you spread upon your horse, so that I come
to no evil."

So he, seeing that he might not rid himself of
his father save by the granting of a gift, and being
desirous above all that he should part, bade his son
to fetch this horsecloth. When the lad heard his
father's call he sprang to him, saying—

"Father, what is your pleasure?"

"Fair son," said he, "get you to the stable, and
if you find it open give my father the covering
that is upon my horse. Give him the best cloth
in the stable, so that he may make himself a mantle
or a habit, or any other sort of cloak that pleases
him."

Then the lad, who was thoughtful beyond his
years, made answer—

"Grandsire, come now with me."

So the merchant went with him to the stable,
exceedingly heavy and wrathful. The lad chose
the best horsecloth he might find in the stable, the
newest, the largest, and the most fair; this he
folded in two, and drawing forth his knife, divided
the cloth in two portions. Then he bestowed on
his grandfather one half of the sundered horsecloth.

"Fair child," said the old man, "what have you
done? Why have you cut the cloth that your
father has given me? Very cruelly have you
treated me, for you were bidden to give me the
G

horsecloth whole. I shall return and complain to
my son thereof."

"Go where you will," replied the boy, "for certainly you shall have nothing more from me."

The merchant went forth from the stable.

"Son," said he, "chastise now thy child, since
he counts thy word as nothing but an idle tale,
and fears not to disobey thy commandment. Dost
thou not see that he keeps one half of the horsecloth ? "

"Plague take thee ! " cried the father; "give him
all the cloth."

"Certes," replied the boy, "that will I never do,
for how then shall you be paid? Rather will I
keep the half until I am grown a man, and then
give it to you. For just as you have chased him
from your house, so I will put you from my door.
Even as he has bestowed on you all his wealth,
so, in my turn, will I require of you all your
substance. Naught from me shall you carry
away, save that only which you have granted to
him. If you leave him to die in his misery, I wait
my day, and surely will leave you to perish in
yours."

The father listened to these words, and at the
end sighed heavily. He repented him of the evil
that he purposed, and from the parable that his
child had spoken took heed and warning. Turning himself about towards the merchant, he said—

"Father, return to my house. Sin and the
Enemy thought to have caught me in the snare,
but, please God, I have escaped from the fowler.
You are master and lord, and I render all that I
have received into your hands. If my wife cannot
live with you in quiet, then you shall be served and
cherished elsewhere. Chimney corner, and carpet,
pillow and bed of feathers, at your ease you shall
have pleasure in them all. I take St. Martin to

witness that never will I drink stoup of wine, never
carve morsel from dish, but that yours shall be the
richer portion.   Henceforth you shall live softly in
the ceiled chamber, near by a blazing fire, clad
warmly in your furred robe, even as I.   And all
this is not of charity, but of your right, for, fair
sweet father, if I am rich it is because of your
substance."

Thus the brave witness and the open remon-
strance of a child freed his father from the bad
thoughts that he harboured.   And deeply should
this adventure be considered of those who are
about to marry their children.   Let them not strip
themselves so bare as to have nothing left.   For
he who gives all, and depends upon the charity of
others, prepares a rod for his own back.

SIR HUGH OF TABARIE

IN the years when Saladin was King, there lived
a Prince in Galilee, who was named Sir Hugh of
Tabarie. On a day he was with other Christian
men who gave battle to the Turks, and, since it
pleased God to cast His chivalry behind Him, Sir
Hugh was taken prisoner, and many another stout
knight with him. When dusk closed down on the
field, the Prince was led before Saladin, who, calling him straightway to mind, rejoiced greatly and
cried—

"Ah, Sir Hugh, now are you taken."

"Sire," answered the brave knight, "the greater
grief is mine."

"By my faith, Hugh, every reason have you for
grief, since you must either pay your ransom or
die."

"Sire, I am more fain to pay ransom than to
die, if by any means I may find the price you
require of me."

"Is that truly so?" said the King.

"Sire," said Sir Hugh, "in the fewest words,
what is the sum you demand of me?"

"I ask of you," replied the King, "one hundred
thousand besants."

"Sire, such a sum is too great a ransom for a
man of my lands to pay."

"Hugh," said the King, "you are so good a
knight, and so hardy, that there is none who hears
of your prison and this ransom, but will gladly send
of his riches for your ease."

"Sire," said he, "since thus it must be, I promise to pay the sum you require, but what time do you grant me to find so mighty a ransom?"

"Hugh," said the King, "I accord you the grace of one year. If within the year you count me out the tale of these besants, I will take it gladly; but if you fail to gain it, then must you return to your prison, and I will hold you more willingly still."

"Sire, I pledge my word and my faith. Now deliver me such a safe conduct that I may return in surety to my own land."

"Hugh, before you part I have a privy word to speak to you."

"Sire, with all my heart, and where?"

"In this tent, close by."

When they were entered into the pavilion, the Emperor Saladin sought to know of Sir Hugh in what fashion a man was made knight of the Christian chivalry, and required of him that he should show it to his eyes.

"Sire, whom then should I dub knight?"

"Myself," answered the King.

"Sire, God forbid that I should be so false as to confer so high a gift and so fair a lordship even upon the body of so mighty a prince as you."

"But wherefore?" said the King.

"For reason, sire, that your body is but an empty vessel."

"Empty of what, Sir Hugh?"

"Sire, of Christianity and of baptism."

"Hugh," said he, "think not hardly of me because of this. You are in my hand, and if you do the thing that I require of you, what man is there to blame you greatly when you return to your own realm. I seek this grace of you, rather than of another, because you are the stoutest and most perfect knight that ever I may meet."

"Sire," said he, "I will show you what you seek to know, for were it but the will of God that you were a christened man, our chivalry would bear in you its fairest flower."

"Hugh," said he, "that may not be."

Thereupon Sir Hugh made ready all things necessary for the making of a knight; and having trimmed the hair and beard of the King in seemly fashion, he caused him to enter within a bath, and inquired—

"Sire, do you understand the meaning of this water?"

"Hugh, of this I know nothing."

"Sire, as the little child comes forth from the waters of baptism clean of sin, so should you issue from this bath washed pure of all stain and villainy."

"By the law of the Prophet, Sir Hugh, it is a fair beginning."

Then Sir Hugh brought the Sultan before an untouched bed, and having laid him therein, he said—

"Sire, this bed is the promise of that long rest in Paradise which you must gain by the toils of chivalry."

So when the King had lain softly therein for a little space, Sir Hugh caused him to stand upon his feet, and having clothed him in a fair white vesture of linen and of silk, said—

"Sire, this spotless stole you first put on is but the symbol of a body held and guarded clean."

Afterwards he set upon the King a gown of scarlet silk, and said—

"Sire, this vermeil robe keeps ever in your mind the blood a knight must shed in the service of his God and the defence of Holy Church."

Then taking the King's feet in his hands, he drew thereon shoes of brown leather, saying—

"Sire, these brown shoes with which you are shod, signify the colour of that earth from which you came, and to which you must return; for whatever degree God permits you to attain, remember, O mortal man, that you are but dust."

Then Sir Hugh raised the Sultan to his feet, and girt him with a white baldrick, saying—

"Sire, this white cincture I belt about your loins is the type of that chastity with which you must be girded withal. For he who would be worthy of such dignity as this must ever keep his body pure as any maid."

After this was brought to Sir Hugh a pair of golden spurs, and these he did upon the shoes with which the Sultan was shod, saying—

"Sire, so swiftly as the destrier plunges in the fray at the prick of these spurs, so swiftly, so joyously, should you fight as a soldier of God for the defence of Holy Church."

Then at the last Hugh took a sword, and holding it before the King, said—

"Sire, know you the three lessons of this glaive?"

"What lessons are these?"

"Courage, justice and loyalty. The cross at the hilt of his sword gives courage to the bearer, for when the brave knight girds his sword upon him he neither can, nor should, fear the strong Adversary himself. Again, sire, the two sharp edges of the blade teach loyalty and justice, for the office of chivalry is this, to sustain the weak against the strong, the poor before the rich, uprightly and loyally."

The King listened to all these words very heedfully, and at the end inquired if there was nothing more that went to the making of a knight.

"Sire, there is one thing else, but that I dare not do."

"What thing is this?"

"It is the accolade."

"Grant me now this accolade, and tell me the meaning thereof."

"Sire, the accolade is a blow upon the neck given with a sword, and the significance thereof is that the newly made knight may always bear in mind the lord who did him that great courtesy. But such a stroke will I not deal to you, for it is not seemly, since I am here your prisoner."

That night Saladin, the mighty Sultan, feasted in his chamber, with the fifty greatest lords of his realm, emirs, governors and admirals, and Sir Hugh of Tabarie sat on a cushion at his feet. At the close of the banquet Sir Hugh rose up before the King and said—

"Sire, grant me grace. I may not forget that you bade me to seek out all fair and honourable lords, since there is none who would not gladly come to my help in this matter of my ransom. But, fair Sir King, in all the world shall I never find a lord so wise, so hardy, and so courteous as yourself. Since you have taught me this lesson, it is but just and right that I should pray you to be the first to grant me aid herein."

Then Saladin laughed loudly out of a merry heart, and said—

"Pray God that the end be as sweet as the beginning. Truly, Sir Hugh, I will not have it on my conscience that you miss your ransom because of any meanness of mine, and therefore, without guile, for my part I will give you fifty thousand good besants."

Then the great Sultan rose from his throne, and taking Prince Hugh with him, came to each of the

lords in turn—emir, governor and admiral—and
prayed of him aid in the business of this ransom.
So all the lords gave largely out of a good heart,
in such measure that Sir Hugh presently acquitted
himself of his ransom, and returned to his own
realm from amongst the Paynim.

THE STORY OF KING FLORUS AND OF THE FAIR JEHANE

HERE begins the story of a certain King who was named King Florus of Ausay. This King Florus was a very stout knight, and a gentleman of proud descent. He was wedded to the daughter of the Prince of Brabant, a gentlewoman of high lineage. Very fair was the maid when she became his dame, slender of shape and dainty of fashion, and the story telleth that she was but fifteen summers old when King Florus became her lord, and he was but of seventeen years. A right happy life they passed together, as becometh bride and groom who wed fondly in their youth; yet because he might have no child of her King Florus was often dolent, and she for her part was vexed full grievously. This lady was very gracious of person, and very devout towards God and Holy Church. She gave alms willingly, and was so charitable that she nourished and clothed the needy, kissing their hands and feet. Moreover, so constant and private in service was she to the lepers of the lazar house, both men and women, that the Holy Ghost dwelt within her. Her lord, King Florus, so long as his realm had peace, rode forth as knight-errant to all the tournaments in Allemaigne and France and many other lands of which the noise reached him; thereon he spent much treasure, and gained great honour thereby.

But now my tale ceases to speak of him, and telleth of a knight who dwelt in the marches of

Flanders and of Hainault. This knight was wise in counsel, and brave of heart, very sure and trusty. He had to wife a right fair lady, of whom he had one daughter, young and fresh, named Jehane, a maid of some twelve years. Many sweet words were spoken of this maiden, for in all the country round was none so fair. Her mother prayed often to her lord that he should grant the girl in marriage, but so given were all his thoughts to the running of tourneys that he considered nothing of the trothing of his child, though his wife admonished him ever on his return from the jousts.

This knight had for squire a man named Robert, the bravest squire in any Christian realm. His prowess and his praise were such that oft he aided his lord to bear away the prize from the tournaments whereat he ran. So great was his praise that his lady spake him thus—

"Robert, more careth my lord for these joustings than for any words I speak, which thing is grievous to me, for I would that he gave care and pains to wed this daughter of mine. I pray you, therefore, for love of me, that if you may, you tell him that very ill he does, and is greatly to be blamed, not to marry his own fair child, for there is no knight of these parts, however rich his state, who would not gladly welcome such a bride."

"Lady," said Robert, "you have well spoken. Very readily will I speak thereof, and since my lord asks often of my counsel, every hope have I that he will take heed to my words."

"Robert," said the lady, "you will find me no niggard, so you do this task."

"Lady," said Robert, "your prayer is guerdon enough for me. Be assured I will do all that I may."

"I am content," returned the lady.

Now within a little space the knight made ready

to fare to a tournament very far from his land.
When he came to the field, he (with a certain
knight in whose company he rode) was joined to
one party, and his banner was carried to the lodging of his lord. The tilting began, and such
deeds did the knight, by the cunning service of his
squire, that he bore off the honour and the prize
of that tourney from the one side and the other.
On the second day the knight prepared to return
to his own country; so Robert took him often to
task and blamed him greatly that he had not
bestowed his fair daughter in marriage. Having
heard this many times, at the end his lord replied—

"Robert, thou and thy lady give me no peace
in the matter of the marriage of my daughter; but
at present I see and know of none in my parts to
whom I am content to give her."

"Ah, sir," cried Robert, "there is no knight in
your realm who would not receive her right
joyously."

"Robert, fair friend, they are worth nothing,
not one of them; neither will I bestow her there
with my good will. I know of no man in the world
who is worthy of her, save one man only, and he,
forsooth, is no knight."

"Sir, tell me his name," answered Robert, "and
I will find means to speak to him so privily that
the marriage shall be made."

"Certes, Robert," returned the knight, "meseems
thou art very desirous that my daughter shall be
wedded."

"Sir," quoth Robert, "you speak truly, for it is
full time."

"Robert," said the knight, "since thou art so hot
to carol at her wedding, she shall soon enough be
married if thou accord thereto."

"Certes, sir," said Robert, "right willingly will
I consent thereto."

"To that you pledge your word?" demanded the knight.

"Truly, sir, yes," answered Robert.

"Robert, thou hast served me very faithfully, and ever have I found thee skilled and true. Such as I am, that thou hast made of me; for by thine aid at the tourneys have I gained five hundred pounds of rent. 'Twas but a short time since that I had but five hundred; whereas now I have one thousand pounds from rent of land. This, therefore, I owe to thee, and I acquit me of my debt by giving thee my fair daughter, so thou art willing to take her at my hand."

"Ah, sir," cried Robert, "for the pity of God, say not thus. I am too low a man to snatch at so high a maiden, nor dare I pretend to one so rich and gracious as my demoiselle, since there is no knight in all the realm, whate'er his breeding, who would not count it honour to be her lord."

"Robert, know of a surety that never shall knight of this country call her his; but I will bestow her on thee, if thou refusest her not, and for her dowry shall she bring thee four hundred pounds from rent of my lands."

"Ah, sir," said Robert, "you are pleased to make a mock of me."

"Robert," said the knight, "be assured this is no jest."

"Ah, sir, neither my lady nor her mighty kin will endure to consent thereto."

"Robert," said the knight, "this matter concerns none of them. Hold, I give thee my glove, and I invest thee with four hundred pounds of my land, and this is my warrant for the delivery thereof."

"Sir," said Robert, "I will not refuse so goodly a gift, since it is given with so true a heart."

"Robert," replied the knight, "the grant is sealed."

So the knight granted him his glove, and invested him with rights in that fair maiden and her land.

Thus they passed upon their ways until it fortuned that this knight returned to his own house. When he was entered therein, his wife—that comely dame—received him right sweetly, and said—

"Husband, for the love of God, give thought at this time to the marriage of our maid."

"Dame," said her lord, "thou hast spoken so often of this matter that I have trothed her already."

"Sir," inquired the lady, "to whom?"

"Certes, dame, I have pledged her to a man who will ever be loyal and true. I have given her to Robert, my squire."

"To Robert! Alas the day," quoth the lady. "Robert is but a naked man, nor is there a knight, however noble, in all this realm who would not have taken her gladly. Certainly Robert shall have none of her."

"Dame, have her he shall, for I have delivered to him as my daughter's portion four hundred pounds in rent of land, and all his rights therein I warrant and will maintain."

When the lady heard this thing she was sore troubled, and said to her lord that of a surety should Robert never possess her maid.

"Dame," said her husband, "have her he shall, with good will or with bad will, for I have made a covenant with him, and will carry out my bargain."

When the lady heard these words of her lord she sought her chamber, and wept and lamented very grievously. After her tears were shed then she sent to seek her brothers and other kinsmen of her house, and showed them of that thing her lord would do, and they said—

"Lady, what have we to do herein? We have no care to go counter to your lord, for he is a stout knight, weighty of counsel and heavy of hand. Moreover, can he not do as he will with his daughter, and his land besides? Know you well that for this cause will none of us hang shield about his neck."

"Alas," said the lady, "never may my heart find happiness again, if thus I lose my child. At the least, fair lords, I pray and require you to show him that should he make this marriage he acts not rightly, nor after his own honour."

"Lady," said they, "this we will do full willingly."

So they sought out the knight and acquitted themselves of their task, and he answered them in courteous wise—

"Fair lords, I will tell you what I can do for your love. So it be your pleasure, I will defer this marriage on such understanding as I now declare. You are great lords, and are rich in gold and lands. Moreover, you are near of kin to this fair maid of mine, whom very tenderly I love. If on your part you will endue her with four hundred pounds of rent on your lands, I, on mine, will disavow this bond of marriage, and will wed the girl according to your wise counsel."

"In the name of God," answered they with one accord, "would you spoil us of all the wealth in our wallets?"

"Since, then," replied the knight, "you may not do this thing, suffer me to do as I will with my own."

"Sir, with right good mind," answered they.

Then the knight sent for his chaplain, and before him affianced Robert and his fair daughter together, appointing a certain day for the marriage. But on the third day Robert prayed his lord that he would dub him knight, since it was not seemly that he should take a wife so fair and of such high station till he was of her degree. His lord agreed thereto with a glad heart, and on the morrow granted him his desire; therefore after the third day he married the fair maid with great joy and festival.

At the hour Messire Robert was made knight he spake thus to his lord—

"Sir, once when I was in grievous peril of death, I vowed to seek St. James's shrine on the morrow of that day I gained my spurs. I pray you be not wroth with me if to-morrow morn it becomes my honour to wend thither directly after this marriage, for in no wise will I fail to observe my vow."

"Certes, Messire Robert, if you do this despite to my daughter, and go lonely upon your road, very rightly will you be held to blame."

"Sir," said he, "so it pleases God, I shall soon return, but go I must on peril of my soul."

When a certain knight of the lord's household heard these words, greatly he reproached Messire Robert for parting from his bride at such an hour, but Robert answered him that he durst not break his oath.

"Truly," said the knight, who was named Raoul, "truly if you wend thus to St. James's shrine, leaving so fair a bride but a wedded maid, very surely will I win her love ere you return. Certain proofs, moreover, will I give that I have had my way with her; and to this will I pledge my lands against the lands our lord has granted you, for mine are fully worth the rents of yours."

"My wife," answered Messire Robert, "does not come of a race to deal me so shrewd a wrong, and since I give no credence to your words, willingly will I make the wager, if so it pleases you."

H

"Yes," said Raoul, "and to this you pledge your faith?"

"Yea," said Messire Robert, "willingly. And you?"

"I, too, pledge my faith. Now let us seek our lord forthwith, and set before him our bargain."

"That is my desire also," said Messire Robert.

Then they went straight to their lord and laid before him this wager, and plighted troth to observe their covenant. So in the morning Messire Robert was married to the fair maiden, and when the bridal Mass was ended, incontinent he parted from the hall, without tasting the wedding meats, and set forth on his way, a pilgrim to Compostella.

Now ceaseth the tale to speak of him, and telleth of Raoul, who was hot in thought as to how he might gain the wager and have to do with the fair lady. So relateth the tale that the lady behaved very discreetly whilst her husband was on pilgrimage, for she spent much time upon her knees in church, praying God to bring her lord again. For his part Messire Raoul was in a heat in what manner he might win the wager, for more and more it seemed to him that he should lose his land. He sought speech with an old dame who attended on the lady, promising that so she brought him in such a place and hour that he might speak privily to Madame Jehane, and have his will, then he would deal so largely with her, that never in her life should she be poor.

"Certes, sir," said the crone, "you are so lovely a knight, so sweet in speech and so courteous, that verily it is my lady's duty to set her love upon you, and it will be my pleasure to toil in your service."

So the knight took forty sous from his pouch, and gave them to her that she might buy a kirtle. The old woman received them greedily, and hiding the money in a secret place promised to speak to her lady. The knight bade farewell, and went his way, but the crone tarried in that place, and when her lady entered from the church said straitly—

"Lady, for God's love, tell me truly, when my lord went to Compostella did he leave you a maid?"

"Why ask you such a question, Dame Hersent?"

"Because, lady, I believe you to be a virgin wife!"

"Certes, Dame Hersent, and that I am, nor do I know woman who would be aught else in my case."

"Lady," returned Dame Hersent, "ah, the pity of it! If you but knew the joy that women have in company of the man they love, you would say that there is no fonder happiness to be found on earth. Greatly I marvel, therefore, that you love not, *par amours,* seeing that every lady loveth with her friend. Were the thing but pleasing to you, fair falleth the chance, for well I know a knight, comely of person, sweet and wise of speech, who asks naught better than to set on you his love. Very rich is he, and lovelier far than the shamed recreant who has left you in this plight. If you are not too fearful to grant him grace, you can have of him all that you please to ask, and such joy moreover as no lady can hope for more."

Whilst the crone was speaking, the lady, who was but a woman, felt her senses stir within. Curiously she inquired who this knight should be.

"Who is he, lady? God above! one has no fear to cry his name! Who should it be but that lovely lord, so courteous, so bold, Messire Raoul, of your father's house, the sweetest heart of all the world."

"Dame Hersent," said the lady, "you will do well to let these words be, for I have no wish to do myself such wrong, neither come I of such stock as goes after shame."

"Dame," replied the old woman, "I know it well; but never can you have the joy of maid with man."

Thus ended their discourse; but presently Sir Raoul came again to the crone, and she made plain to him how she had spoken to her lady, and in what fashion she was answered.

"Dame Hersent," said the knight, "so should a virtuous lady reply; but I pray you speak again with her of this matter, for the archer does not wing the bird with a first arrow; and, stay, take these twenty sous, and buy a lining to your coat."

So that ancient dame took the gift, and wearied the lady with enticing words, but nothing came of all her proffers.

Slowly or quickly thus passed the days, till came the tidings that Sir Robert was on his way from Compostella, and was already near to Paris. Very speedily this news was noised abroad, and Sir Raoul, fearing greatly to lose his lands, again sought speech with the crone. Then said the old woman that in no wise could she snare the bird, but that for the great love she bore him this thing she would do—so he would recompense her service —namely, that she would put matters in such a case that none should be in the house save himself and the lady, and then he could act according to his pleasure, whether she would or whether she would not. So Raoul answered that he desired no other thing.

"This I will do," said the old woman. "Messire shall come again in eight days, and on that day shall my lady bathe within her bower. I will see that all her household are forth from the castle, so may you come privily to her chamber, and have your desire of her, whether she cry yea or whether she cry nay."

"You have fairly spoken," answered he.

Hard upon this came letters from Messire Robert

that he would be at the castle on Sunday. On the
Thursday, therefore, the crone caused the bath to
be heated in the bower, and the lady disarrayed herself to enter therein. Then the old woman sent
messages to Sir Raoul that he should come
speedily, and moreover she caused all the household to go forth from that place. Sir Raoul came
to the bower, and entering, saluted the lady, but
she deigned no reply to his greeting, and said—

"Sir Raoul, of a truth I thank you for this
courtesy, yet you might have asked if such a visit
would be according to my wish. Accursed may
you be for a most ungentle knight."

But Sir Raoul made reply—

"Madame, for God's sake have pity upon me, for
I die for love of you. Lady, as you hope for grace,
so grant grace to me."

"Sir Raoul," cried she, "never for pity will I
grant you this day, or any day, the grace of my
love. Know well that if you do not leave me alone
in peace certainly will I tell your lord, my father,
the honour that you require of me, for I am no such
woman as you think."

"Nay, lady, is it so indeed?"

"Yes, and very surely," replied she.

Then Sir Raoul sprang forward, and clasping
her in his arms (for he was very mighty) bore her
towards her bed. As they strove he saw beneath
her right breast a black spot upon the groin, and
thought within himself that here was certain proof
that he had had to do with her. But as he carried
her towards the bed his spurs caught within the
serge valence about the foot thereof, so that they
fell together, the lord below and the lady above;
whereupon she rose lightly to her feet, and seizing
a billet of wood from the hearth, smote him upon
the head so shrewdly that the blood dropped upon
the rushes from the wound. When Sir Raoul knew

his wound to be both deep and large no more he
desired to play, so he arose from the floor and
departed straightway from that chamber to his own
lodging, a long mile thence, and sought a surgeon
for his hurt. For her part the faithful lady called
upon Dame Hersent, and returning to her bath,
complained to her of this strange adventure with
the knight.

Very great and rich was the feast that the father
of the fair lady ordained against the home-coming
of Sir Robert. Many a lord was bidden to his
hall, and amongst these my lord, Sir Raoul, his
knight; but he sent messages that he might not
come, for reason of his sickness. On the Sunday
came Sir Robert, and was sweetly welcomed of all;
but the father of the fair lady sought out Sir Raoul,
nor would hold him excused from the feast because
of his grievous wound. Therefore he tired his face
and his wound the best that he was able, and went
to hall, where all day long the lords and ladies
sat at meat and drink, and rose for morris and to
dance.

When closed the night Sir Robert sought his
chamber, and very graciously the lady received
him, as it becometh every wife to receive her
husband. On the morrow again the guests were
gathered about the board, but after dinner uprose
Sir Raoul demanding that Messire Robert should
pay his wager, since he had had to do with his
wife, by sign and token of a certain black spot
beneath her right breast.

"Of that I know nothing," answered Sir Robert,
"for I have not looked so boldly upon her."

"I require you by the faith that you have
pledged me to take heed, and to do me justice
herein."

"That will I, truly," answered Sir Robert.

When came the night once more, then Sir Robert

observed his wife curiously, and marked the black spot upon her white body, whereat the greater grief was his.   In the morning he sought out Sir Raoul, and owned before his lord that he had lost the bet. Sick at heart was he throughout the day.   When darkness came he went to the stable, and saddling his palfrey, issued forth from the courtyard, taking with him what he might carry of his wealth.   So he set forth on the road to Paris, and coming to the city sojourned therein for some three days.   There the tale ceaseth to speak of him, and telleth of his wife.

Very dolent and right heavy was the fair lady that thus her lord had fled his house.   Very long and right greatly she considered the reason of his flight.   She wept and lamented her widowhood, even till such time as her father entered her chamber, and said that it were much better that she had never wed, since she had brought him to shame, him, and all her house, and told her how and why.   When she heard this thing she was sick of heart, and swore that never had she done such deed; but her words profited her nothing, for though a woman gave her body to be burned, yet would none believe her clean of sin, once such blame is set upon her.

Very early in the night the lady rose from the bed, and taking what wealth she had in her coffer, saddled a palfrey and took the road.   She had sheared her dainty tresses to the shoulder, and in all points was clad as a boy.   In this manner came she to Paris, seeking for her husband, for to her heart she declared that never would she give over her search until they were met together once more. So she rode at adventure, a squire searching for her lord.   Now on a morning she departed from Paris, and riding on the way to Orleans came to Tombe Isoire, and there met with Sir Robert, her husband.

Her heart was very full as she drew close and saluted him, and he rendered her greeting for greeting, saying—

"Fair friend, God give you heart's desire."

"Sir," said she, "from whence come you?"

"Certes, fair friend, I am of Hainault."

"Sir, and whither go you?"

"Forsooth, fair friend, little I know where my path may lead me, nor have I home where I may dwell. Where Fortune hales me, thither I must go, and the Dame looks not kindly on me, for I have lost the thing that most I loved in all the world, and she hath lost me. Moreover with her went house and lands that were fair and deep. But tell me, what is your name, and whither doth God bring you?"

"Certes, sir," answered Jehane, "I purpose to seek Marseilles, near by the sea, where as I hope there is noise of war. There, if I may, will I enter the service of some hardy captain and learn the trade of arms, so it be God's pleasure. For such is my plight that in nowise can I stay in my own country. To my eyes, sir, you seem a knight whom I would serve very gladly, if such was your will, nor of my fellowship could you take any harm."

"Fair friend," answered Messire Robert, "truly am I a belted knight, and in what place the battle is set, there would I gladly ride. But tell me now, what is your name?"

"Sir, my name is John."

"It is right welcome," said the knight.

"And you, sir, what is your name?"

"John, my name is Robert."

"Sir Robert, join me to your company as squire, and I will serve you to the utmost of my power."

"John, so would I do gladly, but I have so little money in my pouch, that ere three days are gone I must sell my very steed; therefore I may take no squire."

"Sir," said John, "be not troubled thereat, for God will provide, if so it seems good to Him. But where are you set to dine?"

"John, my dinner is a simple business, for I have nothing in my purse save three sous of Paris."

"Sir, be not troubled thereat, for on my part I have with me nearly ten pounds of Tournay money, and these are as your own, since your wallet is not heavy to your wish."

"Fair friend, thanks, and thanks again."

The two comrades rode at a brisk pace to Montlhery, where John found meat for his lord, and they ate together. When they had eaten they sought their chamber, the knight lying in a fair bed, and John sleeping in another, at his feet. Refreshed with sleep, John rose and did the harness upon their horses, so they mounted and passed upon their way. Journeying thus at last they lighted at Marseilles upon the Sea, but to their grief they might not hear the rumour of any war. There for the time my story ceases to speak of the two of them, and returns to Messire Raoul, that false knight, who, by leasing, had wrongly gained the land of Sir Robert.

For more than seven years did Messire Raoul hold the lands of Sir Robert against law and right. Then a sore sickness took hold upon him, and afflicted him so grievously that very near he came to death. Much he feared the wrong he had wrought to that fair lady, the daughter of his lord, and to her husband besides, for by reason of his malice were they utterly undone. So great was his sin that he dared not show the matter to the priest, but tossed upon his bed in utter unrest. On a certain day when his sickness lay too heavy upon him he bade his chaplain draw near his bed, for this priest was a wise confessor, loyal and true, and very close to the sick man's heart.   Then he spake—

"Father—my father in God, if not according to the flesh—the time is come when I must die.   For God's love give me now your counsel, as you are a ghostly man, for on my soul there lies a sin so ugly and so black that scarcely may I hope to be anealed."

The priest prayed him to speak more plainly, so that he might aid him to the utmost of his power, wherefore Sir Raoul brought himself to tell the story that you have heard.   At the end he begged the chaplain for the love of God to show him what he must do to obtain the grace of pardon for a sin so dark.

"Sir," said the priest, "be not altogether cast down, for so you are willing to do such penance as I lay upon you, I will take your sin on me and on my own soul, and you shall be clean."

"Now tell me of this penance," said the knight.

"Sir, within a year of your recovery from this sickness must you take the cross and pass beyond the sea, and in all places where men ask the reason of your pilgrimage, there you must tell the story of this bitter wrong.   Moreover, this day must you give hostages to God that thus you will do."

"All this will I do gladly."

"Sir, what rich pledge can you offer, therefore?"

"The best," replied the knight.   "You, your-self, shall be hostage and surety for me; and on my honour as a knight well will I redeem my pledge."

"Sir," said the priest, "in the hand of God am I set as your pledge."

The sick man turned from death to life, and soon was altogether healed.   A full year passed away, and yet he had not taken the cross.   Right often the holy man reminded him of his bond, but he treated the covenant as a jest.   Then the chaplain told him straitly that except he discharged him as his surety before God, he would tell the whole matter to the father of the fair lady whom he had utterly destroyed.   When the knight heard this he said to the chaplain that within six months would he seek the sea for the springtide crossing, and thereto he plighted faith.   But now the story ceases to speak of Messire Raoul, and returns to King Florus of Ausay, of whom it has told nought for a great while.

A right happy life led King Florus and his wife together, as becomes bride and groom who wed fondly in their youth, but very dolent and sore of heart were they that they might get no child.   The lady caused Masses to be sung, and was urgent in prayer for her desire, but since it was not according to the will of God, no gain she got thereby.   On a day there came to the castle of King Florus a holy hermit who dwelt deep within the great forest of Ausay, in a very desolate place.   The queen received him very gladly, and because he was a wise man and a holy, would be shriven by him of her sins.   So she bared him her secret wound, and told him of her grief that she might have no child by her lord.

"Ah, madame," said the holy man, "it becometh you patiently to suffer the pleasure of our Lord. When it is His will, then shall the barren become a joyful mother of children."

"Certes, sir," said the lady, "would that it were now, for less dear am I to my lord therefor.   Moreover the high barons of this realm cast the thing against me, and give counsel to my lord that he should put the barren woman away and take another bride."

"Truly, madame," said the holy man, "griev-

ously would he sin against God and Holy Church
by such a deed."

"Ah, sir, pray you to God for me that I may bear
a child to my lord, for much I doubt that he will
put me away."

"Madame," said the holy man, "prayers of mine
are little worth, save by the will of God, yet such
as they are you shall have them willingly."

Hardly had this holy man departed from the lady,
when the barons of the realm drew together before
the King, and counselled him that he should put
away his wife, since by her he might have no child,
and take another bride. Moreover, if he would not
abide by their counsel, then would they withdraw
their fealty, for in no case should the kingdom
remain without an heir. King Florus feared his
barons greatly, and gave credence to their word,
so he promised to send his wife to her kindred,
and prayed the lords to seek him another queen,
which thing was accorded between them. When
the lady knew thereof she was stricken to the heart,
but nothing might she do, for well she understood
that her lord was purposed to forsake her. Therefore she sent to seek that hermit who was her confessor, and when he was come she set before him
this business of the barons, and how they would
bring another wife to her husband. "So I pray
you, fair father, to aid me with counsel as to what
I must do."

"Lady," said the holy man, "if it be thus, you
must suffer it as best you may, for against king
and barons you can make no head."

"Sir," said the gentle lady, "you speak truly;
so, if it pleases God, I will dwell as an anchoress
near to you, for then shall I serve God all the
days of my life, and yet draw some stay and comfort from your presence."

"Lady," said the prudent man, "that were too

hazardous a thing, for you are too tender in years, and fair and fresh. But I will tell you what to do. Near by my hermitage is a convent of White Nuns, very quiet and devout. If you go thither, right gladly will they receive you, as well by reason of your blameless life as of your high degree."

"Sir," said she, "wisely have you spoken, and this I will do, since so you counsel me."

On the morrow King Florus spake to his wife, and said—

"Since you may have no child by me, needs must we say farewell. I tell you truly that the parting presses hardly upon me, for never again shall woman lie so nearly to my heart as you have lain."

Then might he speak no more because of tears, and the lady wept with him.

"Husband," said she, "for God's love have pity upon me, for where may I hide myself, and what may I find to do?"

"Wife, so it pleases God, your good days are not yet past, for honourably and in rich estate shall you return to your own friends in your own land."

"Lord," said the dame, "I require none of this gear. So it please you, I will bestow me in a certain convent of nuns, if it will receive me, and there I will serve God all my life; for since I lose your love I am she whose heart shall never harbour love again."

So King Florus and the lady wept together very bitterly.

On the third day the Queen set forth to her convent; and the fresh Queen came to the palace in great pomp, and held revel and festival with her friends. For four years did King Florus possess this lady, yet never might he get an heir. So now the story ceases to speak of King Florus, and turns again to Messire Robert and to John, who were come to Marseilles.

Very sad was Sir Robert when he came to the city that he might hear of no arming in all the land; so he said to John—

"What shall we do? You have lent me much money, for the which I owe you more than thanks. I will give it you again, though I have to sell my very palfrey, to discharge me of the debt."

"Sir," said John, "if it please you give heed to me, and I will show you what we have to do. There remain yet to us one hundred Tournay sous. If you grant me leave, I will turn our two good horses into better money. With this I will make French bread, for I am the lightest baker of whom you have heard, and I doubt but little that we shall gain our money and our livelihood besides."

"John," said Sir Robert, "I am content that you should do according to your will."

The next day John sold his two horses for ten pounds Tournay. With these he bought corn, and carried it to the mill. Afterwards he bought baskets and set to work at his oven to bake good French bread. So white and so fresh were these loaves of his baking that he sold more than the best baker of the town, and prospered so greatly that within two years he had put by well one hundred pounds for their need.

Then said John to his lord—

"Would it not be good to hire a fair large house, with cellarage for wine, that we might offer hostelry and lodging to wealthy folk from home?"

"John," answered Sir Robert, "your will is mine, for every reason have I for content with you."

Then John hired a house, both fair and great, and there gave lodging to honest folk, gaining money very plenteously. He clad his lord in costly raiment, so that Sir Robert bestrode his own

palfrey, and sat at meat and drink with the most
honourable of the town. Moreover John caused
his board to be furnished with all manner of wines
and store, so that his companions marvelled greatly
at the abundance thereof. With all this so bravely
did John prosper that within four years he had put
by more than three hundred pounds, besides the
furnishing of inn and bakery, which very well was
worth another fifty pounds. But here the story
ceases to speak of John and Sir Robert, and turneth
again to tell of Messire Raoul.

Now telleth the tale that the chaplain pressed Sir
Raoul right earnestly that he should pass beyond
the sea, and thus discharge his surety from the
bond, for much he feared that the knight would yet
find reason to remain. So instant was the priest
in pleading, that Sir Raoul saw well that go he
must. He made him ready for his journey, spending money without stint, and at the end set forth
upon the road, him and his three squires. He drew
presently to Marseilles-on-Sea, and there sought
lodging at the French Hostelry owned by Sir Robert
and by John. When John set eyes upon him he
knew him well, because he had seen him many
times, and for reason of the scar of the wound that
he had given him. The knight sojourned in the
town for fifteen days, till he might find passage in
some vessel going oversea. Whilst he was dwelling at the inn John took him apart and asked him
of the purpose of his journey, whereat Messire
Raoul told him openly all the occasion thereof, just
as the tale hath related already. John listened to
his story, but answered naught for good or evil.
Presently Sir Raoul caused his harness and his
gear to be bestowed on the nave, and mounted in
the ship, but for eight days it might not depart
from forth the harbour. On the ninth day the
vessel sailed from port on its way to the Holy

Sepulchre. Thus Sir Raoul did his pilgrimage,
and there made honest confession of his sins.   In
sign of penitence his confessor charged him strictly
to restore to the knight and his lady the fief he held
in scorn of law and right; and Sir Raoul promised
straitly that when he came again to his own land he
would carry out the wishes of his heart.   So parting
from Jerusalem he voyaged to Acre, and took
passage in the first homing ship, as a man who
desires above all things to look upon the face of his
own country. He adventured on the sea, and fared
so speedily, by night as by day, that in less than
three months he cast anchor at the port of Aigues
Mortes. Parting from the harbour he stayed not till
he was come to Marseilles, where he rested eight
days at the inn owned by Sir Robert and John,
which inn men called the French Hostelry; but Sir
Robert did not recall him to mind, for he thought
but little of Sir Raoul. At the end of eight days he
set forth from Marseilles with his three squires,
and at length returned to his own home, where his
household received him gladly, for he was a great
lord, very rich in land and in store. His chaplain
inquired of him if any had asked the reason for his
journey.

"Yes," said he, "in three places, to wit, Marseilles, Acre, and Jerusalem. Moreover that priest
who shrived me counselled me to give back his
lands to my lord, Sir Robert, so I may find him, or
if I may not hear of him, to his wife or his heirs."

"Certes," said the chaplain, "he gave you godly
counsel."

So Messire Raoul dwelt in his own house for a
great while in peace and ease; and there the tale
ceaseth to speak of him, and returns to Messire
Robert and to John.

Sir Robert and John dwelt as citizens in Marseilles for the space of six years. At the end of

six years had they put by in a sure place the sum of six hundred pounds. John and his business prospered exceedingly, for so gentle was he and diligent, that he was beloved of all his neighbours. Men spake almost too well of him, and he maintained his lord in such estate and worship that it was marvellous to see. When the end of the seventh year drew near, John sought occasion to speak soberly to Sir Robert his lord, and said—

"Sir, we have dwelt a great while in this city, and have been so fortunate in our dealings that we have gained nearly six hundred pounds in money and in silver vessels."

"Certes," said Sir Robert, "all this, John, is not mine, but yours, for you have earned it."

"Sir," said John, "saving your grace, it is not mine, but yours, for you are my own true lord, and never, please God, will I take another."

"John, I thank you heartily," said Robert. "I hold you not as servant, but as comrade and as friend."

"Sir," said John, "all my days have I given you loyal service, and so will I ever do."

"By my faith," said Sir Robert, "what you require of me, that is my pleasure. But as to returning to my own country, I know not what to say. So much have I lost there that never can it be made up to me."

"Sir," answered John, "fret not over your loss, for, so God pleases, you shall hear good news when you come into your own land. And be not fearful of anything, for in whatever place we shall be, please God, I shall gather enough for me and for you."

"Certes, John," said Sir Robert, "I will do that which pleases you, and lodge wheresoe'er you will."

I

"Sir," said John, "now will I sell our goods and make ready for the journey, for we shall part within fifteen days."

So John sold all the fair furnishing of his houses, and bought thereout three horses, a palfrey for his lord, another for himself, and a pack horse for the road. Then they bade farewell to their neighbours and to the most worshipful citizens of the town, who grieved sorely at their going.

Sir Robert and John travelled so hardily that in less than three weeks they drew to their own country, and Sir Robert caused it to be told to his lord, whose daughter he had wedded, that he was near at hand. The lord was merry at heart, for much he hoped that his daughter might be with her husband; and so she was, but hid in the trappings of a squire.

The lord greeted Robert warmly, but when he could learn no tidings of his daughter, his mirth was turned into sorrow; nevertheless he made a rich banquet for Sir Robert, and bade his knights and his neighbours to the feast. Amongst these came Sir Raoul who held Sir Robert's land in his despite. Great was the merriment on that day and the morrow, and during all this joy Sir Robert told to John the story of his wager, and of the manner in which Sir Raoul spoiled him of his land.

"Sir," said John, "challenge him to combat as a false traitor, and I will fight the battle in your stead."

"John," said Sir Robert, "this you shall not do."

Thus they left the matter till the morrow, when John came to Sir Robert, and said that he was purposed to speak to the father of his wife. So they sought the lord, and John spake him thus—

"Sir, you are, after God, the lord of my master Sir Robert, who in the years that are gone married

your child. As you know, a wager was made
between him and Sir Raoul, who said that ere Sir
Robert came home from St. James's shrine he
would gain the lady to his wish. Sir Raoul spake
falsely, and is a most disloyal and traitor knight,
for never had he part or share in your daughter's
love. All which I am ready to prove upon his
body."

Then Robert strode forth and said—

"John, fair friend, this business is mine alone,
nor because of it shall you hang shield about your
neck."

So Sir Robert held forth his gage to his lord,
and Sir Raoul tendered gage of battle in return,
though but fearfully; for needs must he defend
himself, or be proclaimed recreant and traitor.
Thus were the pledges given, and the day for the
ordeal by battle pronounced to be fifteen days
thence without appeal.

Now hearken well to this strange story of John,
and what he did. John, who more sweetly was
named Madame Jehane, had in the house of her
father a certain cousin, who was a fair demoiselle
of some twenty-five years. To this cousin Jehane
went and discovered the whole matter, telling her
all the story, from the first thing to the last. She
prayed her, moreover, to keep the business hidden,
until such time and hour as she should make herself known to her father. The cousin—to whom
Jehane was very well known—promised readily to
conceal the matter, saying that never should the
secret be made plain by her fault. Then was the
chamber of her cousin made fresh and ready for
Madame Jehane. Therein for the two weeks before
the battle Jehane bathed and perfumed her, and
took her ease as best she might, for well had she
reason to look her fairest. Also she caused women
to shape closely to her figure four goodly gowns;

one was of scarlet, one of vair, one of peacock blue, and one of trailing silk. Thus with rest and peace she came once more to the fulness of her beauty, and was so dainty, fresh and fair, that no lady showed her peer in all the world.

As for Sir Robert, very greatly was he discomforted during all these fifteen days at the loss of John his squire, for he knew nothing of his fate. Nevertheless on the appointed day he got himself into his harness, and prepared him for the battle stoutly and with a good heart.

On the appointed day the two knights entered within the lists together. Drawing apart for a little space, they rushed furiously the one on the other, and gave such mighty strokes with the blades of their great swords that their horses were borne to the ground beneath them. Sir Raoul was wounded lightly in the left side, so Sir Robert getting first upon his feet came swiftly to him, and smote him with all his force upon the helm. So mighty was the blow that the sword sheared clear through the helmet to the coif of steel, but the coif was so strong that the head was not wounded; nevertheless of that stroke he reeled so that had he not caught at his saddle, certainly he had fallen to the earth. Then Sir Raoul, who was a very stout champion, struck Sir Robert so fiercely upon the headpiece that he was all bemused, and the sword glancing downwards upon the shoulder hacked off the mail of the hauberk, but did him no hurt. Thereat Sir Robert smote him again with all the strength that he was able, and the blow lighting upon the buckler carried away a quarter of the shield. When Sir Raoul knew the hardiness of his foe much he feared for the issue of the combat, and well he wished himself once more beyond the sea, and Sir Robert settled safely on his land. However, he put forward all his prowess, and

pressed Sir Robert so grimly that with one great
stroke he clove to the boss upon the very middle
of Sir Robert's shield. For his part Sir Robert
struck fairly at Sir Raoul's helm, but he thrust
his shield before him, and that mighty blow
passing clean through the buckler came full upon
the charger's neck, so that horse and rider
tumbled to the ground. Messire Raoul climbed
stoutly to his feet, as a valiant man who had often
ridden with the spears, but Sir Robert lighted
from his steed, for he would not deign to fight at
vantage with a foe on foot.

Now strove the two knights together, hand to
hand, in such fashion that shield and helm and
hauberk were hewn in pieces, and the blood ran
from their bodies by reason of their trenchant
glaives. Had they been able to deal such blows
as in the first passage of their arms, very quickly
both one and the other had been slain, for of their
shields scarce enough held together to cover their
gauntlets. The fear of death or shame was now
before their eyes, and the nearness of their persons
summoned them to bring this judgment to an end.
Sir Robert gripped his sword in both hands, and
with all the greatness of his strength smote Sir
Raoul upon the helm. Half the shattered headpiece fell upon his shoulders, and the sword cutting through the coif made a grisly wound. So
bewildered was Sir Raoul at the stroke that he was
beaten to the knee; but he rose lightly again,
though, since he knew that his head was naked,
very fearful was he of death. He ran therefore
at Sir Robert, smiting with all his power at the
remnants of his shield. Through shield and
helmet went the glaive to the depth of full three
fingers, but the wearied sword coming full upon
the coif of steel brake in pieces, for the armourer's
work was very strong. When Sir Raoul looked

upon the shards of his sword, and remembered
that his head was naked, much he doubted of his
end.   Nevertheless he stooped to the ground, and
seizing a great stone in both his hands flung it at
Sir Robert with all his might.   Sir Robert stepped
aside quickly, avoiding the cast, and ran in upon
his adversary, who turned his back and took to
flight about the lists.   So Sir Robert cried that
save his foe admitted himself recreant and shamed
he would slay him with the sword.

"Gentle knight," answered Sir Raoul, "I yield
thee what remaineth of my sword, and throw
myself entirely on thy grace. Show mercy on me,
gentle knight, and pray thy lord and mine that he
have pity upon me, and spare my life. Take back
thy land that I have held against both law and
right, and therewith take my own; for all I said
against that fair and spotless lady was just foul
lies."

When my lord, Sir Robert, heard these words he
thought within himself that Sir Raoul might do
no more.   Therefore he prayed his lord so urgently
to pardon Sir Raoul for this felony, that his
prayer was accorded on such terms that Sir Raoul
should abide over sea for all his days.

In such fashion Sir Robert won back his land,
and added that of Sir Raoul besides. But in this
thing he found little comfort, for grief of heart
over the fair and faithful lady from whom he had
parted. Moreover, in no wise could he forget
John, his squire, who was lost to him also.   His
lord, too, shared in his sorrow, for reason that
he might never gain tidings of his one fair
child.

But Madame Jehane, who had spent two weeks
in her cousin's chamber in all ease and comfort,
when she heard that her husband had gained the
battle, was greatly content. As we know, she had

caused her women to shape closely to her person
four goodly gowns, and of these she arrayed herself in the most rich, which was of cloth of silk,
banded with fine Arabian gold. So shapely was
she of body, so bright of face, and so gracious
of address that nothing more lovely could be found
in all the world, so that her very cousin, even,
marvelled at her exceeding beauty. For the bathing, the tiring, and ease of mind and body of the
past fifteen days had given her back her early
freshness, as was wonderful to see. Very sweet,
very ravishing showed Madame Jehane in her
silken robe banded with gold. So when she was
ready she called to her cousin, and said—

"How seem I to thee?"

"Why, dame, the prettiest person in all the
world."

"Now, fair cousin, I will tell thee what thou
shalt do. Go thou straight to my father, and tell
him to be heavy no more, but rather merry and
glad, because thou bringest him good news of his
daughter. Tell him that she is sound and well,
and that so he come with thee, he shall see her
with his eyes. Then lead him here, and he will
greet me again, I deem, right willingly."

The maiden answered that gladly would she give
the message, so she sought out the father of
Madame Jehane, and said as she was bidden.
When the lord heard thereof he wondered at this
strange thing, and going after the damsel found
his daughter in her chamber. When he saw her
face he cast his arms about her neck, shedding
tears of joy and pity, yea, such was his happiness
that scarcely could he find a word. When he
might speak he asked where she had been so long
a while.

"Fair father," said the lady, "you shall hear it
in good time. But, for the love of God, cause my

mother to come to me speedily, for I die till I see her once again."

The lord sent incontinent for his wife, and when she was come into the chamber where her daughter lay, and saw and knew her face, straight she fell down in a swoon for joy, and might not speak for a great space. But when her senses were come to her again no man could conceive the joy and festival she made above her child.

Whilst mother and daughter held each other fast, the father of the fair lady went in quest of Sir Robert, and meeting him said thus—

"Fair sweet son, very joyful news have I to share with you."

"Certes," said Sir Robert, "of joy have I great need, but God alone can help my evil case, for sad at heart am I for the loss of my sweet wife, and sad, besides, for the loss of him who did me more good than any other in the world, for John, my faithful squire."

"Sir Robert," said the lord, "spoil not your life for John; squires can be met with at every turning. But as to your wife, I have a certain thing to tell, for I come from her but now, and know well that she is the most peerless lady in all the world."

When Messire Robert heard this he fell a-trembling with joy, and said to his lord—

"Ah, sir, for God's love bring me to see that this is true!"

"Right willingly," said the lord, "come now with me."

The lord went before and Robert followed after, till they were come to the chamber where mother and daughter yet clasped each other close, weeping with joy the one upon the other. When they knew their husbands near they drew apart, and as soon as Sir Robert saw his wife he ran to her with

open arms, and embraced her. So they kissed each
the other with many little kisses, and wept for joy
and pity. Yea, they held each to the other in this
fashion whilst a man might run ten acres of land,
nor ceased enlacing. Then the lord commanded
that the tables should be spread for supper; so
they ate with mirth and merriment.

After supper, when the songs and the dances
were done, they went to their beds, neither was
Sir Robert parted from the Lady Jehane, for they
were right happy to be met together again, and
talked of many things. At the last Sir Robert
asked of her where she had been so great a time,
and she said—

"Husband, it is over long a story to tell, but
you shall hear it all at a more convenient season.
Tell me, rather, what you have done, and where
you have been all this while."

"Wife," said Sir Robert, "I will tell you
gladly."

So he told her all the tale she knew by rote,
and of John his squire, who gained him bread,
and said that so distressed was he at the loss of his
companion that never would he give over the
search till he had found him, yea, that he would
saddle with the morn and part.

"Husband," said the lady, "that would be mad-
ness. Are you set again to leave me, and what
shall I do thereof?"

"Certes, lady, I can do none other; for never
man did such things for his friend as he has done
for me."

"Husband," said the wife, "what he did for you
was but his duty; he did no more than what he
should have done."

"Wife," said Messire Robert, "by your speech
you should have known him."

"Truly," answered the lady, "truly, I should

know him well, for never aught of what he did
was hid from me."

"Lady," said Sir Robert, "I marvel at such
words."

"Sir," said she, "there is no need for wonder.
If I tell you, yea and verily, that such a thing
is true, will you honestly believe my word?"

"Wife," said he, "on my honour."

"Believe, then, what I am about to tell you, for
know assuredly that I am that very John whom
you would seek, and this is how it happed. When
I was told the matter of the wager, and of the
treason of Messire Raoul; when, too, I knew that
you were fled because of your grief at my faith-
lessness, and by reason of the land that for ever
you had lost, then was I more cast down than any
woman since woman first was made. So I clipped
my hair close to my head, and taking all the
money in my chest, about ten pounds Tournay, I
arrayed me in the guise of a squire, and followed
after you to Paris, coming up with you at Tombe
Isoire. From there we companied together, even
to Marseilles, where I served you as my own liege
lord for near seven years, nor do I grudge you
varlet's service. And know for truth that I am
innocent and clean of that deed the foul knight
fastened upon me, as clearly now appears, for he
has been put to shame in open field, and has
publicly confessed his treason."

Having spoken thus, Madame Jehane embraced
Sir Robert, her lord, and kissed him very sweetly
on the mouth. When Messire Robert was persuaded that she, indeed, was John, his faithful
squire, his joy was greater far than thought or
words may express, and much he marvelled that
so high a lady could prove so lowly and so service-
able. For which thing he loved her the more
dearly all the days of his life.

Thus came together these two parted lovers; thus, on their own domain, which was both broad and fair, they lived a happy life, as becometh lovers in their youth. Often Sir Robert rode to tournaments in the train of his lord, and much honour he gained and such wealth, moreover, that his land became twice as great as that he had. After the death of the father and mother of Lady Jehane he became the heir to all their substance. So stout a knight was he, that by his prowess he was made a double banneret, and was worth four thousand pounds in land. Yet always must he be a childless man, to his exceeding grief, though for more than ten years he was with his wife after the combat with Sir Raoul.

After the term of ten years, by the will of God—which is mightier than the strength of man—the pains of death gat hold upon him. He met death like a brave knight, assoiled by the rites of Holy Church, and was laid in his grave with great honour. His wife, the fair lady, mourned so grievously upon him, that all about her felt pity for her sorrow. Yet, during the days, the sharpness of her grief was assuaged, and she came to take a little comfort, though as yet it was but a little.

The Lady Jehane bore herself during her widowhood as a devout and kindly lady, devoted to God and Holy Church. Very humble was she and right charitable, dearly cherishing the poor and needy. So good was she that no tongue might say aught of her but praise; and so fair that all who looked upon her owned that she was the mirror of all ladies in the world for beauty and for virtue. But now for a little space the tale ceases to speak of her, and returns to tell of King Florus, for it has been dumb of him o'erlong.

King Florus of Ausay lay at his own castle

sorely grieved and vexed at the departure of his first wife, for she whom the barons had seated in her chair, though fresh and gracious, might not bring that peace of heart which was that lady's gift. Four years they lived together, yet never might have an heir. At the end thereof the pains of death seized the lady, so she was buried amidst the weeping of her friends, and with such fair state and service as were fitting to the dignity of a queen.

King Florus remained a widower for above two years. He was yet a young man, for he was no more than forty-five years of age, and his barons prayed him that he would seek another wife.

"Certes," answered King Florus, "I desire not greatly to do this thing, for I have had two wives, yet might not get an heir by either. Moreover the first wife that I had was so virtuous and so fair, and so dearly did I love her in my heart for her exceeding goodlihead, that never is she absent from my thoughts. I tell you truly that never again will I wed till I may meet a woman sweet and good as she. God rest her soul, for as I hear she passed away in that White convent where she was withdrawn."

"Ah, sire," said a knight who was in his private counsel, "many a comely dame goes about the realm whom you have never seen. One at least I know who for kindness and for beauty has not her like in all the world. If you but saw her fairness, if you but knew her worth, you would own that fortunate indeed were he—yea, though a king —who might own such rich treasure. She is a gentlewoman, discreet, and rich in money and in lands, and, if you will, I can tell you many a tale of her discretion and of her worth."

The King replied that gladly would he hear; so

the knight related how the lady set out to follow
after her lord, how she came up with him and
brought him to Marseilles, and the many kind-
nesses and the great services she rendered him,
just as the tale hath told before. Thereat King
Florus marvelled much, and said privily to the
knight that very gladly would he become the
husband of such a wife.

"Sire," answered the knight, who was near
neighbour to Madame Jehane, "I will seek the
lady, if such is your good pleasure, and will speak
her so fairly, if I may, that in marriage you twain
may be one."

"Yea," said King Florus, "get you speedily to
horse, and I pray you to be diligent in your
embassy."

The knight passed straightway upon his errand,
and without any tarrying came to the land where
dwelt that lovely lady whom the tale calls Madame
Jehane. He found her in a certain castle of hers,
and she welcomed him gladly as a neighbour and
a friend. When they might have some private
speech together, the knight conveyed to her the
commandment of King Florus, that she should
ride to him and be wedded as his wife. When the
lady heard his word she smiled more sweetly than
ever siren sang, and answered softly to the
knight—

"Your king knows less of women, nor is he so
courteous, as fame has bruited, to command that I
should hasten to him that he may take me as his
wife. Certes, I am not a handmaid to ride to him
for wages. But tell your king rather to come to
me if he finds my love so desirable and sweet, and
woo me to receive him as husband and as spouse.
For truly the lord should pray and require the lady,
and not the lady the lord."

"Lady," answered the knight, "all that you have

told me will I tell him again; but I doubt that he
will come for pride."

"Sir knight," said the lady, "he will do the
thing that pleases him; but in this matter he shows
neither courtesy nor reason."

"Lady," said the knight, "in God's name, so let
it be. With leave I take farewell to seek my lord
the King, and will tell him as I am bidden. So if
there is any over-word give it me before I part."

"Yea," said the lady. "Take to him my greeting, and add my fairest thanks for the honour to
which he calls me."

The knight parted from the lady forthwith, and
on the fourth day returned to King Florus of
Ausay, whom he found in his chamber, deep in
business with his privy council. The knight
saluted the King, who gave him his salutation
again, and seating him by his side, asked how it
chanced in this matter of the lady. Then the
knight gave the message with which she charged
him; how she would not come, for she was no
kitchen-maid to haste at his bidding for her wages;
but that rather should a lord pray and require of a
lady; how that she sent him her fairest greeting,
and her sweetest thanks for the honour he craved
of her.

When King Florus heard these words, he pondered in his seat, nor did any man speak for a
great space.

"Sire," said a knight, who was of his inmost
mind, "what do you consider so deeply? Certes,
all these words most richly become a discreet and
virtuous lady, and—so help me God—she is both
wise and brave. In good faith you will do well
to fix upon a day when you can seek her, and send
her greetings and letters that on such a day you
will arrive to do her honour, and to crave her as
your bride."

"Certes," said King Florus, "I will send her letters that I will lie at her castle for Easter, and that she make all ready to receive her husband and her King."

Then King Florus bade the knight who was his messenger to prepare himself within three days to carry these tidings to his lady. On the third day the knight set forth, and, riding hard, brought messages to the lady that the King would spend Easter at her castle. So she answered that since it was God's will it was woman's too, and that she would take counsel with her friends, and would array herself to receive him as the honour of a lady and his greatness required. At these words the knight returned to his lord, King Florus, and gave him the answer of the fair lady as you have heard. So King Florus of Ausay made him ready for his journey, and with a great company set forth to the country of this fair dame. When he was come there he took and married her with great pomp and festival. Then he brought her to his own realm, where she was welcomed of all most gladly. And King Florus joyed exceedingly over his wife because of her great beauty, and because of the right judgment and high courage that were in her.

Within the year that the King had taken her to wife the fair Jehane was delivered of a daughter, and afterwards she rejoiced as the mother of a son. The boy was named Florence, and the girl Flora. The boy Florence was very goodly to see, and after he was made knight was esteemed the hardiest warrior of his day, insomuch that he was chosen to be Emperor of Constantinople. A mighty prince was he, and wrought great mischief and evil to the Paynims. As to the Princess Flora, she became the Queen of her father's realm, and the son of the King of Hungary took her as wife, so was she lady of two kingdoms.

Such honour as this God gave to the fair lady because of her true and loyal heart. For many years King Florus lived happily with his virtuous wife, and when it was the will of God that his days should end, he took back to his Maker a stainless soul. The lady endured to live but six months after him, and departed from this world as became so good and loyal a dame with a quiet mind.

Here finishes the tale of King Florus and the fair Jehane.

OF THE COVETOUS MAN AND OF
THE ENVIOUS MAN

ONCE upon a time, more than one hundred years
ago, there lived two companions, who spent their
days together very evilly. The one of these comrades was so brimmed with envy, that you might
find no heart so rank with the gall of bitterness.
The other was so filled with covetousness, that
nothing sufficed of all that could be given to him.
Now covetousness is so foul a vice, that often she
bringeth many men to shame. Covetousness lendeth out her money upon usury, and deceiveth with
her balances, so that he who lendeth may have the
greater gain. But envy is the worser sin, since she
grudges joy to others, and is desirous of all the
wealth of all the world.

On a day the envious man and the covetous man
were about their business together, and they came
upon St. Martin walking in the fields. But the
saint had been but a little space in their company
when he perceived very clearly the evil desires that
were rooted in the hidden places of their hearts.
Thus they fared till they lighted on two beaten
paths, one going this way, and the other that, and
a chapel stood between the ways. There St. Martin
stayed his steps, and beckoned to these evil-minded
men.

"Lords," said he, "I take this path to the right
that I may enter within the church. I am St.
Martin, who bestowed his cloak on the beggar, and
that you may always keep in mind this meeting I
will give, in turn, to each of you a gift. He who

K   129

makes known to me his prayer shall have his desire granted forthwith. But to him who refrains from words, straightway shall be given twice as much as is bestowed upon his fellow."

So when St. Martin was gone, the covetous man considered within himself that if he left his companion to require a gift, he would receive twice as much as him, and sweetly enjoy a double gain.

"Make your prayer, fair fellow, to the holy saint," said he, "for very surely you will receive of him all that you may ask. Ask largely of him, for he will largely give. If you go prudently about the matter you will be wealthy all your life."

But he whose heart was brimmed with venom and envy dared not to ask according to his desire, for reason that he feared to die of grief and malice that his comrade's portion should be larger than his. Thus for a great while they kept their tongues from speech, turning the business over, this way and that.

"Wait no longer, lest a mischief befall you," cried at last the covetous man. "Yea you or nay you, I must have the double of your share, for all your cunning and caution. Ask, or I will beat you more grievously than ever yet was beaten donkey at Pont."

"Sire," answered the envious man, "pray I will, since it is better to receive a gift than stripes. If I require of the saint, money or houses or lands, very surely will you receive of his bounty twice that he giveth to me. But, so I am able, of all these shall you get nothing. Holy St. Martin, I pray and require of your clemency that I may lose one of my eyes, so that my fellow may lose both of his; thus shall he be pained and grieved in double measure."

Very careful was the saint to observe his covenant, and of four eyes these comrades lost three,

since the envious man became one-eyed, and the
covetous man a poor blind beggar. Thus these fair
friends were ruined by their gain. But sorrow may
he have who lets his heart be troubled by their
wretched plight, for these men were not of sterling
gold, but of false alloy.

OF A JEW WHO TOOK AS SURETY THE IMAGE OF OUR LADY

So many marvels are written of the sweet miracles of Our Lady, that amongst them I scarce know which to choose. Yet, alas! I have not that long leisure to set them forth before you every one. Then must it be with me as with him who walks abroad through summer meadows deep in flowers. Before, behind, on either side, he sees the countless blossoms of the field. Blue, vermeil, gold, they dance upon the green. Then, since he may not gather all, he plucks a rose, a lily, here and there, as he may find them to his hand. So from amongst the number of Our Lady's lovely deeds I pluck a leaf, one here, one there, and wreathe this artless garland, lest I have naught to cast before her feet.

In days long past—as the scribe hath truly written—there lived in the strong city of Byzantium a certain citizen, who held Our Lady very dear. Rich he was, and of great worship, because of his wealth and of the praise of men. To keep his station in the eyes of his fellows, he spent his substance so largely, and thereto so wantonly, that in a little while he had wasted all his goods, and naught remained to do but that he must sell his very lands. Yet so rich of heart was this burgess that not poverty even might make him knot his purse. He still kept open house, and gave goodly cheer to all, ever borrowing more and more, spending and vending, wasting and hasting to scatter everything he had. For of poverty he had neither

heed nor fear, so long as he might find a man to
lend. But at the last he was utterly undone. All
his friends passed him by when they saw how
deeply he was sunk in debt, and that to no lender
did he e'er repay what he owed. For he who bor-
rows, never paying back again, neither seeking
from others that which is his due, very quickly
loses his credit, yea, though he be the King of
France.

The good citizen was sore vexed, and knew not
what to do or say, when he found that his creditors
pressed him hardly, and that he was wholly disap-
pointed of those friends in whom he put his trust.
Sore was his sorrow, deep his distress, and bitter
his shame, his wrath and sadness, when by no
means whatever might he grant his customary
bounty, nor of his charity give alms and benefits
to the poor. So long as he was a man of worship,
with store of gold and silver, great were his doles
to those of low estate. But such was the malice
wherewith Dame Fortune pursued him, and such
the shame and loss she set upon him, that he had
nothing left to give to others, or to keep for himself. And since Dame Fortune looked upon him
with a frowning countenance, there was none to
welcome him with a smiling face.

Now this unhappy burgess knew not what to
do, for some of his acquaintance gazed the other
way, whilst men, to whom he had done naught but
good, jested upon him openly in the street.
Doubtless such is the way of the world to those
honest folk who are cast beneath at the turn of
Fortune's wheel. Therefore those to whom he had
shown the greatest kindness requited him with the
utmost despite, counting him viler than a dog; and
those, who in his day of prosperity loved and
affected his company, were the very men who now
mocked and despised him. Well say the Scrip-

tures, Put not your trust in man. For in these
days faith is so rare and so forgetful, that the son
fails the father in his peril, and the mother may
not count upon her maid. Mad is he who
strips himself for others, for so soon as he comes
before them naked, then they cry, "Beggar,
begone!"

When this citizen, who for so long a while had
known such great honour, saw himself so scorned,
and found that in all the town he had neither kinsman nor friend, he knew not what to say or do,
nor whom to take for counsel in his need. So,
by the will of God, he turned in his despair to a
certain Jew, the richest in all the city. Him he
sought out straightway, with a face aflame, and
said—

"Master Jew, here is my case. All my daughters,
all my sons, all my friends, and, very surely, all of
those to whom I have done most good in this
world, have failed me utterly and every one. I am
stripped of all my substance. Foolish have I been,
and unlucky, since I wasted all I had on those very
clerks and laymen who desert me now. I am a
merchant of great knowledge, and so you will lend
me of your treasure, I count to gain so largely,
that never shall I have to pray another for a loan;
for of your wealth will I make such usage that all
will think the more of me thereby."

"Because you have dealt so generously with
others," answered the Jew, "in this very hour will
I lend you freely of my moneys if you can give me
pledge or surety for them."

But the Christian made answer to him—

"Fair, sweet friend, all my kinsfolk and acquaintance have cast me utterly behind them, neither
care they for me any more, notwithstanding that
they thrive by reason of my gifts and toil. I can
offer no kinsman as surety, nor have I a friend

in the world. But though I can give neither pledge
nor surety, strive how I may, yet I swear to you
now on my faith and conscience, that, without
fail, I will repay you your loan and your substance
on the very day that the debt becomes due."

"If things are thus, I can lend you nothing,"
answered the Jew; "for grievously I doubt that you
may not carry out your bargain."

"Fair, sweet friend," he made reply, "since then
I neither have, nor think to have, a pledge to offer,
take now in pledge, I pray you, my Maker, in
whom is all my faith, this Jesus Christ, the King
of Heaven, the King of kings, the God of gods.
If you have not your money returned on the very
day that you shall name, I swear to you by God,
fair brother Jew, and by His Mother, so tender
and so dear, that I will become your villein and
your serf, in such wise and fashion as any other
slave of yours; so that with a ring about my neck
you may sell me in the market-place, just as any
brute beast."

Now in his heart the Jew greatly desired and
longed to make this Christian his bondsman.
Therefore, laughing, he replied—

"I believe but little that Jesus Christ, the son of
Mary, whom our forefathers crucified on a cross
of wood, was truly God. But inasmuch as He was
doubtless a holy man, and a prophet of mighty
name, if you will put Him in pledge in such manner that you will serve me all your life should you
fail me in this our bargain, why, I will take your
pledge without demur."

"Fairly have you spoken," said he, "by my
soul. Let us go straightway to the church of Our
Lady, the most glorious Mother of God."

A great company of Christians and of Jews went
with them to the church, and many a clerk and
layman was witness to their device and covenant.

Without any delay, the wretched merchant kneeled him down before the Statue, whilst the hot tears rushed to his eyes, and over-ran and wetted all his face, because of the poverty which drove him to this deed. The unhappy man knew not what to do in his plight, but he cast his burden upon the Lord, and, weeping, prayed God's precious Mother that she would deign to set wretchedness and bondage far from him. But very fearful was he, and sore adread in his heart.

When he had prayed his prayer to Our Lady, he sprang lightly to his feet, and said—

"Friend Jew, by my soul see here my Surety. In giving you this Child and this Image, I give you Jesus Christ, Himself, as pledge. He created me, and He fashioned me. 'Tis He Who is my bond for your moneys. A richer pledge you may not think to have, so help me God, now and for evermore."

He placed the hand of the Child in that of the Jew, and forthwith delivered the pledge and plighted faith. Then, yet upon his knees, most pitifully, with eyes all wet, he cried aloud in the hearing of Christian and of Jew—

"Fair Lord God, most merciful, most mighty and most sure, at the end of this business, I beseech Thee with clasped hands, fair, kindest Father, that by the pleadings of Thy sweet Mother, if it should happen that on the appointed day for any cause I may not give again the wealth I owe the Jew, then of Thy courtesy pay Thou my debt, and without an hour's delay redeem Thy pledge and faith. For if but one single day I fail to keep faith, then his serf must I be all the days of my life, save only that I break my oath sworn on this Image."

He rose lightly to his feet, though with a tearful face, and the Jew straightway counted out to him a great sum of money, to deal with in the future as he had dealt with his own. But he had lost the desire to play, for he remembered too plainly that of such mirth comes bitterness. The scalded man hates boiling water, and well he knew, and clearly he perceived, that he who is in rags goes shivering in the wind.

The honest merchant—whom God kept in charge—went forth with a light heart, that leaped and fluttered in his breast, because of the wealth he had in seisin. He bargained for a bark that lay in harbour, and since he had much skill in such business, he stored the ship with divers kinds of merchandise. Then putting his trust in God, and commending body and goods to His keeping, he hoisted sail, and set forth upon the water. He voyaged to divers lands, and trafficked with the merchants thereof to such purpose, that before the year had gone by he was no more in dread of beggary. God increased his store, so that he prospered in every market. But the gains and riches of the merchant in nowise made him grudging of his substance. Freely was given to him, freely he gave to others, for the love of God Who for every man ripens His harvest.

In a short while the merchant became very rich. One market opened another market, and money made more money. So greatly did his substance multiply that at the end, the story tells us, he might not keep the count of his wealth. So to set field by field, and house by house, he travelled in many strange lands. One day darkened, and the next day dawned, but he never gave thought to that certain day when he must return to the Jew the loan of which he had made so fruitful a use. He called it not to mind until there was but one single day between him and the appointed time, and as it chanced he bethought him thereof when

he was at sea. He well-nigh swooned when the
day came to his heart and memory.

"Ah, gentle Lady of the King of Glory! sweet
Maid and debonair!" cried he; "unhappy wretch,
what can I do?"

So sore was his grief that with clenched hands
he beat upon his breast, and presently with locked
teeth fell fainting to the deck, where he lay sense-
less for a great space. The sailors ran to his
succour, and, pressing about him, cried out and
lamented his evil case, for certainly they deemed
that he was dead. Passing heavy were they at this
sad mischance, for not one word could they draw
from his lips, nor for all their pains might they
find in him either pulse or breath. When he was
returned a little from his swoon, he addressed himself to prayer, weeping and sighing for a great
while, because for grief he found no words to say.

"Alas!" cried he, "alas, my luckless lot! What
a besotted merchant have I been! How foully has
misfortune stolen upon me! How has the Adversary beguiled me, and snared my thoughts, that I
might not better mark the appointed day! Surely
on the tables of my heart should it have been
written that for pledge I gave Jesus Christ, and
His Mother, sweet and dear. Alas! very right is
it that I should go heavy, and that my heart should
be sick and sad, since never by day nor by night
have I taken thought how to return that mighty
debt which so affrights me now. Affrighted, alas!
much cause have I to fear. Were a bird now to
quit the ship, yet should he not wing to Byzantium in thirty days—no, nor in forty. Foul fall the
day, for I am quite undone. Alas! for the shame
I have brought upon my kin. Very great riches
are very little worth, since thus am I snared and
taken."

In this manner the good merchant made his

complaint, and with many sighs bewailed his wretched plight. But when he had eased his heart with words, the Holy Spirit wrought upon him, so that his courage came to him again, and he said—

"What is here for tears? Rather should I take comfort in that He, Who hath power over all, is holden as my pledge. Let me place the matter in His mighty hand, nor concern myself overmuch with what is His business more than mine. I owe the money, but He will pay my debt; and thus by His balm shall I be healed. On the morrow must I repay the money that I owe, but there is yet a full night before the money need be counted to the Jew. I will not concern myself greatly with this matter, but commend myself humbly to His will. No other thing is there to do, for none can deliver me from my trouble, save Him alone. He is my Surety, and very surely will He discharge me from this debt, for without Him there is no redemption."

Then straightway the merchant took a strong, clamped coffer, and sealed within it the debt which he must now restore the Jew. Without waiting for the morrow, he cast it into the sea with his own hand, and with tears commended it to that great Lord and God Who holds every man in His good keeping, and to Whom earth and sea are ministers and servants alike. So He Who is of such high and puissant majesty, that naught He wills to do is burdensome or heavy to Him, was pleased to steer that coffer with its precious load of besants through the waters, so that it made more than a thousand leagues in that one night. Thus with the dawn it drew right to Byzantium, and on the appointed day the casket and the treasure came to the shore.

Now by the will of God it chanced that the rich Jew, who lent the Christian of his moneys, lived in a fair dwelling near by the sea. A certain

servant of his rose early from his bed to walk on
the shore in the cool summer dawn, and spied the
casket, which had but just drawn to land. So,
without taking off his raiment, he sprang into the
sea that he might lay hold upon it; but he was not
able, for the coffer tossed grievously whenever he
would make it his own. Very covetous was the
varlet of this coffer, yet might he never set his hand
upon it. For the casket moved warily, as though
it would say, "Go your road, since in nowise am
I yours."

So presently the servant sought his lord, and
returned with him to the shore. And forthwith
the coffer drew to the very feet of the Jew, and
seemed to him to say—

"Fair Sir Jew, receive your own. By me God
redeems the merchant from his debt, and henceforth
he is free, quite free of you."

Then the Jew entered swiftly within his door,
bearing the casket with him, and when he had
counted over its great riches, he hid the treasure
in a privy place at the foot of his bed, so that none
might know of the matter. Moreover, he found
within a certain letter news that, very soon, this
merchant, who so far had voyaged in so many
lands, would seek Byzantium in ships laden with
tissues and broideries and all manner of stuffs and
merchandise. So the friends and acquaintance of
the merchant rejoiced greatly at his prosperity, and
the whole city welcomed him with mirth and
festival. All men made much of his home-coming,
and clerk and layman joined alike in the feast.

When the Jew heard the noise of the joyous
greeting vouchsafed to the citizen, he rose up
quickly, and sought him out without delay. They
spoke at great length together, and many words
passed between the twain. At the last the Jew
made mention of his money, as if he sought to

know when payment should be made. For presently in his merry talk, yet laughing, he took the
Christian by the hand, and wagging his head
from side to side, said—

"Oh, faithful Christian ! oh, faithful Christian ! "

Thereat the burgess began to smile, and made
reply that he would learn the meaning of those
words.

"By the Law, it means that I have lent you
monies in heaped-up measure from my wealth, to
be repaid me on a day now gone. Since you have
failed in bond and faith, now holds the bargain,
that should you break your covenant, though but
for one single day, then all the years of your life
must you labour as my serf. If now you throw me
back your bond, then I must reckon your Holy
Faith and your plighted word as worth just two
grains of dust upon a balance."

Then he, whose only hope was in God, made
answer to the Jew, and said—

"I owe you nothing, since all that was your due
has been paid to the uttermost doit."

Very cunning was this Jew; therefore he
replied—

"Many an honest man was witness to the loan,
but what witness can you bring to the payment of
the debt? There is little new in such a plea as
yours."

"Right easily can I find proof of quittance, and
to spare. All this would make me fear, indeed,
were not such a mighty Surety at my side. But
so you will come with me to the church, where my
pledge was taken, very surely will I show you proof
of the redemption of my bond."

So they, and a great company with them, went
to the minster, which was filled altogether with the
press.

Then the citizen, hoping all things of his God,

and rooted deeply in his trust, bowed himself down with clasped hands right humbly to the floor before the Image of Our Lady. From his very heart, with all his soul, he prayed and required of her that she would obtain of her sweet Son to hearken to his prayer, and his words were broken by his sighs. Afterwards he cried with a clear voice in the hearing of them all, and said—

"Lord Jesus, so truly as Thou art the very Son of God, witness for me to this Hebrew of the truth as it is known to Thee. Very God of Very God, exalt now Thine honour, and for the glory of Thy Name make clear whether I have discharged me of this debt or not."

Then the Image made answer in these very words—

"It is a true testimony that to the appointed day this Jew has been paid in full whatsoever you have had of him. In proof whereof the casket yet remains hid in a privy place beneath his bed, from whence he took the debt I paid him in your place."

When the Jew heard this marvel he was filled with confusion, and was greatly astonied, so that he knew not what to say, nor what to do. So by the grace and lovingkindness of the Holy Spirit that very day he was baptized, and became a christened man, nor did he ever after waver in that faith.

So every year it was the gracious custom of all good citizens to keep this wonder in remembrance with dances and midnight revelry, with feast and high solemnity. And this holy day was observed in Byzantium, the mighty city, which Constantine, the noble Emperor, afterwards called Constantinople.

THE LAY OF GRAELENT

Now will I tell you the adventure of Graelent, even as it was told to me, for the lay is sweet to hear, and the tune thereof lovely to bear in mind.

Graelent was born in Brittany of a gentle and noble house, very comely of person and very frank of heart. The King who held Brittany in that day made mortal war upon his neighbours, and commanded his vassals to take arms in his quarrel. Amongst these came Graelent, whom the King welcomed gladly, and since he was a wise and hardy knight, greatly was he honoured and cherished by the Court. So Graelent strove valiantly at tourney and at joust, and pained himself mightily to do the enemy all the mischief that he was able. The Queen heard tell the prowess of her knight, and loved him in her heart for reason of his feats of arms and of the good men spake of him. So she called her chamberlain apart, and said—

"Tell me truly, hast thou not often heard speak of that fair knight, Sir Graelent, whose praise is in all men's mouths?"

"Lady," answered the chamberlain, "I know him for a courteous gentleman, well spoken of by all."

"I would he were my friend," replied the lady, "for I am in much unrest because of him. Go thou and bid him come to me, so he would be worthy of my love."

"Passing gracious and rich is your gift, lady, and doubtless he will receive it with marvellous joy.

Why, from here to Troy there is no priest even, however holy, who in looking on your face would not lose Heaven in your eyes."

Thereupon the chamberlain took leave of the Queen, and seeking Graelent within his lodging, saluted him courteously, and gave him the message, praying him to come without delay to the palace.

"Go before, fair friend," answered the knight, "for I will follow you at once."

So when the chamberlain was gone, Graelent caused his grey horse to be saddled, and mounting thereon, rode to the castle, attended by his squire. He descended without the hall, and passing before the King, entered within the Queen's chamber. When the lady saw him she embraced him closely, and cherished and honoured him sweetly. Then she made the knight to be seated on a fair carpet, and to his face praised him for his exceeding comeliness. But he answered her very simply and courteously, saying nothing but what was seemly to be said. Then the Queen kept silence for a great while, considering whether she should require him to love her for the love of love; but at the last, made bold by passion, she asked if his heart was set on any maid or dame.

"Lady," said he, "I love no woman, for love is a serious business, not a jest. Out of five hundred who speak glibly of love, not one can spell the first letter of his name. With such it is idleness, or fulness of bread, or fancy, masking in the guise of love. Love requires of his servants chastity in thought, in word and in deed. If one of two lovers is loyal, and the other jealous and false, how may their friendship last, for love is slain! But sweetly and discreetly love passes from person to person, from heart to heart, or it is nothing worth. For what the lover would, that would the beloved; what

she would ask of him, that should he go before to
grant. Without accord such as this, love is but a
bond and a constraint. For above all things love
means sweetness, and truth, and measure; yea,
loyalty to the loved one and to your word. And
because of this I dare not meddle with so high a
matter."

The Queen heard Graelent gladly, finding him
so tripping of tongue, and since his words were
wise and courteous, at the end she discovered to
him her heart.

"Friend, Sir Graelent, though I am a wife, yet
have I never loved my lord. But I love you very
dearly, and what I have asked of you, will you not
go before to grant?"

"Lady," said he, "give me pity and forgive-
ness, but this may not be. I am the vassal of
the King, and on my knees have pledged him
loyalty and faith, and sworn to defend his life
and honour. Never shall he have shame because
of me."

With these words Sir Graelent took his leave
of the Queen, and went his way.

Seeing him go in this fashion, the Queen commenced to sigh. She was grieved in her very heart,
and knew not what to do. But whatever chanced she
would not renounce her passion, so often she required his love by means of soft messages and costly
gifts, but he refused them all. Then the Queen turned
from love to hate, and the greatness of her passion
became the measure of her wrath, for very evilly
she spoke of Graelent to the King. So long as the
war endured, Graelent remained in that realm. He
spent all that he had upon his company, for the
King grudged wages to his men. The Queen persuaded the King to this, counselling him that by
withholding the pay of the sergeants, Graelent
might in no wise flee the country, nor take service

with another lord. So at the end Graelent was
wonderfully downcast, nor was it strange that he
was sad, for there remained nothing which he
might pledge, but one poor steed, and when this
was gone, no horse had he to carry him from the
realm.

It was now the month of May, when the hours
are long and warm. The burgess with whom
Graelent lodged had risen early in the morning,
and with his wife had gone to eat with neighbours
in the town. No one was in the house except
Graelent, no squire, nor archer, nor servant, save
only the daughter of his host, a very courteous
maid. When the hour for dinner was come she
prayed the knight that they might sit at board
together. But he had no heart for mirth, and seeking out his squire, bade him bridle and saddle his
horse, for he had no care to eat.

"I have no saddle," replied the squire.

"Friend," said the demoiselle, "I will lend you
bridle and saddle as well."

So when the harness was done upon him,
Graelent mounted his horse, and went his way
through the town, clad in a cloak of sorry fur,
which he had worn overlong already. The townsfolk in the street turned and stared upon him,
making a jest of his poverty, but of their jibes he
took no heed, for such act but after their kind, and
seldom show kindliness or courtesy.

Now without the town there spread a great forest,
thick with trees, and through the forest ran a river.
Towards this forest Graelent rode, deep in heavy
thought, and very dolent. Having ridden for a
little space beneath the trees, he spied within a leafy
thicket a fair white hart, whiter even than snow on
winter branches. The hart fled before him, and
Graelent followed so closely in her track that man
and deer presently came together to a grassy lawn,

in the midst of which sprang a fountain of clear,
sweet water. Now in this fountain a demoiselle
disported herself for her delight. Her raiment was
set on a bush near by, and her two maidens stood
on the bank, busied in their lady's service. Graelent forgot the chase at so sweet a sight, since never
in his life had he seen so lovely a dame. For the
lady was slender in shape and white, very gracious
and dainty of colour, with laughing eyes and an
open brow—certainly the most beautiful thing in
all the world. Graelent dared not draw nigh the
fountain for fear of troubling the dame, so he came
softly to the bush to set hands upon her raiment.
The two maidens marked his approach, and at their
fright the lady turned, and calling him by name,
cried with great anger—

"Graelent, put my raiment down, for it will profit
you little even if you carry it away, and leave me
naked in this wood. But if you are indeed too
greedy of gain to remember your knighthood, at
least return me my shift, and content yourself with
my mantle, since it will bring you money, as it is
very good."

"I am not a merchant's son," answered Graelent
merrily, "nor am I a huckster to sell mantles in a
booth. If your cloak were worth the spoil of three
castles I would not now carry it from the bush.
Come forth from your bathing, fair friend, and
clothe yourself in your vesture, for you have to say
a certain word to me."

"I will not trust myself to your hand, for
you might seize upon me," answered the lady;
"and I tell you frankly that I put no faith in
your word, nor have had any dealings with your
school."

Then Graelent answered still more merrily—

"Lady, needs must I suffer your wrath. But at
least I will guard your raiment till you come forth

from the well; and, fairest, very dainty is your body in my eyes."

When the lady knew that Graelent would not depart, nor render again her raiment, then she demanded surety that he would do her no hurt. This thing was accorded between them, so she came forth from the fountain, and did her vesture upon her. Then Graelent took her gently by the left hand, and prayed and required of her that she would grant him love for love. But the lady answered—

"I marvel greatly that you should dare to speak to me in this fashion, for I have little reason to think you discreet. You are bold, sir knight, and overbold, to seek to ally yourself with a woman of my lineage."

Sir Graelent was not abashed by the dame's proud spirit, but wooed and prayed her gently and sweetly, promising that if she granted him her love he would serve her in all loyalty, and never depart therefrom all the days of his life. The demoiselle hearkened to the words of Graelent, and saw plainly that he was a valiant knight, courteous and wise. She thought within herself that should she send him from her, never might she find again so sure a friend. Since then she knew him worthy of her love, she kissed him softly, and spoke to him in this manner—

"Graelent, I will love you none the less truly, though we have not met until this day. But one thing is needful that our love may endure. Never must you speak a word by which this hidden thing may become known. I will furnish you with deniers in your purse, with cloth of silk, with silver and with gold. Night and day will I stay with you, and great shall be the love between us twain. You shall see me riding at your side, you may talk and laugh with me at your pleasure, but I must

never be seen of your comrades, nor must they
know aught concerning your bride. Graelent, you
are loyal, brave and courteous, and comely enough
to the view. For you I spread my snare at the
fountain; for you shall I suffer heavy pains, as
well I knew before I set forth on this adventure.
Now must I trust to your discretion, for if you
speak vainly and boastfully of this thing, then am
I undone. Remain now for a year in this country,
which shall be for you a home that your lady loves
well. But noon is past, and it is time for you to
go. Farewell, and a messenger shortly shall tell
you that which I would have you do."

Graelent took leave of the lady, and she sweetly
clasped and kissed him farewell. He returned to
his lodging, dismounted from his steed, and entering within a chamber, leaned from the casement,
considering this strange adventure. Looking towards the forest, he saw a varlet issue therefrom
riding upon a palfrey. He drew rein before Graelent's door, and taking his feet from the stirrup,
saluted the knight. So Graelent inquired from
whence he rode, and of his name and business.

"Sir," answered he, "I am the messenger of
your lady. She sends you this destrier by my
hand, and would have me enter your service, to
pay your servitors their wages and to take charge
of your lodging."

When Graelent heard this message he thought it
both good and fair. He kissed the varlet upon the
cheek, and accepting his gift, caused the destrier—
which was the noblest, the swiftest and the most
speedy under the sun—to be led to the stable. Then
the varlet carried his baggage to his master's chamber, and took therefrom a large cushion and a rich
coverlet which he spread upon the couch. After this
he drew thereout a purse containing much gold and
silver, and stout cloth fitting for the knight's

apparel. Then he sent for the host, and paying him what was owing, called upon him to witness that he was recompensed most largely for the lodging. He bade him also to seek out such knights as should pass through the town to refresh and solace themselves in the company of his lord. The host was a worthy man. He made ready a plenteous dinner, and inquired through the town for such poor knights as were in misease by reason of prison or of war. These he brought to the hostelry of Sir Graelent, and comforted them with instruments of music, and with all manner of mirth. Amongst them sat Graelent at meat, gay and debonair, and richly apparelled. Moreover, to these poor knights and the harpers Graelent gave goodly gifts, so that there was not a citizen in all the town who did not hold him in great worship, and regard him as his lord.

From this moment Graelent lived greatly at his ease, for not a cloud was in his sky. His lady came at will and pleasure; all day long they laughed and played together, and at night she lay softly at his side. What truer happiness might he know than this? Often, besides, he rode to such tournaments of the land as he was able, and all men esteemed him for a stout and worthy knight. Very pleasant were his days and his love, and if such things might last for ever he had nothing else to ask of life.

When a full year had passed by, the season drew to the feast of Pentecost. Now it was the custom of the King to summon at that tide his barons and all who held their fiefs of him to his Court for a rich banquet. Amongst these lords was bidden Sir Graelent. After men had eaten and drunk the whole day, and all were merry, the King commanded the Queen to put off her royal robes, and to stand forth upon the daïs. Then he boasted before the company—

"Lord barons, how seems it to you? Beneath the sky is there a lovelier queen than mine, be she maid, dame or demoiselle?"

So all the lords made haste to praise the Queen, and to cry and affirm that in all the world was neither maid nor wife so dainty, fresh and fair. Not a single voice but bragged of her beauty, save only that of Graelent. He smiled at their folly, for his heart remembered his friend, and he held in pity all those who so greatly rejoiced in the Queen. So he sat with covered head, and with face bent smiling to the board. The Queen marked his discourtesy, and drew thereto the notice of the King.

"Sire, do you observe this dishonour? Not one of these mighty lords but has praised the beauty of your wife, save Graelent only, who makes a mock of her. Always has he held me in envy and despite."

The King commanded Graelent to his throne, and in the hearing of all bade the knight to tell, on his faith as vassal to his liege, for what reason he had hid his face and laughed.

"Sire," answered Graelent to the King, "sire, hearken to my words. In all the world no man of your lineage does so shameful a deed as this. You make your wife a show upon a stage. You force your lords to praise her just with lies, saying that the sun does not shine upon her peer. One man will tell the truth to your face, and say that very easily can be found a fairer dame than she."

Right heavy was the King when he heard these words. He conjured Graelent to tell him straightly if he knew a daintier dame.

"Yes, sire, and thirty times more gracious than the Queen."

The Queen was marvellously wrathful to hear this
thing, and prayed her husband of his grace to com-
pel the knight to bring that woman to the Court of
whose beauty he made so proud a boast.

"Set us side by side, and let the choice be made
between us. Should she prove the fairer, let him
go in peace; but if not, let justice be done on him
for his calumny and malice."

So the King bade his guards to lay hands on
Graelent, swearing that between them never should
be love nor peace, nor should the knight issue
forth from prison, until he had brought before him
her whose beauty he had praised so much.

Graelent was held a captive. He repented him
of his hasty words, and begged the King to grant
him respite. He feared to have lost his friend, and
sweated grievously with rage and mortification.
But though many of the King's house pitied him
in his evil case, the long days brought him no relief,
until a full year went by, and once again the King
made a great banquet to his barons and his lieges.
Then was Graelent brought to hall, and put to
liberty, on such terms that he would return bringing
with him her whose loveliness he had praised before
the King. Should she prove so desirable and dear
as his boast, then all would be well, for he had
nought to fear. But if he returned without his lady,
then he must go to judgment, and his only hope
would be in the mercy of the King.

Graelent mounted his good horse and parted from
the Court, sad and wrathful. He sought his lodging, and inquired for his servant, but might not
find him. He called upon his friend, but the lady
did not heed his voice. Then Graelent gave way to
despair, and preferred death to life. He shut himself within his chamber, crying upon his dear one
for grace and mercy, but from her he got neither
speech nor comfort. So, seeing that his love had

withdrawn herself from him by reason of his grievous fault, he took no rest by night or day, and held
his life in utter despite. For a full year he lived
in this piteous case, so that it was marvellous to
those about him that he might endure his life.

On the day appointed, the sureties brought
Graelent where the King was set in hall with his
lords. Then the King inquired of Graelent where
was now his friend.

"Sire," answered the knight, "she is not here,
for in no wise might I find her. Now do with me
according to your will."

"Sir Graelent," said the King, "very foully have
you spoken. You have slandered the Queen, and
given all my lords the lie. When you go from my
hands never will you do more mischief with your
tongue."

Then the King spoke with a high voice to his
barons.

"Lords, I pray and command you to give judgment in this matter. You heard the blame that
Graelent set upon me before all my Court. You
know the deep dishonour that he fastened on the
Queen. How may such a disloyal vassal deal
honestly with his lord, for as the proverb tells,
' Hope not for friendship from the man who beats
your dog ! ' "

The lords of the King's household went out from
before him, and gathered themselves together to
consider their judgment. They kept silence for a
great space, for it was grievous to them to deal
harshly with so valiant a knight. Whilst they thus
refrained from words a certain page hastened unto
them, and prayed them not to press the matter,
for (said he) "even now two young maidens, the
freshest maids in all the realm, seek the Court.
Perchance they bring succour to the good knight,
and, so it be the will of God, may deliver him from

peril." So the lords waited right gladly, and
presently they saw two damsels come riding to the
palace. Very young were these maidens, very
slender and gracious, and daintily cloaked in two
fair mantles. So when the pages had hastened to
hold their stirrup and bridle, the maidens dismounted from their palfreys, and entering within
the hall came straight before the King.

"Sire," said one of the two damsels, "hearken
now to me. My lady commands us to pray you to
put back this cause for a while, nor to deliver judgment therein, since she comes to plead with you
for the deliverance of this knight."

When the Queen heard this message she was
filled with shame, and made speed to get her from
the hall. Hardly had she gone than there entered
two other damsels, whiter and more sweetly flushed
even than their fellows. These bade the King to
wait for a little, since their mistress was now at
hand. So all men stared upon them, and praised
their great beauty, saying that if the maid was so
fair, what then must be the loveliness of the dame.
When, therefore, the demoiselle came in her turn,
the King's household stood upon their feet to give
her greeting. Never did woman show so queenly
to men's sight as did this lady riding to the hall.
Passing sweet she was to see, passing simple and
gracious of manner, with softer eyes and a daintier
face than girl of mother born. The whole Court
marvelled at her beauty, for no spot or blemish
might be found in her body. She was richly
dressed in a kirtle of vermeil silk, broidered with
gold, and her mantle was worth the spoil of a
king's castle. Her palfrey was of good race, and
speedy; the harness and trappings upon him were
worth a thousand livres in minted coin. All men
pressed about her, praising her face and person,
her simplicity and queenlihead. She came at a

slow pace before the King, and dismounting from
the palfrey, spoke very courteously in this fashion—

"Sire," said she, "hearken to me, and you, lord
barons, give heed to my pleading. You know the
words Graelent spake to the King, in the ears of
men, when the Queen made herself a show before
the lords, saying that often had he seen a fairer
lady. Very hasty and foolish was his tongue,
since he provoked the King to anger. But at
least he told the truth when he said that there is
no dame so comely but that very easily may be
found one more sweet than she. Look now boldly
upon my face, and judge you rightly in this quarrel
between the Queen and me. So shall Sir Graelent
be acquitted of this blame."

Then gazing upon her, all the King's household,
lord and lackey, prince and page, cried with one
voice that her favour was greater than that of the
Queen. The King himself gave judgment with his
barons that this thing was so; therefore was Sir
Graelent acquitted of his blame, and declared a free
man.

When judgment was given the lady took her
leave of the King, and attended by her four damsels
departed straightway from the hall upon her
palfrey. Sir Graelent caused his white horse to be
saddled, and mounting, followed hotly after her
through the town. Day after day he rode in her
track, pleading for pity and pardon, but she gave
him neither good words nor bad in answer. So far
they fared that at last they came to the forest, and
taking their way through a deep wood rode to the
bank of a fair, clear stream. The lady set her
palfrey to the river, but when she saw that Graelent
also would enter therein she cried to him—

"Stay, Graelent, the stream is deep, and it is
death for you to follow."

Graelent took no heed to her words, but forced

his horse to enter the river, so that speedily the waters closed above his head. Then the lady seized his bridle, and with extreme toil brought horse and rider back again to land.

"Graelent," said she, "you may not pass this river, however mightily you pain yourself, therefore must you remain alone on this shore."

Again the lady set her palfrey to the river, but Graelent could not suffer to see her go upon her way without him. Again he forced his horse to enter the water; but the current was very swift and the stream was very deep, so that presently Graelent was torn from his saddle, and being borne away by the stream came very nigh to drown. When the four maidens saw his piteous plight they cried aloud to their lady, and said—

"Lady, for the love of God, take pity on your poor friend. See how he drowns in this evil case. Alas, cursed be the day you spake soft words in his ear, and gave him the grace of your love. Lady, look how the current hurries him to his death. How may your heart suffer him to drown whom you have held so close! Aid him, nor have the sin on your soul that you endured to let the man who loved you die without your help."

When the lady heard the complaint of her maidens, no longer could she hide the pity she felt in her heart. In all haste she turned her palfrey to the river, and entering the stream clutched her lover by the belt. Thus they won together to the bank. There she stripped the drowned man of his raiment, and wrapping him fast in her own dry mantle cherished him so meetly that presently he came again to life. So she brought him safely into her own land, and none has met Sir Graelent since that day.

But the Breton folk still hold firmly that Graelent yet liveth with his friend. His destrier, when he escaped him from the perilous river, grieved greatly for his master's loss. He sought again the mighty forest, yet never was at rest by night or day. No peace might he find, but ever pawed he with his hoofs upon the ground, and neighed so loudly that the noise went through all the country round about. Many a man coveted so noble a steed, and sought to put bit and bridle in his mouth, yet never might one set hands upon him, for he would not suffer another master. So each year in its season, the forest was filled with the cry and the trouble of this noble horse which might not find its lord.

This adventure of the good steed and of the stout knight, who went to the land of Faery with his love, was noised abroad throughout all Brittany, and the Bretons made a lay thereof which was sung in the ears of many people, and was called a Lay of the Death of Sir Graelent.

THE THREE THIEVES

THIS story tells that once upon a time there were three thieves faring together, who had robbed many people, both church folk and lay. One of these thieves was named Travers, but though he was in the company of two robbers, yet he was not altogether such as they. They, indeed, were thieves by descent as well as by choice, for their father was hanged for his misdeeds. The one was called Haimet, and the other Barat, but which was the more cunning workman at his trade it would be hard to tell.

The three companions were passing one day through a high and leafy wood, when Haimet spied a magpie's nest hidden within an oak. He went beneath the tree, and his sharp eyes quickly perceived that the bird was sitting upon her eggs. This thing he showed to Travers, and afterwards to his brother.

"Friends," said he, "would not he be a good thief who might take these eggs, and so softly descend the tree that the magpie knew nought thereof?"

"There is no man in the world who can do such a feat," answered Barat.

"Certes, there is such a man," said Haimet, "and you shall see him at his task, if you will only look at me."

Haimet set hands upon the oak, and climbed lightly up the great tree, as one who had no fear to fall. He came to the nest, and parting the straw softly from beneath, drew forth the eggs coyly and delicately. Then he descended to the ground with

a merry heart, and addressing himself to his comrades, showed the eggs that he had stolen.

"Friends," said he, "here are the eggs, ready
for boiling upon a fire!"

"Truly," said Barat, "no man's fingers are
nimbler than yours, and if you can only return the
eggs to the nest, why I will own freely that you are
the most cunning thief of us all."

"Certes," answered Haimet, "they shall be set
again beneath the bird, and not a shell of them
all shall be broken."

So he came again to the oak, and mounted
swiftly into the tree, hand over hand. Now he had
gone but a little way when Barat hastened to the
tree, and climbed therein even more lightly and
surely than his brother. He followed him secretly
from branch to branch, for Haimet was intent upon
his task, and gave no thought to those he had left
below. Then, whilst Haimet returned the eggs to
the rifled nest, he stole the very breeches from his
legs, and forthwith descended to the ground. When
Travers saw this he was sick at heart, because he
knew well he might never do such feats as these.
Presently Haimet came down to his companions,
and said—

"Friends, how seems it to you? Fingers like
mine should pick up a good living."

"I know not how it looks to me," answered Barat.
"Your fingers are quick enough, but your brains
must be very dull, since they cannot procure you
even hosen for your legs."

"Yes, truly, I have hosen, and those altogether
new, for it was but the other day I laid hands upon
the cloth, and they reach to my very ankles."

"Are they so long as that?" said Barat; "shew
them to us, and hide them not away."

Then Haimet lifted his tunic and stared upon
his legs, for he was without breeches.

"Lord!" said he, "how can this have chanced?
Where, then, are my hosen?"

"I do not think that you have any, fair fellow,"
said Travers. "There is no such thief as Barat,
from here to Nevers, or so it seems to me. Cunning
indeed is the thief who can steal from a thief. But
for my part I am not meant for your trade, for I
cannot spell even its A B C. A hundred times should
I be taken in my simplicity, where you would escape
by guile. I will return to my own village where
I was married to my wife. Mad must I have been
to forsake it to become a thief. I am neither fool
nor idler, and know well how to toil in the fields,
to winnow and to reap. With the help of God I
am yet strong enough to gain my bread, so I go
my way, and commend you to God His keeping."

So Travers parted from the company of the two
thieves, and travelled by hill and dale till he came
at last to his own country. His comely wife, Dame
Maria, bore him no grudge for his absence, but
welcomed his return with much joy, as was her
husband's due. He settled down amongst his
friends and acquaintance, and earned his living
honestly and well. He prospered greatly, so that
he had enough and to spare, both of this and of
that. Now, towards Christmas, Travers killed a pig
which he had fattened all the year. He hung the
bacon from a rafter of his house, but better had
he done, and much trouble would he have escaped,
had he sold it in the village, as you will see who
read this story.

On a day when Travers was cutting fagots
within a coppice, Haimet and Barat, seeking what
they might find, lighted on his house, and found
Dame Maria spinning at her wheel. Then said
these rogues whose business it was to cozen the
simple—

"Dame, where is your husband?"

"Gentles," answered she, unknowing of these cheats, "he is in the wood, gathering fagots for the fire."

"May God prosper his work," said they devoutly.

So they seated themselves, and looked about the house, high and low, at larder and hearth-stone, in every nook and corner. Presently Barat, raising his head, saw the side of bacon hanging from the rafters. He drew the attention of Haimet to the meat, saying—

"Travers pains himself greatly to hide this bacon in his room. He fears lest we should live a little at his cost, or taste his savoury meat. Yet taste we will, if so we may."

Then they took their leave, and going a short distance, hid themselves behind a hedge, where each set to work upon the sharpening of a stake.

When Travers returned to his home—

"Husband," said his wife, Dame Maria, "two men have sought you who frightened me greatly, for I was alone in the house, and they would not tell me their business. They were mean and shifty to look upon, and there is not a thing in all the room that they have not taken stock of—not the bacon, nor anything else—knife, reaping-hook, nor axe, for their eyes were in every place at once."

"Well I know who they are and what they want of me," said Travers, "for they have seen me often. We have lost our bacon, I promise you, since Barat and Haimet have come to seek it for themselves. It is to no purpose that we have cured it in the smoke, of that I am very sure. In an evil hour I killed my pig, and certainly it were better to have sold it last Saturday when I was able."

"Husband," answered the wife, "if you take the

bacon down from the ceiling, perchance these thieves may not find it when they come."

Therefore, because of the importunity of his wife, Travers mounted on a stool and cut the cord, so that the bacon fell upon the floor. But not knowing where to bestow the meat, they let it remain even where it had fallen, having first covered it with the vessel in which they kneaded their bread. Then, sad at heart, they went to bed to take what rest they might.

When the night was come, those who were so desirous of the bacon came to the house, and with their stakes made a hole in the wall near to the threshold, a hole so large that you might have trundled a mill-stone therein. Thereby they entered softly, and groped warily about the house. Now Barat went from stool to table till he came beneath the rafter from whence the bacon hung. He knew by touch that the cord was severed, and he whispered in his brother's ear that he had not found the meat, "But," said the thief, "Travers is a fool if he thinks to conceal it for long."

Then they listened in the darkness of the room to the breathing of those upon the bed.

Travers did not dare to sleep, and finding that his wife was becoming drowsy, roused her, saying—

"Wife, this is no time for sleep. I shall go about the house to see that all is fast."

"Do not leave me," answered his wife.

But Travers, who was a prudent man, rose from his bed to make sure of all his goods. He came to the kneading trough, and raising it a little from the ground, felt the bacon safely beneath. Then taking a great axe in his hand he went out to visit his cow in her byre.

Barat came swiftly to the bed, like the bold and cunning thief he was.

"Marion," said he, "fair sister, I have a certain thing to ask you, but dare not do so, for fear you think me mad."

"That I will never deem you, husband, by St. Paul; but I will counsel you to the best of my power."

"I slept so soundly that I cannot remember where we bestowed the bacon yester night, so bemused am I with dreams."

"God help you, husband, to find more seasonable jests; is it not hid beneath the bin upon the floor?"

"In God's name, sister, you speak truly, and I will go to feel if it is yet there."

Being desirous to keep his word, Barat lifted the trough and drew forth the bacon. Then he rejoined Haimet, who was near by, and the two thieves hastened towards the coppice, making much of each other because of the success of their trick.

Now Travers returned to his bed, first carefully fastening his doors.

"Certes," said his wife, "dazed you must have been to ask me what had become of our bacon."

"God help me," cried Travers, "when did I ask you this question?"

"Why, but now, husband."

"Sister, our bacon has walked off. Never shall we see it more, unless I may steal it from these thieves. But they are the most cunning robbers in all the land."

Travers went out forthwith in quest of the rogues who had carried off his bacon. He took a short cut through a field of wheat, and following the path very swiftly, presently found himself between the tricksters and the wood. Haimet was very near to cover, but Barat went more heavily, seeing that his load was right heavy. So Travers, being anxious to take his own again, quickened his steps, and coming to him said—

"Give it to me, for you are weary, seeing you have carried it so long a road. Sit down now, and take a little rest."

Barat, thinking that he had met with Haimet, gladly placed the bacon on the shoulders of Travers, and went his way. But Travers turned him back to his own house, and hastened towards his home by the nearest path. Now Barat, deeming that Haimet followed after, ran towards the wood until he overtook his brother. When he knew him again he had great fear, because he thought him behind. But when Haimet saw him stagger, he cried out, "Let me bear the bacon for a while. I think it little likely that I shall fall beneath its weight, as you are near to do. Certainly you are overdone."

"God give me health," answered Barat, "for Travers has made a fool of us. It is he who carries his bacon on his own shoulders. But the game is not finished yet, and I have yet a throw to make."

Travers proceeded on his way in quietness and peace, as one who had nought to fear from any man. But Barat, wet with haste, overtook him in the end. He had taken off his shirt and wrapped it about his head like a coif, and as much as he was able bore himself in the semblance of a woman.

"Alas," cried he, "very nearly am I dead by reason of the loss and mischief dealt me by these wicked men. God, what has become of my husband, who has suffered so many things at their hands?"

Thinking that his wife was speaking to him, Travers held forth the bacon.

"Sister," said he, "God is yet above the Devil. You see we have again our own."

Then he, who never thought to lay hands upon the meat, seized upon it greedily.

"Do not wait for me, husband, but get to bed as quickly as you can, for now you may sleep without any fear."

So Travers returned to his own house, and Barat hastened to his brother, bearing the bacon with him.

When Travers found his wife in tears—

"Certes, Mary," said he, "all this has come upon us by reason of our sins. I thought to charge your shoulders with our bacon in the garden, but now I know well that these rogues have bestowed it upon theirs. Heavens, I wonder where he learned to play the part of a woman so bravely in manner and in speech! Hard is the lesson I am set to learn in school, because of a flitch of bacon. But, please God, I will find them this night, yea, though I walk till I have no sole to my shoe, and supplant them yet."

Travers took the path leading to the wood, and entering in the coppice, saw the red blaze of a fire which these two thieves had litten. He heard their voices lifted in dispute, so he concealed himself behind an oak, and listened to their words. At the end Barat and Haimet agreed that it were better to eat the bacon forthwith, lest a new cast of the dice should go against them. Whilst they went to seek dry cones and brushwood for the fire, Travers crept privily to the oak beneath which it was burning. But the wood was damp and green, so that more smoke and smother came from that fire than flame. Then Travers climbed into the tree, and by the aid of bough and branch came at last to the place where he would be. The two thieves returned presently with cones and brambles. These they threw upon the fire in handfuls, saying that very soon it would grill their bacon, and Travers hearkened to their speech. He had stripped himself to his shirt, and hung from a limb of the oak by his arm. Now, in a while, Haimet lifted his eyes to the tree, and saw above him the hanged man, tall, grotesque and horrible to see, naked in his very shirt.

"Barat," whispered he, "our father is spying upon us. Behold him hanging from this branch in a very hideous fashion. Surely it is he come back to us, is it not?"

"God help me," cried Barat, "it seems to me that he is about to fall."

Then because of their fear the two thieves fled from that place, without leisure to eat, or to bear away, the bacon they had stolen.

When Travers marked their flight he tarried no longer in the oak, but taking his bacon, returned straightway to his house, with none to give him nay. His wife praised him to his face, saying—

"Husband, you are welcome home, for you have proven your worth. Never did there live a braver man than you."

"Sister," said he, "take wood from the cellar, and make a fire. Certainly we must eat our bacon, if we would call it our own."

Dame Maria lighted a fire with fagots upon the hearth; she put water in the cauldron, and hung it on the hook above the fire. Travers for his part carefully cut the bacon for which he had suffered so great trouble, and put it in the pot till all was full. When this was done—

"Fair sister," said he, "watch by the fire, if you can keep awake. I have not slept this night, and will rest a little on the bed. But I will not take off my clothes, because I still am troubled of these thieves."

"Husband," answered she, "ill luck go with them. Sleep soundly and in peace, for there is none to do you wrong."

So Dame Maria kept vigil whilst Travers slept, for very greatly had he need of rest.

During this time Barat lamented in the wood, for well he knew, when he found the bacon gone, that Travers had played this trick upon them.

"Certes," said he, "we have lost the meat because of our fearful hearts, and it belongs to Travers by right of courage. A good breakfast he will make, for he deems that none can take it from him. He will look upon us as dirt, if we leave it in his hands. Let us go to his house and mark where he has bestowed it."

The two thieves hastened to the door of Travers' house. Barat set his eye to a crevice therein, and saw a sight which gave him little joy, for the pot was boiling upon the fire.

"Haimet," said he, "the bacon is cooking, and much I grieve that there is none for us."

"Let it boil in peace till it is fit for eating," answered Haimet. "I shall not give Travers quittance in this matter till he has paid me wages for my toil."

Haimet sought a long stake which he cut from a hazel tree, and sharpened it with his knife. Then he climbed upon the roof of the house, and uncovered a little space above the spot where the cauldron boiled upon the fire. Through this opening he could see the wife of Travers sound asleep, for she was weary of her vigil, and nodded over the hearth. Haimet lowered the rod, which he had sharpened like a dart, and struck it in the pot so adroitly that he drew forth a portion of the bacon from out the cauldron. This he raised cunningly to the roof, and had great joy of his fishing. Then awoke Travers from his sleep, and saw this thing, and marked the thief, who was both malicious and strong.

"Gossip, upon my roof," said he, "it is not reasonable of you to strip the covering from over my head. In this manner we shall never come to

an end. Climb down; let us give and take. Let
each of us have his share of the bacon."

So Haimet descended from the roof, and the
bacon was taken from the cauldron. Dame Maria
divided the meat into three portions, for the thieves
had no care to let Travers part the lots. The two
brothers took two portions, and Travers one; but
his was not the best, for all that he had nourished
the pig.

For this reason was the proverb made, oh,
gentles, that "Bad is the company of thieves."

THE FRIENDSHIP OF AMIS AND AMILE

IN the days of Pepin, King of the Franks, a boy
was born in the Castle of Bericain to a father of
Allemaigne, of noble descent and of great holiness.
His father and mother, who had no other child,
vowed to God and to St. Peter and St. Paul that
if God vouchsafed him breath he should be carried
to Rome for his baptism. At the same hour a
vision was seen of the Count of Alverne—whose
wife was near her day—in which he saw the Apostle
of Rome, who baptized many children in his
palace, and confirmed them with the anointing of
holy oil. When the Count awoke from his sleep
he inquired of the wise men of those parts what
this thing might mean. Then a certain wise old
man, having heard his words, by the counsel of
God made answer, and said—

"Rejoice greatly, Count, for a son shall now
be born to thee great in courage and in virtue, and
thou shalt carry him to Rome, so that he may be
baptized by the Apostle."

So the Count rejoiced in his heart, and he
and his people praised the counsel of that ancient
man.

The child was born, and cherished dearly, and
when he was of the age of two years his father
prepared to carry him to Rome, according to his
purpose. On his way he came to the city of Lucca,
and there fell in with a certain nobleman of
Allemaigne who was on pilgrimage to Rome, that
there he might baptize his son. Each greeted the
other, and inquired of his name and business; and

when they knew they were in the like case, and
bound on the same errand, they took each other
as companion with a kind heart, and voyaged
together to Rome.   The two children, also, loved
so dearly, that one would not eat save the other
ate with him; so that they fed from the same dish,
and lay in the one bed.   In such manner as this
the fathers carried the boys before the Apostle at
Rome, and said to him—

"Holy Father, whom we believe and know to be
seated in the chair of St. Peter the Apostle, we,
the Count of Alverne, and the Chatelain of Castle
Bericain, humbly pray your Holiness that you
would deign to baptize the sons they have carried
here from a distant land, and to accept this humble
offering from their hands."

Then the Pope made answer—

"It is very meet to come with such a gift before
me, but of such I have no need.   Give it, therefore,
to the poor, who cry for alms.   Right willingly
will I baptize the children, and may the Father, the
Son and the Holy Ghost ever fold them close in the
love of the Holy Trinity."

So at that one time the Apostle baptized the two
children in St. Saviour's Church, and he gave to
the son of the Count of Alverne the name of Amile,
and to the son of the Chatelain of Castle Bericain
gave he the name of Amis.   Many a knight of
Rome held them at the font, and answered in their
name as god-parents, according to the will of God.
Then, when the Sacrament of Baptism was at an
end, the Apostle commanded to be brought two
wooden cups, fair with gold and set with costly
stones, of one workmanship, size and fashion, and
these he handed to the children, saying—

"Take this gift in witness that I have baptized
you in St. Saviour's Church."

So the knights received the cups with great joy,

and rendered him grace for his gift, and parting
from thence repaired each to his own home in all
comfort and solace.

To the child of the Knight of Bericain God also
gave a gift, the gift of such wise understanding that
men might almost believe that he was another
Solomon.

When Amis was of the age of thirty years a fever
seized upon his father, and he began to admonish
his son in words such as these—

"Fair, dear son, my end is near at hand, but
thou shalt tarry for a season, and be thine own
lord.   Firstly, fair son, observe the commandments
of God, and be of the chivalry of Jesus Christ.
Keep faith with thy overlords, and turn not thy
back on thy companions and thy friends.   Defend
the widow and the orphan; be pitiful to the captive
and to all in need; think every day upon that day
which shall be thy last.   Forsake not the society
and friendship of the son of the Count of Alverne,
for the Apostle of Rome baptized you together on
one day, and graced you with one gift.   Are you
not alike in all things—in beauty, in comeliness,
and in strength, so that whosoever sees you, thinks
you to be sons of one mother?"

Having spoken these words, he was houselled of
the priest, and died in our Lord; and his son gave
him fitting burial, and paid him all such service as
is meetly required for the dead.

After the death of his father divers evil persons
wrought Amis much mischief, because of the envy
they felt towards him; but nevertheless he bore
them no ill will, and patiently suffered all the wrong
and malice that they did.   Let me tell you, then,
without more words, that such was his case that he
and his servants were cast forth from the heritage
of his fathers, and driven from the gate of his own
keep.   But when he had called to mind the words

of his father, he said to those who journeyed with him in the way—

"The wicked have spoiled me wrongfully of my inheritance, yet have I good hope that the Lord is on my side. Come now, let us seek the Court of Count Amile, my comrade and my friend. Peradventure he will give us of his goods and lands; but if not, then will we gather to Hildegarde, the Queen, wife of King Charles of France, the stay and support of the disinherited."

So those of his company made answer that they would follow where he led, and would serve him as his men. They rode, therefore, to the court of the Count, but might not find him, for reason that he had passed to Bericain to comfort Amis, his companion, because of the death of his father. When Amile might not find Amis, he departed from the castle, greatly vexed, and resolved within himself that he would not solace himself in his own fief until he had met with Amis, his friend. Therefore he rode on this quest through France and Allemaigne, seeking news of him from all his kindred, but finding none.

Now Amis, together with his company, for his part sought diligently for Amile his friend, until it chanced that on a day a certain lord gave him harbourage, and at his bidding Amis told him of this adventure. Then said the nobleman—

"Dwell ye with me, sir knights, and I will give my daughter to your lord, because of the wisdom men report of him, and you, for your own part, shall be made rich in silver, in gold and in lands."

They rejoiced greatly at his word, and the wedding feast was celebrated with marvellous joy. But when they had tarried in that place for one year and six months, Amis called together his ten companions and spake to them.

"We are recreant, inasmuch as we have forgotten all this while to seek for Amile."

So he left two men-at-arms, together with his precious cup, and set forth towards Paris.

Now for the space of nearly two years Amile had sought for Amis without pause or rest. Drawing near to Paris he lighted upon a pilgrim and asked of him if perchance he knew aught of Amis, whom evil men had hunted from his lands. The palmer said "Nay," wherefore Amile divested himself of his cloak, and gave it to the pilgrim, saying—

"Pray thou to our Lord and His saints for me that they give me grace to meet Amis, my friend."

So he saluted the pilgrim, and went his way to Paris, seeking in every place for news of Amis his friend, and finding none. But the pilgrim, passing swiftly upon his road, came upon Amis about the hour of vespers, and they saluted each the other. Then Amis inquired of the palmer whether he had seen or heard, in any land or realm, aught of Amile, the son of the Count of Alverne.

"What manner of man art thou," answered the palmer all astonied, "that thou makest mock of a pilgrim? Thou seemest to me that very Amile who but this morn sought of me if I had seen Amis, his friend. I know not for what reason thou hast changed thine apparel, thy company, thy horses and thy arms, nor why thou askest of me the same question thou didst require at nine hours of the morn when thou gavest me this cloak."

"Be not angry with me," said Amis, "for I am not the man you deem; but I am Amis who searches for his friend Amile."

So he gave him money from his pouch, and prayed him that he would require of our Lord that He might grant him grace to find Amile.

"Hasten quickly to Paris," said the pilgrim,

N

"and there shalt thou find him whom so fondly thou seekest."

So Amis hastened instantly to the city.

It chanced upon the morrow that Amile departed from Paris, and took his ease within a daisied meadow near by the pleasant waters of the Seine. Whilst he ate there with his knights there came that way Amis with his men-at-arms. So Amile and his company armed themselves forthwith, and rode forth before them at adventure. Then Amis said to his companions—

"Behold these French knights who seek to do us a mischief. Stand stoutly together, and so shall we defend our lives. If we but escape this peril soon shall we be within the walls of Paris, and sweetly shall we be entreated at the palace of the King."

Then drew the two companies together with loosened rein, with lance in rest, and with brandished sword, in such fashion that it seemed as if none might escape alive from the fury of that onset. But God, the all powerful, Who knoweth all, and bringeth to a good end the travail of the just, suffered not that spears should meet in that encounter. So when they were near at hand Amis cried aloud—

"Who are you, knights, that are so eager to slay Amis the Banished and his companions?"

When Amile heard these words he knew well the voice of Amis, his comrade, so he answered him—

"Oh thou, Amis, most dear, sweet as rest to my labour, know me for Amile, son of the Count of Alverne, who have not given over my quest for thee these two whole years."

Then forthwith they lighted from their steeds, and clasped and kissed each the other, giving grace to God Who granteth the treasure to the seeker.

Moreover, upon the guard of Amile's sword, wherein was set a holy relic, they swore faith, and friendship, and fellowship to death, the one with the other. So set they forth from that place, riding together to the Court of Charles, the King of France. There they moved amongst the lords, young, discreet and wise, fair to see, shapen wondrously alike in form and face, beloved of all men and held of all in honour. There, too, the King received them with much courtesy, making of Amis his treasurer, and to Amile gave he the office of seneschal.

In this fashion they tarried long with the King, but at the end of three years Amis said to Amile—

"Fair, sweet companion, I desire greatly to see my wife, whom I have left so long. Stay thou at Court, and for my part I will return so soon as I may. But have thou no dealings with the daughter of the King, and, more than all, beware and keep thee from the malice of Arderay the felon knight."

"I will observe thy bidding," answered Amile, "but make no long tarrying from my side."

On these words Amis departed from the Court; but Amile for his part saw with his eyes that the daughter of the King was fair, and knew the princess, in love, as soon as he was able. Thus the commandment and the warning of Amis, his companion, passed quickly from his mind; yet think not too hardly of the young man, forasmuch that he was not more holy than David, nor wiser than Solomon, David's son.

Whilst Amile was busied with these matters there came to him Arderay, the traitor, full of envy, and said—

"Thou dost not know, comrade, thou dost not know that Amis has stolen gold from the King's treasury, and therefore hath he taken flight. Since things are thus I require that you swear to me fealty

of friendship and of brotherhood, and I will swear
to you the like oath on the holy Gospels."

Having pledged such troth as this, Amile feared
not to betray his secret to the felon knight. Now
when Amile bore bason and ewer to the King, that
he might wash his hands, then said that false
Arderay to his lord—

"Take no water from the hands of this recreant,
Sir King, for he is worthier of death than of life,
since he has plucked from the Queen's daughter the
flower of her maidenhood."

When Amile heard this thing he was so fearful
that he fell upon the floor, and answered not a word,
so that the courteous King raised him to his feet,
and said—

"Have no fear, Amile, but stand up and acquit
thee of this blame."

Then Amile stood upon his feet and said—

"Sir King, give no ready credence to the lies of
this traitor Arderay, for well I know that you are
an upright judge, turning neither for love nor hate
out of the narrow way. Grant me, therefore, time
for counsel with my friends, so that I may purge
myself of this charge before you, and in single
combat with Arderay, the traitor, prove him to be a
liar before all your Court."

The King gave to both champions till three
hours after noon that each might take counsel with
his friends, and bade that at such time they should
stand before him to fulfil their devoir. At the
appointed hour they came before the King. With
Arderay for friend and witness came Herbert the
Count; but Amile found none to stand at his side,
save only Hildegarde, the Queen. So sweetly did
the lady plead his cause that she prevailed upon
her lord to grant Amile such further respite for
counsel that he might seek Amis, his friend; yet
nevertheless only on such covenant that if Amile

returned not on the appointed day the lady should
be banished ever from the royal bed.

Whilst Amile was on his way to take counsel
with his friend, he chanced on Amis, his comrade,
who repaired to the Court of the King. So he
alighted from his steed, and kneeling at the feet
of his companion, said—

"Oh thou, my one hope of surety, I have not
obeyed the charge you laid upon me, and am truly
blamed by reason of my dealings with the daughter
of the King. Therefore must I endure ordeal of
battle with the false Arderay."

"Let us leave here our companions," returned
Amis, sighing, "and enter in this wood to make the
matter clear."

Then Amis, having heard, reproached Amile,
and said—

"Let us now exchange our garments and our
horses, and thou, for thy part, get thee gone to my
house, whilst I ride to do judgment by combat for
thee upon this traitor."

But Amile answered him—

"How then may I go about thine house, seeing
that I know not thy wife nor thy household, nor
ever have looked upon their face?"

And Amis replied—

"Very easily mayest thou do this thing, so thou
dost but walk prudently; but take thou good heed
to have no dealings with my wife."

Thereupon the two companions departed one
from the other, with tears; Amis riding to the Court
of the King in the guise of Amile, and Amile to the
house of his comrade in the guise of Amis. Now
the wife of Amis, seeing him draw near, hastened
to embrace him whom she thought was her lord,
and would have kissed him. But Amile said—

"Is this a time for play? I have matter for tears
rather than for claspings, for since I parted from

thee have I suffered many bitter griefs, yea, and yet must suffer."

And that night as they made ready to lie together in one bed, Amile set his naked sword between the twain, and said to his brother's wife—

"Beware lest thy body draw near in any wise to mine, for then will I slay thee with this sword."

In such fashion passed the night, and every night, until Amis repaired secretly to the castle to know certainly whether Amile kept faith and word in this matter of his wife.

The day appointed for the combat now was come, and the Queen awaited Amile, sick of heart; for Arderay, that traitor, cried aloud, that certainly ought she never to come near the King's bed, since she had suffered and consented to Amile's dealings with her maid. Whilst Arderay boasted thus, Amis entered within the Court of the King at the hour of noon, clad in the apparel of his comrade, and said—

"Right debonair and Lord Justicier of this realm, here stand I to seek ordeal of battle with this false Arderay, because of the blame he has laid upon me, the Queen, and the Princess, her child."

Then answered the King right courteously—

"Be stout of heart, oh Count, for if you prove Arderay to be false I will give thee my daughter Belisant to wife."

On the morning of the morrow Arderay and Amis rode into the lists, armed from plume to heel, in the presence of the King and of much people. But the Queen with a great company of maidens and widows and dames went from church to church, giving gifts of money and of torches, and praying God for the safety of the champion of her daughter. Now Amis considered in his heart that should he slay Arderay he would be guilty of his blood before the eyes of God, and if he were overthrown then

would it be a shame to him for all his days. So he
spake in such manner as this to Arderay.

"Foul counsel hast thou followed, Sir Count, so
ardently to seek my death, and to thrust this life
of thine into grievous peril of hurt. So thou wilt
withdraw the reproach thou hast fastened upon me,
and avoid this mortal strife, thou canst have of me
friendship and loyal service."

But Arderay was right wroth at these words,
and replied—

"No care have I for friendship or service of thine;.
rather will I swear to the truth as that truth is, and
smite thy head from thy shoulders."

Then Arderay swore that his foe had done wrong
to the daughter of the King, and Amis made oath
that he lied. Thereupon, incontinent they drove
together, and with mighty strokes strove one
against the other from the hour of tierce till it was
nones. And at nones Arderay fell within the lists;
and Amis struck off his head.

The King lamented that Arderay was dead, but
rejoiced that his daughter was proved clean from
stain. He gave the Princess to Amis for dame,
and with her, as dowry, a mighty sum in gold and
silver, and a city near by the sea where they might
dwell. So Amis rejoiced greatly in his bride; and
returned as quickly as he might to the castle where
he had hidden Amile, his companion. When Amile
saw him hastening homewards with many horsemen, he was sore adread that Amis was overthrown,
and made ready to escape. But Amis sent messages
to him that he should return in all surety, since he
had avenged him upon Arderay, and thus, by
proxy, was he married to the daughter of the King.
So Amile repaired from that place, and dwelt with
his dame in that city which was her heritage.

Now Amis abode with his wife, but by the per-
mission of God he became a leper, and his sickness

was so heavy upon him that he could not leave his
bed, for whom God loveth him He chasteneth. His
wife—who was named Obias—for this cause hated
him sorely, and sought his death many a time in
shameful fashion. When Amis perceived her
malice he called to him two of his men-at-arms,
Azonem and Horatus, and said to them—

"Deliver me from the hands of this wicked
woman, and take with you my cup secretly, and
bear us to the tower of Bericain."

When they drew near to the castle men came out
before them asking of the sickness and of the man
whom they carried there.   Then they answered that
this was Amis, their lord, who was a leper, for
which cause they prayed them to show him some
pity.   But mercilessly they beat the sergeants, and
tumbled Amis forth from the litter in which he was
borne, crying—

"Flee swiftly from hence, if ye care aught for
your lives."

Then Amis wept grievously, and said—

"Oh Thou, God most pitiful and compassionate,
grant me to die, or give me help in this my
extremity."

Again he said to the men-at-arms—

"Carry me now to the church of the Father of
Rome; perchance God of His loving kindness will
there give alms to the beggar."

When they were come to Rome, Constantine the
Apostle, full of pity and of sanctity, together with
many a knight of those who had held Amis at the
font, came before him and supplied the wants of
Amis and his servants.   But after three years a
great famine came upon the city—a famine so
grievous that the father put his very offspring from
the door.   Then Azonem and Horatus spake to
Amis—

"Fair sir, bear witness how loyally we have

served you from the death of your father, even to this day, and that never have we done against your bidding. But now we dare no longer to bide with you, since we have no heart to die of hunger. For this cause we pray you to acquit us of our service, so that we may avoid this mortal pestilence."

Then answered Amis in his tears—

"Oh, my dear children, not servants but sons, my only comfort, I pray you for the love of God that you forsake me not here, but that you bear me to the city of my comrade, Count Amile."

And these, willing to obey his commandment, carried him to that place where Amile lay. Now when they came before the court of Amile's house they began to sound their clappers, as the leper is wont to do; so when Amile heard the sound thereof he bade a servitor of his to carry to the sick man bread and meat, and the cup which was given to him at Rome brimmed with rich wine. When the man-at-arms had done the bidding of his lord, he came to him again, and said—

"Sir, by the faith which is your due, if I held not your cup within my hand, I should believe it to be the cup that the sick man beareth even now, for they are alike in workmanship and height."

And Amile said to him—

"Go quickly, and bring him hither to me."

When the leper was come before his comrade, Amile inquired of him who he was, and how he came to own such a cup.

"I am of Castle Bericain," said he, "and the cup was given me by the Apostle of Rome who baptized me."

When Amile heard these words he knew within himself that this was Amis, his comrade, who had delivered him from death, and given him the daughter of the King of France as dame. So at once he fell upon his neck, and began to weep and lament his evil case, kissing and embracing him. When his wife heard this thing she ran forth with fallen hair, weeping and making great sorrow, for she bore in mind that this was he who had done judgment on Arderay. Forthwith they set him in a very fair bed, and said to him—

"Tarry with us, fair sir, until the will of God is done on you, for all that we have is as thine own."

So he dwelt with them, he and his two men-at-arms likewise.

Now on a night when Amis and Amile lay together in a chamber, without other company, God sent Raphael, His angel, to Amis, who spake him thus—

"Amis, sleepest thou ? "

And he, deeming that Amile had called him, answered—

"I sleep not, fair dear companion."

And the angel said to him—

"Thou hast well spoken, for thou art the companion of the citizens of Heaven, and like Job and Tobit hast suffered all things meekly and with patience. I am Raphael, an angel of our Lord, who am come to show thee medicine for thy healing, for God hath heard thy prayers. Thou must bid Amile, thy comrade, to slay his two children with the sword, and wash thee in their blood, that thus thy body may become clean."

Then Amis replied—

"This be far from me, that my comrade be blood-guilty for my health."

But the angel said—

"It is meet that he should do this thing."

On these words the angel departed from him.

Now Amile also, in his sleep, had heard these words, and he awoke, and said—

"Comrade, who is this who hath spoken to thee ? "

And Amis answered that no man had spoken. "But I prayed our Lord, as is my wont."

But Amile said—

"It is not thus, but some one hath spoken with thee."

Then he rose from the bed, and went to the door of the chamber, and finding it fast, said—

"Tell me, fair brother, who hath said to thee these hidden words."

Then Amis began to weep bitterly, and denied not that it was Raphael, the angel of our Lord, who had said to him, "Amis, our Lord sends word to thee that thou biddest Amile to slay his two children with the sword, and to wash thee in their blood, that thou mayest be clean of thy leprosy."

And Amile was sorely distressed on hearing these words, and said—

"Amis, gladly have I given thee sergeant and damsel and all the riches that I had, and in fraud thou feignest that the angel hath bidden me to slay my two little ones with the sword."

Then Amis broke out into weeping, and said—

"I know that I have told thee of a grievous matter, but not of mine own free will; I pray thee therefore that thou cast me not forth from thy house."

And Amile answered him that the covenant he had made with him he would not depart from till the hour of death. "But I adjure thee by the faith between me and thee, and by our fellowship, and by the baptism given to us twain at Rome, that thou tell me truly whether it was man or angel who spoke to thee of this thing."

And Amis made reply—

"So truly as the angel hath held converse with me this night, so may God make me clean of my infirmity."

Then Amile began to weep privily, and to consider within his heart. "If this man was willing to die in my stead before the King, why then should I not slay mine own for him! He hath kept faith with me even unto death: shall I not therefore keep faith with him! Abraham was saved by faith, and by faith have the saints proved mightier than kings. Yea, God saith in the Gospel, 'Whatsoever ye would that men should do unto you, even so do unto them.'"

Then Amile delayed no more, but went to his wife's chamber, and bade her to attend the Divine Office; so the Countess sought the church, as was her wont to do, and the Count took his sword and went to the bed where lay the children, and they were asleep. And bending above them he wept bitterly, and said—

"Hath any man heard of such father who was willing to slay his child? Alas, alas, my children, no longer shall I be your father, but your cruel murderer."

The children awoke because of their father's tears which fell upon them, and looking upon his face began to laugh. Since therefore they were about the age of three years he said to them—

"Your laughter will turn to tears, for now your innocent blood shall be shed."

He spoke thus, and cut off their heads; and making straight their limbs upon the bed, he set their heads to their bodies, and covered all with the coverlet, as if they slept. So he washed his companion with the blood of that slaying, and said—

"Lord God, Jesus Christ, Who hast bidden men to keep faith on earth, and didst cleanse the leper with Thy word, deign Thou to make clean my comrade, for love of whom I have shed the blood of my children."

Straightway was Amis made whole of his

leprosy, and they gave grace to our Lord with great joy, saying—

"Blessed be God, the Father of our Lord Jesus Christ, who saveth those who put their trust in Him."

And Amile clad his comrade from his own rich apparel; and passing to the church to render thanks in that place, the bells rang without ringers, as was the will of God. When the people of the city heard thereof they hastened to behold this marvel. Now the wife of the Count, when she saw the twain walking together, began to question which was her husband, and said, "Well I know the vesture which they wear, but which is Amile, that I know not," and the Count said—

"I am Amile, and this, my companion, is Amis, who is healed."

Then the Countess marvelled greatly, and said—

"Easy is it to see that he is healed, but much desire I to know the manner of that healing."

"Render thanks to our Lord," returned the Count, "nor seek curiously of the fashion of that cleansing."

The hour of tierce was now come, and neither of the parents had yet entered in the chamber where the children lay, but the father went heavily for reason of their death. The Countess asked therefore for her sons that they might share in the joy, but the Count replied—

"Nay, dame, but let the children sleep."

Then entering by himself within the chamber to bewail his children, he found them playing in the bed; and about their necks, in the place of that mortal wound, showed as it were a crimson thread. So he clasped them in his arms, and bore them to their mother, saying—

"Dame, rejoice greatly, for thy sons whom I had slain with the sword, at the bidding of the

angel, are alive, and by their blood is Amis
cleansed and healed."

When the Countess heard this thing she said—

"Count, why was I not with thee to gather the
blood of my children, that I too might have washed
Amis, thy comrade and my lord?"

And the Count answered her—

"Dame, let be these words; rather let us dedicate
ourselves to our Lord, who hath wrought such
marvels in our house."

So from that day, even unto their deaths, they
lived together in perfect chastity; and for the space
of ten days the people of that city held high
festival. But on that very day that Amis was made
clean, the devil seized upon his wife, and breaking
her neck, carried off her soul.

After these things Amis rode to the castle of
Bericain, and laid siege thereto, and sat before it
for so long a time that those within the castle
yielded themselves into his hand. He received
them graciously, forgetting his anger against
them, and forgiving them the wrongs that they
had done, so that from thenceforth he dwelt peace-
ably amongst them, and with him, in his own
house, lived the elder son of Count Amile. There
he served our Lord with all his heart.

Now Adrian, being at this time Pope of Rome,
sent letters to Charles, King of France, praying
him to come to his aid against Didier, King of the
Lombards, who wrought much mischief to him
and the Church. Now Charles lay in the town of
Thionville, and to that place came Peter, the envoy
of the Apostle, with messages from the Pope praying him to hasten to the succour of Holy Church.
For this cause Charles sent letters to the said
Didier requiring him to render to the Holy Father
the cities and all other things which he had wrongfully seized, and promising that if he would do

this thing the said Charles would send him in
return the sum of forty thousand pieces of gold, in
gold and silver. But he would not do right, neither
for prayers nor for gifts.

Then the stout King Charles summoned to his
aid all his men—bishops, abbots, dukes, princes,
marquises, and other stout knights. Divers of
these he sent to Cluses to guard the pass, and of
this number was Albin, Bishop of Angers, a man
of great holiness.

King Charles himself, with a large company of
spears, drew towards Cluses by the way of Mont
Cenis, and he sent Bernard, his uncle, with other
knights, thither by way of Mont Saint-Bernard.
The vanguard of the host said that Didier, with all
his strength, lay at Cluses, which town he had
made strong with iron chains and works of stone.
Whilst Charles approached to Cluses he sent
messengers to Didier, requiring him to render to
the Holy Father the cities which he had taken,
but he would not heed his prayer. Again Charles
sent him other letters demanding three children
of the Justices of Lombardy as hostages, until such
time as he had yielded up the cities of the Church;
in which case for his part he would return to
France with all his spears, without battle and
without malice. But neither for this nor for that
would he stint.

When God the All-powerful had beheld the hard
heart and the malice of this Didier, and found that
the French desired greatly to return, He put so
fearful a trembling in the hearts of the Lombards
that they took to flight, though there was none
that pursued, leaving behind them their tents and
all their harness. So Charles and his host followed
after them, and Frenchman, German, Englishman
and divers other people entered hot after them into
Lombardy.

Amis and Amile were of the host, and very near
to the person of the King. Always they strove to
follow our Lord in good works, and were constant
in fast, in vigil, in giving of alms, in succouring
the widow and the orphan, in assuaging often the
wrath of the King, in patient suffering of evil
men, and in piteous dealings within the Roman
realm.

But though Charles had a great army drawn
together in Lombardy, King Didier feared not to
come before him with his little host—for there
where Didier had a priest, Charles had a bishop;
where one had a monk, the other had an abbot;
if this had a knight, that had a prince; if Didier
had a man-at-arms, then Charles had a duke or a
count. What shall I tell you; for a single knight
on the one side Charles could number thirty
pennons. And the two hosts fell each upon the
other with a tumult of battle cries, and with
banners in array; and the stones and arrows flew
from here and there, and knights were smitten
down on every side.

For the space of three days the Lombards strove
so valiantly that they slew a very great company
of Charles's men. But on the third day Charles
set in order the hardiest and bravest of his host
and said to them—

"Go now, and win this battle, or return no
more."

So King Didier together with the host of the
Lombards fled to the place called Mortara, which
was then known as Belle-Forêt, because the
country was so fair, there to refresh themselves and
their horses. On the morning of the next day
King Charles with his army drew near the town,
and found the Lombards arrayed for the battle.
So fierce was the combat that a great multitude
of men were slain, both of one party and the other,

and for reason of this slaying was the place named
Mortara. There, too, on that field died Amis and
Amile, for as it had pleased God to make their
lives lovely and pleasant together, so in their
deaths they were not divided. There also many
another hardy knight was slain with the sword.
But Didier, together with his Justiciary, and all
the multitude of the Lombards, fled to Pavia; and
King Charles followed closely after him and lay
before the city, and invested it on every side; and
lying there he sent to France to seek the Queen
and his children. But St. Albin, the Bishop of
Angers, and many another bishop and abbot
counselled the King and Queen that they should
bury those who fell in that battle, and build in
that place a church. This counsel greatly pleased
the King, so that on the field were built two
churches, one by bidding of Charles in honour of
St. Eusebius of Verceil, and the other by bidding
of the Queen in honour of St. Peter.

Moreover the King caused to be brought the two
coffins of stone wherein were buried Amis and
Amile, and Amile was carried to the church of
St. Peter, and Amis to the church of St. Eusebius.
But on the morrow the body of Amile in his coffin
of stone was found in the church of St. Eusebius
near by the coffin of his comrade, Amis. So have
you heard the story of this marvellous fellowship
which could not be dissevered, even by death.
This miracle did God for His servants—that God
Who gave such power to His disciples that in His
strength they might move even mountains. Because of this wonder the King and Queen tarried
there for thirty days, giving fit burial to the bodies
of the slain, and honouring those ministers with
many rich gifts.

But all this while the host of Charles toiled
mightily for the taking of the city before which it

o

lay. Our Lord also tormented those within the
walls so grievously that they might not bear their
harness by reason of weakness and of death. At the
end of ten months Charles took Didier the King,
and all those who were with him, and possessed
himself of the city and of all that realm. So Didier
the King and his wife were led as captives into
France.

But St. Albin, who in his day gave life to the
dead and light to the blind, ordained clerks, and
priests and deacons in the aforesaid church of St.
Eusebius, and bade them always to hold in tireless
keeping the bodies of those two comrades, Amis
and Amile, who suffered death under Didier, King
of Lombardy, the 12th day of October, and are
now with our Lord Jesus Christ, Who liveth and
reigneth with the Father and the Holy Ghost,
world without end. Amen.

OF THE KNIGHT WHO PRAYED WHILST
OUR LADY TOURNEYED IN HIS
STEAD

SWEET Jesus, what brave warfare doth he make, and how nobly doth he joust, whose feet devoutly seek the church where the Divine Office is rendered, and who assists at the holy mysteries of Him, the spotless Son of the Mother Maid. For this cause will I tell you a certain story, even as it was told to me, for a fair ensample.

There was once a knight, esteemed of all as a wise and courteous lord, stout and of great valour, who dearly loved and honoured the Virgin Mary. The fame of this knight was bruited about all chivalry; so to make proof alike of lisping squire and burly man-at-arms, he set forth to a tourney, together with a strong company. Now by the will of God it chanced that when the day of the tournament was come he fared speedily towards the field, because he would be first at the breaking of the spears. Near by the road was builded a little church, and the bells thereof rang loud and clear to call men to the singing of the holy Mass. So without doubt or hesitation this knight dismounted at the door, and entered within the church to hearken to the service of God. At an altar therein a priest chanted meetly and with reverence a Mass of the holy Virgin Mary. Then another Mass was begun, the good knight yet kneeling devoutly on his knees, and praying our Lady with an earnest heart. When the second Mass came to its appointed end, straightway a third Mass was commenced, forthwith and in the selfsame place.

"Sir, by the holy Body of God," said the squire
to his lord, "the hour to tourney hurries by. Why
tarry you here? Depart from hence, I pray you.
Let us keep to our own trade, lest men deem you
hermit or hypocrite, or monk without the cowl!"

"Friend," answered the knight, "most worship-
fully doth he tourney who hearkens to the service
of God upon his knees. When the Masses are
altogether at an end, we will go upon our way.
Till then, please God, part from here will I not.
But so that all are said, then will I joust to the
very utmost of my might, according to the will of
God."

With these words the knight refrained from
further speech, and turning himself again towards
the altar took refuge in the holy liturgy, till the last
prayer came to a close with the last chant. Then
they got to horse, as was their bounden duty, and
rode with speed towards that place where the lists
were set for the great play. So, presently, the
knights who were returning from the tournament,
discomfited and overborne, met him who had
carried off all the prizes of the game. They saluted
the knight who was on his way from the Divine
Offerings, and, joining themselves to his company,
praised him to his face, affirming that never before
had knight done such feats of arms as he had
wrought that day, to his undying fame. Moreover
many amongst them drew near and yielded themselves his captives, saying—

"We are your prisoners, for truly we may not
deny that you have overthrown us in the field."

Then, taking thought, the knight was amazed no
more, for quickly he perceived that She had been
upon his business in the press, about whose business he had been within the chapel.

So he called these knights and his fellowship
around him, and said right courteously—

"I pray you, one and all, to hearken to my words, for I have that to tell you which never has been heard of ears."

Then he told over to them, word for word, how that he had not jousted in the tournament, neither had broken lance nor hung shield about his neck, by reason of those Masses he had heard, but verily he believed that the Maiden, whom humbly he had besought within the chapel, had worn his harness in the lists. "Altogether lovely in my eyes is this tournament wherein She has done my devoir; but very foully shall I requite such gracious service if I seek another Lady, or in my folly return to the vanities of the world. Therefore I pledge my word to God in truth, that henceforth I will never fight, save in that tourney where He sits, the one true Judge, Who knows the loyal knight, and recompenses him according to his deeds."

Then he bade them farewell right piteously, and many of his company wept tenderly as they took their leave. But he, parting from them, went his way to an abbey, to become the servant of the Handmaid of the Lord, and to follow in that path which leadeth to a holy end.

So, clearly we may perceive from this ensample, that the gracious God, in Whom we put our faith, loves, cherishes, and delights to honour that man who gladly tarries before His holy altar at the offering of the Mass, and who willingly serves His Mother, so gentle and so dear. Of much profit is this custom, and he who is quiet in the land and wise, will always continue to walk in the way his feet were set in youth, yea, even to that time when he is old and grey-headed.

THE PRIEST AND THE MULBERRIES

A CERTAIN priest having need to go to market, caused his mare to be saddled and brought to his door. The mare had carried her master for two years, and was high and well nourished, for during these years never had she known thirst nor hunger, but of hay and of oats ever had she enough and to spare. The priest climbed to the saddle and set out upon his journey, and well I remember that it was the month of September, for in that season mulberries grow upon the bushes in great plenty and abundance. The priest rode upon his way repeating his hours, his matins and his vigils. As he drew near the gate of the town the path ran through a certain deep hollow, and raising his eyes from his book the priest marked a bush thick with mulberries, bigger, blacker and more ripe than any he had ever seen. Desire entered his heart, for very covetous was he of this fair fruit, and gradually checking the pace of his mare, he presently caused her to stand beside the bush. Yet one thing still was wanting to his delight. The mulberries near the ground were set about with spines and thorns, whilst the sweetest of all hung so high upon the tree that in no wise could he reach them from his seat. This thing the priest saw, so in a while he climbed up, and stood with his two feet upon the saddle, whence by leaning over a little he could pluck the fruit. Then he chose the fairest, the ripest, and the sweetest of all these mulberries, eating them as swiftly and greedily as he might, whilst the mare beneath him moved never a whit. Now, when this priest had eaten as many mulberries as he was able, he glanced downwards, and saw that the mare was standing still and coy, with her head turned towards the bank of that deep road. Thereat the priest rejoiced very greatly, for his two feet were yet upon the saddle, and the mare was very tall.

"God!" said he, "if any one now should cry ' Gee up!'" He thought and spoke the words at the same moment, whereat the mare was suddenly frighted, and springing forward on the instant tumbled the luckless priest into the bush where the thorns and briars grew sharpest and thickest. There he lay in that uneasy bed, nor might move from one side to the other, backwards or forwards, for all the money in the mint.

The mare galloped straight to her own stable, but when the priest's household saw her return in this fashion they were greatly discomforted. The servants cursed her for an evil and a luckless jade, whilst the cook maid swooned like any dame, for well she believed that her master was dead. When they were returned a little to themselves they ran to and fro, here and there, about the country searching for the priest, and presently on their way to the market town they drew near to that bush where their master yet lay in much misease. On hearing their words bewailing his piteous case, the priest raised a lamentable voice, and cried—

"Diva, Diva, do not pass me by. This bush is an uneasy bed, and here I lie very hurt and troubled and utterly cast down. Do you not see how my blood is staining these thorns and briars a vermeil red?"

The servants hurried to the bush, and stared upon the priest.

"Sir," said they, "who has flung you herein?"

"Alas," answered he, "'tis sin that has undone me. This morning when I rode this way reading

in my Book of Hours, I desired over greatly to eat
of the mulberries growing hereon, and so I fell
into the sin of gluttony. Therefore this bush gat
hold upon me. But help me forth from this place,
for I wish now for no other thing but to have a
surgeon for my hurts, and to rest in my own house."

Now by this little story we may learn that the
prudent man does not cry aloud all he may think
in his heart, since by so doing many an one has
suffered loss and shame, as we may see by this fable
of the Priest and the Mulberries.

THE STORY OF ASENATH

In the first of the seven years of great plenty
Pharaoh sent forth Joseph to lay up corn, and
gather food within the cities. So Joseph went out
over all the land of Egypt, and came in the country
of Heliopolis, where lived Poti-pherah, the priest,
and chief counsellor of the great King. His
daughter, Asenath, was the fairest of all the virgins
of the earth; and seemed rather to be a daughter of
Israel than an Egyptian. But Asenath was scorn-
ful and proud, and a despiser of men. No man of
all the sons of men had seen her with his eyes, for
she lodged within a strong tower, tall and wide,
near by the habitation of Poti-pherah, the priest.
Now high upon this tower were ten chambers. The
first chamber was fair and great, and was builded
of marble blocks of divers colours; the walls were
of precious stones set in a chasing of gold, and
the ceiling thereof was golden. There stood the
gods of the Egyptians in metal of silver and gold,
and Asenath bowed before them and offered sacri-
fice, every day of all the days. The second chamber
was the habitation of Asenath, and was adorned
cunningly with ornaments of gold and silver, with
costly gems, and with arras and stuffs most
precious. In the third chamber was brought
together the wealth of all the world, and in that
place also were set the aumbries of Asenath. Seven
virgins, her fellows, lodged in the seven other
chambers. They were very fair, and no man had
spoken with them, nor any male child.

The chamber of Asenath was pierced with three

windows; the first, which was very wide, looked
towards the east, the second looked towards the
south, and the third was set towards the north.
Here was spread a couch of gold, covered with a
purple coverlet, embroidered with golden thread,
and hemmed with jacinths. There slept Asenath,
with no bed-fellow, neither had man sat ever upon
her bed. About this house was a goodly garden,
closed round with a very strong wall, and entered
by four iron gates. Each door had for warders
eighteen men, very mighty and young, well armed
and full of valour. At the right side of the garden
sprang a fountain of living water, and near by the
fountain a cistern which gave of this water to all
the trees of the garden, and these trees bore much
fruit. And Asenath was queenly as Sarah,
gracious as Rebecca, and fair as Rachel.

*How Joseph rebuked Asenath because she
worshipped idols.*

Joseph sent a message to Poti-pherah that he
would come to his house. So Poti-pherah rejoiced
greatly, saying to his daughter, "Joseph, the friend
of God, enters herein. I would give thee to him as
his wife."

But Asenath was sore vexed when she heard
these words, and said—

"No captive shall ever be my husband, but only
the son of a king."

Whilst they spake thus together, a messenger
came before them and cried, "Joseph is here"; so
Asenath fled to her chamber high within the tower.
Now Joseph was seated in Pharaoh's own chariot of
beaten gold, and it was drawn by four horses, white
as snow, with bridles and harness of gold. Joseph
was clad in a vesture of fine linen, white and glister-

ing, and his mantle was of purple, spun with gold. He wore a golden circlet upon his head, and in this crown were set twelve stones, most precious, each stone having for ornament a golden star.   Moreover he held in his hand the royal sceptre, and an olive branch charged with fruit.   Poti-pherah and his wife hastened to meet him, and bowed before him to the ground.   They led him within the garden, and caused the doors to be shut.   But when Asenath regarded Joseph from on high the tower, she repented her of the words she spoke concerning him, and said—

"Behold the sun and the chariot of the sun! Certainly this Joseph is the child of God; for what father could beget so fair an offspring, and what womb of woman could carry such light."

Joseph entered in the house of Poti-pherah, and whilst they washed his feet he asked what woman had looked forth from the window of the tower.

"Let her go forth from the house," he commanded.

This he said because he feared lest she should desire him, and should send him messages and divers gifts, even as other women of her nation, whom he had refused with holy indignation.   But Poti-pherah replied—

"Sire, this is my daughter, who is a virgin, and hateth men; neither hath she seen any man save me, her father, and thyself this very day.   If thou wilt, she shall come before thee and salute thee."

Then Joseph thought within himself, "Since she hateth man, she will not cast her eyes upon me." So he answered to her father—

"Since your daughter is a virgin, I will cherish her even as my sister."

Then her mother went out to seek Asenath, and brought her before Joseph.

"Salute thy brother," said Poti-pherah, "who

hateth the strange woman, even as thou hatest man."

"God keep thee," replied Asenath, "for thou art blessed of God most high."

And Joseph answered, "May the God of life bless thee evermore."

Then commanded Poti-pherah that she should kiss Joseph; but as she drew near Joseph set his hand against her breast and said—

"It is not meet that a man who worships the living God, and eateth the bread of life and drinketh from the chalice without corruption, should embrace the strange woman, who bows down before deaf and dumb idols; who serves them with the kisses of her mouth; is anointed with their reprobate oil, and eats an accursed bread, and drinks unsanctified wine from their table."

Of the penitence of Asenath, and of the consolation of an angel; how he came from Heaven to the chamber of Asenath, and spake with her and sweetly comforted her.

When Asenath heard Joseph speak these words she was sore vexed, even unto tears; wherefore Joseph took pity upon her and blessed her, laying his hand upon her head. Asenath rejoiced greatly at the benediction. She sought her bed, sick with fear and joy, and renounced the gods before whom she bowed, and humbled herself to the ground. So Joseph ate and drank, and when he rose to go Poti-pherah prayed him to tarry till the morrow; but he might not, and parted, having promised to return within eight days.

Then Asenath put on sad raiment, such as she wore at the death of her brother, and went clothed in a garment of heaviness. She closed the doors of her chamber upon her and wept. Moreover she

flung forth all her idols by the window set towards
the north; all the royal meat she gave to the dogs;
she put dust upon her head, lay upon the ground,
and lamented bitterly for seven days.

But the eighth morning, at the hour when the
cock crows and the dogs howl at the breaking of the
day, Asenath looked forth from the window giving
to the east, and saw a star shining clear, and the
heavens open, and there appeared a great light.
She fell to earth with her face in the dust, and a
man descended from the heavens and stood by her
head, calling on her by her name. But Asenath
answered nothing, because of the greatness of her
fear.   Then the man called her a second time, saying, "Asenath! Asenath!" and she replied—
"Lord, here am I. Tell me whom thou art."

And he said—

"I am Prince of the House of God and Captain
of His Host. Rise, stand upon thy feet, for I have
to speak with thee."

Then Asenath raised her head, and saw a man by
her side who in all points was, as it were, Joseph. He
was clad in a white stole, and bore the royal sceptre
in his hand, and a crown was upon his brow. His
face was as the lightning, his eyes as rays of the
sun, and the hair of his head like a flame of fire.
At the sight of him Asenath was sore afraid, and
hid her face upon the ground. But the Angel raised
her to her feet, and comforted her, saying—

"Put off this black raiment with which thou art
clothed, and this girdle of sadness. Remove the
sackcloth from thy body, and the dust from thine
head; cleanse thy face and thy hands with living
water, and adorn thee with fair apparel, for I have
somewhat to say to thee."

So she adorned herself with speed, and when she
came to him again he said—

"Asenath, take off this ornament from thine

head, for thou art virgin. Rejoice, and be of good
cheer, for thy name is written in the Book of Life,
and shall never be taken away.   Thou art born
again this very day and quickened anew.   For thou
shalt receive the Bread of Blessing, and drink of
the Wine without corruption; and be anointed
with the Holy Chrism.   Yea, I have given thee for
wife to Joseph, and thou no more shall be called
Asenath, but a name shall be given thee of fair
refuge, for thy Penitance hath come before the High
King, of whom she is the daughter, and thou shalt
ever live before Him in mirth and gladness."

Then inquired she of the Angel his name, but he
answered—

"My name is written by the finger of God in the
Book of the most high King, but all that is written
therein may not be told, neither is it proper for
the hearing of mortal man."

*Of the table and of the honey that Asenath set
    before the Angel, and how the Angel blessed
    Asenath.*

But Asenath caught the angel by his mantle,
and said—

"If I have found favour in thine eyes, sit for a
little space upon this bed, where never man has sat,
and I will spread the table before my lord."

And the Angel replied, "Do quickly."

So Asenath set a fair linen cloth upon the table,
and put thereon new bread of a sweet savour. Then
said the Angel—

"Give me also a little honey in the honeycomb."

So Asenath was grievously troubled because she
had no honey to set before her guest. But the Angel
comforted her, saying—

"Look within thine aumbrey, and thou shalt find
withal to furnish thy table."

Then she hastened thereto, and found a store of virgin honey, white as snow, of sweetest savour. So she spake to the Angel—

"Sire, I had no honey, but thou spakest the word, and it is there, and the perfume thereof is as the breath of thy mouth."

The Angel smiled at the understanding of Asenath, and placed his hand upon her head, and said—

"Blessed be thou, O Asenath, because thou hast forsaken thy idols, and believed in our living Lord. Yea, blessed are they whom Penitence bringeth before Him, for they shall eat of this honey gathered by the bees of Paradise from the dew of the roses of Heaven; and those who eat thereof shall never see death, but shall live for evermore."

Then the Angel stretched forth his hand and took of the honeycomb and break it; and he ate a little, and gave the rest to the mouth of Asenath, saying—

"This day hast thou eaten of the Bread of Life, and art anointed with the Holy Chrism. Beauty is given thee for ashes; for virtue shall never go from thee, neither shall thy youth wither, nor thy fairness fail; but thou shalt be as the strong city builded as a refuge for the children of our Lord, Who is King for ever more."

Then the Angel touched the honeycomb, and it became unbroken as before. Again he stretched forth his hand, and with his finger signed the cross thereon, and there where his finger touched came forth blood. So he spake to Asenath, and said—

"Behold this honey!"

Whilst she gazed thereon, she saw bees come forth from that honey, some white as snow, others vermeil as jacinths, and they gathered about her, and set virgin honey in the palm of her hand; and she ate thereof, and the Angel with her.

P

"Bees," said the Angel, "return now to your own place."

So they passed through that window which gave upon the east, and took their way to Paradise.

"Faithful as these bees are the words which I have spoken."

Then the Angel put forth his hand three times, and touched the honey, and fire came forth and consumed the honey without singeing the table, and the perfume which came from the honey and the fire was very sweet.

Of the blessing of the seven maidens, and of the marriage of Asenath, as set forth in the story.

Asenath said to the Angel—

"Lord, I have with me seven virgins, born in one night, and nourished with me from my childhood until now. I will seek them, and thou shalt bless them, even as thou hast blessed me."

So she brought them before him, and he blessed them, saying—

"May the most high God bless you, and make you to be seven strong columns of the City of Refuge."

Afterwards he bade Asenath to carry forth the table, and whilst she went about her task, the Angel vanished from her eyes. But looking towards the east she saw, as it were, a chariot drawn by four horses ascending towards Heaven. So Asenath prayed to God right humbly that He would pardon the boldness with which she had spoken to the Captain of His Host.

Whilst she prayed thus a messenger came to Poti-pherah saying that Joseph, the friend of God, sought his house, and was even then at his door. Asenath hastened to meet him, and awaited his coming before the offices of the house. When

Joseph entered the garden she bowed herself before him, and washed the dust from his feet, telling him the words which the Angel had spoken concerning her. The next day Joseph prayed Pharaoh that he might have Asenath to wife, and Pharaoh gave him the woman. He set also garlands of gold upon their heads, the fairest that cunning smiths could fashion, and caused them to embrace in the sight of men. So for seven days was kept high feast and festival, nor might any man labour for those days. He also gave them new names, calling Joseph, the Son of God, and Asenath, Daughter of the Most High King.

Before the time of the seven lean years Asenath bore two sons. And Joseph called the name of the firstborn Manasseh, which is to say Forgetfulness; "For," said he, "God hath made me to forget all my toil, and all my father's house." And the name of the second was called Ephraim, which is to say Fruitfulness; "For," said he, "God hath caused me to be fruitful in the land of my affliction."

THE PALFREY

THAT men may bear in mind the fair deeds that
woman has done, and to tell of her sweetness and
frankness, this tale is here written. For very right
it is that men should hold in remembrance the
excellent virtues that can so easily be perceived in
her. But grievous is it, and very heavy to me, that
all the world does not laud and praise women to
the height which is their due. Ah, God, if but they
kept their hearts whole and unspotted, true and
strong, the world would not contain so rich a
treasure. The greater pity and sorrow, then, that
they take not more heed to their ways, and that so
little stay and stability are to be found in them. Too
often the heart of a woman seems but a weathercock
upon a steeple, whirled about in every wind that
blows; so variable is woman's heart, and more
changeable than any wind. But the story that I
have taken upon me to narrate shall not remain
untold because of the fickle-hearted, nor for reason
of those who grudge praise to the frank and pure;
therefore, give ear to this Lay of the Marvellous
Palfrey.

Once upon a time a certain knight, courteous and
chivalrous, rich of heart, but poor in substance,
had his dwelling in the county of Champagne. So
stout of heart was this lord, so wise in counsel, and
so compact of honour and all high qualities, that
had his fortune been equal to his deserts he would
have had no peer amongst his fellows. He was the
very pattern of the fair and perfect knight, and his

praise was ever in the mouth of men. In whatever land he came he was valued at his proper worth, since strangers esteemed him for the good that was told of him, and rumour but increased his renown. When he had laced the helmet on his head, and ridden within the lists, he did not court the glances of the dames, nor seek to joust with those who were of less fame than he, but there where the press was thickest he strove mightily in the heart of the stour. In the very depths of winter he rode upon his horse, attired in seemly fashion (since in dress may be perceived the inclinations of the heart) and this although his substance was but small. For the lands of this knight brought him of wealth but two hundred pounds of rent, and for this reason he rode to tourneys in hope of gain as well as in quest of honour.

This knight had set all his earthly hope and thoughts on gaining the love of a certain noble lady. The father of the damsel was a puissant Prince, lacking nought in the matter of wealth, and lord of a great house furnished richly as his coffers. His fief and domain were fully worth one thousand pounds a year, and many an one asked of him his fair daughter in marriage, because her exceeding beauty was parcel of the loveliness of the world. The Prince was old and frail; he had no other child than the maiden, and his wife had long been dead. His castle was builded in a deep wood, and all about it stretched the great forest, for in the days of my tale Champagne was a wilder country then than now.

The gentle knight who had set his heart on the love of the fair lady was named Messire William, and he lived within the forest in an ancient manor some two miles from the palace of the Prince. In their love they were as one, and ever they fondly dreamed one upon the other; but the Prince liked the matter but little, and had no mind that they should meet. So when the knight would gaze upon the face of his mistress, he went secretly by a path that he had worn through the profound forest, and which was known of none save him. By this path he rode privily on his palfrey, without gossip or noise, to visit the maiden, many a time. Yet never might these lovers see each other close, however great was their desire, for the wall of the courtyard was very high, and the damsel was not so hardy as to issue forth by the postern. So for their solace they spoke together through a little gap in the wall, but ever between them was the deep and perilous fosse, set thickly about with hedges of thorn and spine, so that never closer might they meet. The castle of the Prince was builded upon a high place, and was strongly held with battlement and tower; moreover bridge and portcullis kept his door. The ancient knight, worn by years and warfare, seldom left his lodging, for he might no longer get him to horse. He lived within his own house, and ever would have his daughter seated at his side, to cheer his lonely age with youth. Often this thing was grievous to her, for she failed to come to that fair spot where her heart had taken root. But the brave knight in nowise forgot the road that he had worn, and asked for nothing more than to see her somewhat closer with his eyes.

Now the tale tells that in spite of his poverty the knight owned one thing that was marvellously rich. The palfrey on which he rode had not his like in all the world. It was grey and of a wonderful fair colour, so that no flower was so bright in semblance, nor did any man know of so beautiful a steed. Be assured that not in any kingdom could be discovered so speedy a horse, nor one that carried his rider so softly and so surely. The knight loved his palfrey very dearly, and I tell you truly that in nowise

would he part with him for any manner of wealth,
though the rich folk of that country, and even from
afar, had coveted him for long. Upon this fair
palfrey Messire William went often to his lady,
along the beaten path through the solitary forest,
known but to these two alone. Right careful was
he to keep this matter from the father of the demoiselle; and thus, though these two lovers had such
desire one of the other, they might not clasp their
arms about the neck, nor kiss, nor embrace, nor
for their solace, even, hold each other by the hand.
Nought could they do but speak, and hearken softly
to such sweet words, for well they knew that should
the old Prince know thereof, very swiftly would he
marry his daughter to some rich lord.

Now the knight considered these things within
himself, and day by day called to remembrance the
wretched life that was his, for he might not put
the matter from his mind. So at the end he summoned all his courage, and for weal or woe resolved
that he would go to the aged Prince and require of
him his daughter for his wife, let that betide what
may. For very clear it was to him that such a life
he could not lead for every day of the week. On a
certain day he made himself ready, and repaired
to the castle where the demoiselle dwelt with her
father. He was welcomed very gladly by the
Prince and his company, for he was esteemed a
courteous and gentle knight, and bragged of by all
men as a valiant gentleman, who was lacking in no
good qualities.

"Sire," said the knight, "I ask you of your grace
to listen to my words. I enter in your house to
crave of you such a gift as may God put it in your
heart to bestow."

The old man looked upon him fixedly, and afterwards inquired—

"What is it you would have? Tell me now, for

by my faith I will aid you if I may, yet in all things saving my honour."

"Yea, sire, very easily you may do this thing, if so you please. May God but grant that such is your pleasure."

"I will grant you the gift if it seems to me well, and I will refuse you the boon if it seems to me ill. Nothing will you get from me, neither gift, nor promise, nor blame, that it is not fitting for me to bestow."

"Sire," answered he, "I will tell you the gift I crave at your hand. You know who I am, and right well you knew my father. Well, too, you know my manor and my household, and all those things wherein I take my pleasure and delight. In guerdon of my love, I pray—so it may please you, sire—your daughter as my wife. God grant that my prayer may not disturb your heart, and that my petition may not be refused to my shame. For I will not hide from you that although I am not of her fellowship, yet have I spoken from afar with my demoiselle, and perceived those fair virtues which all men praise. Greatly is my lady loved and esteemed in these parts, for truly there is not her like in all the world. I have been too rash, since I have dared to require so gracious a gift, but so you deign to give to my asking, joyous and merry shall I go for all my days. Now have I told you my petition; so answer me according to my hope and your good pleasure."

The old man had no need for counsel in this matter, so without delay he made answer to the knight—

"I have heard with patience what you had to tell. Certes, and without doubt, my daughter is fair, and fresh, and pure, and a maiden of high descent. For myself, I am a rich vavasour, and come of noble ancestry, having fief and land worth fully one thou-

sand pounds each year in rent. Think you I am so
besotted as to give my daughter to a knight who
lives by play ! I have no child but one, who is close
and dear to my heart, and after I am gone all my
wealth will be hers. She shall wed no naked man,
but in her own degree; for I know not any prince of
this realm, from here even to Lorraine, however
wise and brave, of whom she would not be more
than worthy. It is not yet a month agone since
such a lord as this prayed her at my hand. His
lands were worth five hundred pounds in rent, and
right willingly would he have yielded them to me,
had I but hearkened to his suit. But my daughter
can well afford to wait, for I am so rich that she may
not easily lose her price, nor miss the sacrament of
marriage. Too high is this fruit for your seeking,
for there is none in this realm, nor from here to
Allemaigne, however high his race, who shall have
her, save he be count or king."

The knight was all abashed at these proud words.
He did not wait for further shame, but took his
leave, and went as speedily as he might. But he
knew not what to do, for Love, his guide, afflicted
him very grievously, and bitterly he complained
him thereof. When the maiden heard of this
refusal, and was told the despiteful words her father
had spoken, she was grieved in her very heart, for
her love was no girl's light fancy, but was wholly
given to the knight, far more than any one can
tell. So when the knight—yet heavy and wrathful—
came to the accustomed trysting place to speak a
little to the maiden, each said to the other what was
in the mind. There he opened out to her the news
of his access to her father, and of the disaccord
between the twain.

"Sweet my demoiselle," said the knight, "what
is there to do? It seems better to me to quit my
home, and to dwell henceforth amongst strangers

in a far land, for my last hope is gone. I may never
be yours, neither know I how these things will end.
Cursed be the great wealth with which your father
is so puffed up. Better had it been that you were
not so rich a dame, for he would have looked upon
my poverty with kinder eyes if his substance were
not so great."

"Certes," answered she, "very gladly would I be
no heiress, but only simple maid, if all things were
according to my will. Sire, if my father took heed
only to your good qualities, by my faith he would
not pain himself to prevent your coming to me.
If he but weighed your little riches in the balance
against your great prowess, right soon would he
conclude the bargain. But his heart cannot be
moved : he does not wish what I would have, nor
lament because I may wring my hands. If he
accorded with my desire, right speedily would this
matter be ended. But age and youth walk not
easily together, for in the heart is the difference
between the old and young. Yet so you do according to my device, you shall not fail to gain what
you would have."

"Yea, demoiselle, by my faith, I will not fail
herein ; so tell me now your will."

"I have determined on a thing to which I have
given thought many a time and oft. Very surely
you remember that you have an uncle who is right
rich in houses and in goods. He is not less rich
than my father; he has neither child, wife nor
brother, nor any kindred of his blood nearer than
you. Well is it known that all his wealth is yours
when he is dead, and this in treasure and in rent is
worth sixty marks of virgin gold. Now go to him
without delay, for he is old and frail; tell him that
between my father and yourself is such a business
that it may not come to a good end unless he help
therein. But that if he would promise you three

hundred pounds of his land, and come to require grace of my father, very soon can the affair be ended. For my father loves him dearly, and each counts the other an honourable man. Your uncle holds my father as prudent and wise : they are two ancient gentlemen, of ripe years, and have faith and affiance the one in the other. Now if for love of you your uncle would fairly seek my father and speak him thus, ' I will deliver to my nephew three hundred pounds of my lands, so that you give him your child,' why, the marriage will be made. I verily believe that my father would grant your uncle his request, if only he would ask me of him. And when we are wedded together, then you can render again to your uncle all the land that he has granted you. And so sweetly do I desire your love, that right pleasing I shall find the bargain."

"Fairest," cried the knight, "verily and truly there is nothing I crave in comparison with your love; so forthwith I will find my uncle, and tell him this thing."

The knight bade farewell, and went his way, yet thoughtful and bewildered and sad, by reason of the shame which had been put upon him. He rode at adventure through the thick forest upon his grey palfrey. But as he rode fear left him, and peace entered in his heart, because of the honest and wise counsel given him by the fair maiden. He came without hindrance to Medet, where his uncle had his dwelling, but when he was entered into the house he bewailed his lot, and showed himself all discomforted. So his uncle took him apart into a privy chamber, and there he opened out his heart, and made plain to him all this business.

"Uncle," said he, "if you will do so much as to speak to her sire, and tell him that you have granted me three hundred pounds of your land, I will make this covenant with you, and plight you my faith, my hand in yours, that when I have wedded her who is now denied me, that I will render again and give you quittance for your land. Now I pray that you will do what is required of you."

"Nephew," answered the uncle, "this I will do willingly, since it pleases me right well. By my head, married you shall be, and to the pearl of all the country, for good hope have I to bring this matter to an end."

"Uncle," said the knight, "put your hand to my task, and so press on with the business that time may go swiftly to the wedding. For my part I will arm me richly, and ride to the tournament at Galardon, where, by the aid of God, I trust to gain such ransom as will be helpful to me. And I pray you to use such diligence that I may be married on my return."

"Fair nephew, right gladly," answered he, "for greatly it delights me that so gracious and tender a lady shall be your bride."

So without further tarrying Messire William went his way, merry of heart because of his uncle's promise that without let he should have as wife that maid whom so dearly he desired. For of other happiness he took no heed. Thus blithe and gay of visage he rendered him to the tournament, as one who had no care in all the world.

On the morrow, very early in the morning, the uncle got to horse, and before the hour of prime came to the rich mansion of that old Prince, and of her whose beauty had no peer. He was welcomed with high observance, for the ancient lord loved him very dearly, seeing that they were both of the same years, and were rich and puissant princes, near neighbours in that land. Therefore he rejoiced greatly that one so high in station did honour to his house, and spread before him a fair banquet, with many sweet words, for the old Prince was

frank and courteous of heart, and knew to praise
meetly where honour was due.   When the tables
were cleared, the two spake together of old faces
and old stories, shields, and swords and spears,
and of many a doughty deed, in the most loving
fashion.   But the uncle of the good knight would
not forget his secret thought, and presently discovered it to the Prince in saying—

"What go I now to tell you?   I love you very
truly, as you may easily perceive.   I am come to
require a favour at your hand.   May God put it into
your heart to lend your ear to my prayer in such
a fashion that the matter may be brought to a right
fair end."

"By my head," answered the old Prince, "you
are so near to my heart that you are not likely to
be refused aught that you may ask of me.   Tell me,
that I may grace you with the gift."

"Sire, thanks and thanks again, for I would do
the same by you," returned the uncle of the knight,
who no longer cared to hide his privy mind.   "I am
come to pray of you, fair sire, the hand of your
virtuous maid in marriage.   When we once were
wed I would endow her with my wealth to the
utmost of my power.   You know well that I have
no heir of my body, which troubles me sorely; and
I will keep good faith with you herein, for I am
he who loves you dearly.   When your daughter is
bestowed upon me, it would not be my care to
separate father and child, nor to withdraw my
wealth from yours, but all our substance should be
as one, and we would enjoy together in common
that which God has given us."

When he whose heart was crafty heard these
words, he rejoiced greatly, and made reply—

"Sire, I will give her to you right gladly, for
you are a loyal and an honourable man.   I am more
content that you have required her of me than if

the strongest castle of these parts had been rendered
to my hand. To none other in the world would I
grant my maid so willingly as to you, for you are
prudent and hardy, and many a time have I proved
ere now that I may have confidence in your faith."

Then was promised and betrothed the damsel to
a husband of whom she had little envy, for she was
persuaded that another had asked her as his wife.
When the maiden knew the truth thereof she was
altogether amazed and sorrowful, and often she
swore by St. Mary that never should she be wedded
of him. Right heavy was she, and full of tears,
and grievously she lamented her fate.

"Alas, unhappy wretch, for now I am dead.
What foul treason has this old traitor done, for
which he justly should be slain! How shamefully
he has deceived that brave and courteous knight,
whose honour is untouched by spot. By his wealth
this aged, ancient man has bought me at a price.
May God requite it to his bosom, for he purposes to
commit a great folly, since the day we are wed he
takes his mortal foe to wife. How may I endure
that day! Alas, may God grant that I shall never
see that hour, for too great is the anguish that I
suffer because of this treason. If I were not fast in
prison, right swiftly would I get quit of this trouble,
but nought is there for me to do, since in no wise
can I flee from this manor. So stay I must, and
suffer as my father wills, but truly my pain is more
than I can bear. Ah, God, what will become of
me, and when shall he return who so foully is
betrayed. If he but knew the trick his uncle has set
on him, and how, too, I am taken in the snare, well
I know that he would die of grief. Ah, if he but
knew! Sure I am that he would ride with speed,
and that soon these great woes would be as they
had never been. Too sorely is my heart charged
with sorrow, and better I love to die than to live.

Alas, that this old man ever should cast his thought upon me, but none may deliver me now, for my father loves him because of his wealth. Fie on age! Fie upon riches! Never may bachelor wed with loving maid save he have money in his pouch. Cursed be the wealth which keeps me from him wherein I have my part, for truly my feet are caught in a golden net."

In this wise the maiden bewailed her lot, by reason of her great misease. For so sweetly was her heart knit in the love of her fair bachelor, that in nowise might she withdraw her thoughts from him. Therefore she held in the more despite him to whom her father had given her. Old he was, very aged, with a wrinkled face, and red and peering eyes. From Chalons to Beauvais there was no more ancient knight than he, nor from there to Sens a lord more rich, for that matter. But all the world held him as pitiless and felon; whilst so beautiful and brave was the lady, that men knew no fairer heiress, nor so courteous and simple a maiden, no, not within the Crown of France. How diverse were these twain. On one side was light, and on the other darkness; but there was no spot in the brightness, and no ray within the dark. But the less grief had been hers had she not set her love on so perilous a choice.

Now he to whom the damsel was betrothed, because of his exceeding content, made haste to appoint some near day for the wedding. For he knew little that she was as one distraught by reason of the great love she bore his nephew, as you have heard tell. So her father made all things ready, very richly, and when the third day was come he sent letters to the greybeards, and to those he deemed the wisest of that land, bidding them to the marriage of his daughter, who had bestowed her heart elsewhere. Since he was

well known to all the country round, a great
company of his friends came together to the number
of thirty, to do honour to his house, since not one
of them but owed him service for his lands. Then
it was accorded between them that the demoiselle
should be wedded early on the morrow, and her
maidens were bidden to prepare their lady for the
wedding on the appointed day and hour. But very
wrathful and troubled in heart were the maidens by
reason of this thing.

The Prince inquired of the damsels if his daughter
was fitly arrayed against her marriage, and had
content therein, or was in need of aught that it
became her state to have.

"Nothing she needs, fair sire," made answer one
of her maidens, "so far as we can see; at least so
that we have palfreys and saddles enow to carry us
to the church, for of kinsfolk and of cousins are a
many near this house."

"Do not concern yourself with the palfreys,"
replied the Prince, "for I trow we shall have to
spare. There is not a lord bidden to the wedding
whom I have not asked to lend us from his stables."

Then, making no further tarrying, he returned to
his own lodging, with peace and confidence in his
heart.

Messire William, that brave and prudent knight,
had little thought that this marriage was drawing
so near its term. But Love held him so fast that he
made haste to return, for ever the remembrance of
her face was before his eyes. Since love flowered so
sweetly within his heart, he parted from the tournament in much content, for he deemed that he rode
to receive the gift he desired beyond all the world.
Such he hoped was the will of God, and such the
end of the adventure. Therefore he awaited in his
manor, with what patience he might, the fair and
pleasant tidings his uncle must presently send him,

Q

to hasten to the spousal of his bride.   Since he had
borne off all the prizes of the tourney, he bade a
minstrel to his hall, and sang joyously to the playing of the viol.   Yet, though all was revelry and
merriment, often he looked towards the door to see
one enter therein with news.   Much he marvelled
when the hour would bring these welcome words,
and often he forgot to mark the newest refrains of
the minstrel, because his thoughts were otherwhere.
At the time hope was growing sick a varlet came
into the courtyard.   When Messire William saw him
the heart in his breast leaped and fluttered for joy.

"Sire," said the varlet, "God save you. My lord,
your friend, whom well you know, has sent me to
you in his need. You have a fair palfrey, than
which none goes more softly in the world. My lord
prays and requires of you that for love of him you
will lend him this palfrey, and send it by my hand
forthwith."

"Friend," answered the knight, "for what
business?"

"Sire, to carry his lady daughter to the church,
who is so dainty-sweet and fair."

"For what purpose rides she to church?"

"Fair sire, there to marry your uncle to whom she
is betrothed. Early to-morrow morn my lady will
be brought to the ancient chapel deep within the
forest. Hasten, sire, for already I tarry too long.
Lend your palfrey to your uncle and my lord. Well
we know that it is the noblest horse within the
realm, as many a time has been proved."

When Messire William heard these words—

"God," said he, "then I am betrayed by him in
whom I put my trust; to whom I prayed so much
to help me to my hope. May the Lord God assoil
him never for his treasonable deed. Yet scarcely
can I believe that he has done this wrong. It is
easier to hold that you are telling me lies."

"Well, you will find it truth to-morrow at the ringing of prime; for already is gathered together a company of the ancient lords of these parts."

"Alas," said he, "how, then, am I betrayed and tricked and deceived."

For a very little Messire William would have fallen swooning to the earth, had he not feared the blame of his household. But he was so filled with rage and grief that he knew not what to do, nor what to say. He did not cease lamenting his evil case till the varlet prayed him to control his wrath.

"Sire, cause the saddle to be set forthwith on your good palfrey, so that my lady may be carried softly to the church."

Then Messire William considered within himself to know whether he should send his grey palfrey to him whom he had cause to hate more than any man.

"Yea, without delay," said he, "since she who is the soul of honour has nothing to do with my trouble. My palfrey shall bear her gladly, in recompense of the favours she has granted me, for naught but kindness have I received of her. Never shall I have of her courtesies again, and all my joy and happiness are past. Now must I lend my palfrey to the man who has betrayed me to my death, since he has robbed me of that which I desired more than all the world. No man is bound to return love for treason. Very rash is he to require my palfrey of me, when he scrupled not to take the sweetness, the beauty and the courtesy with which my demoiselle is endowed. Alas, now have I served her in vain, and my long hope is altogether gone. No joy in my life is left, save to send her that thing which it breaks my heart to give. Nevertheless, come what may, my palfrey shall go to the most tender of maidens. Well I know that when she sets her eyes upon him she will bethink

her of me; of me and of my love, for I love and
must love her all the days of my life, yea, though
she has given her heart to those who have wounded
mine.   But sure am I that this thing is not seemly
to her, for Cain, who was brother to Abel, wrought
no fouler treason."

In this manner the knight bewailed his heavy
sorrow.   Then he caused a saddle to be set upon
the palfrey, and calling the servitor delivered the
horse to his keeping.   So the varlet forthwith went
upon his way.

Messire William, yet heavy and wrathful, shut
himself fast within his chamber to brood upon his
grief.   He charged his household that if there was
a man so bold as to seek to hearten him in his sorrow
he would cause him to be hanged.   For his part he
had no care for mirth, and would live withdrawn
from men, since he might never lose the pain and
sorrow that weighed upon his heart.

But whilst the knight was in this case, the servant
in custody of the palfrey returned with all the speed
he might to the castle of the old Prince, where all
was merriment and noise.

The night was still and serene, and the house
was filled with a great company of ancient lords.
When they had eaten their full, the Prince commanded the watch that, without fail, all men should
be roused and apparelled before the breaking of the
day.   He bade, too, that the palfrey and the horses
should be saddled and made ready at the same
hour, without confusion or disarray.   Then they
went to repose themselves and sleep.   But one
amongst them had no hope to sleep, because of the
great unrest she suffered by reason of her love.   All
the night she could not close her eyes.   Others
might rest : she alone remained awake, for her heart
knew no repose.

Now shortly after midnight the moon rose very

bright, and shone clearly in the heavens. When
the warder saw this thing, being yet giddy with the
wine that he had drunken, he deemed that the dawn
had broken.

"Pest take it," said he, "the lords should be
about already."

He sounded his horn and summoned and cried—
"Arouse you, lords, for day is here."

Then those, yet drowsy with sleep, and heavy with
last night's wine, got them from their beds all bewildered. The squires, too, made haste to set saddles
upon the horses, believing that daybreak had come,
though before the dawn would rise very easily might
the horses go five miles, ambling right pleasantly.
So when the company which should bring this demoiselle to the chapel deep within the forest were got
to horse, her father commended his maid to the most
trusty of his friends. Then the saddle was put upon
the grey palfrey; but when it was brought before
the damsel her tears ran faster than they had fallen
before. Her guardian recked nothing of her weeping, for he knew little of maidens, and considered
that she wept because of leaving her father and her
father's house. So her tears and sadness were
accounted as nought, and she mounted upon her
steed, making great sorrow. They took their way
through the forest, but the road was so narrow that
two could not ride together side by side. Therefore
the guardian put the maiden before, and he followed
after, because of the straitness of the path. The
road was long, and the company were tired and
weary for want of sleep. They rode the more
heavily, because they were no longer young, and
had the greater need for rest. They nodded above
the necks of their chargers, and up hill and down
dale for the most part went sleeping. The surest
of this company was in charge of the maiden, but
this night he had taken so little sleep in his bed

that he proved an untrusty warder, for he forgot
everything, save his desire to sleep. The maiden
rode, bridle in hand, thinking of nought except her
love and her sorrow. Whilst she followed the
narrow path, the barons who went before had
already come forth upon the high road. They dozed
in their saddles, and the thoughts of those few who
were awake were otherwhere, and gave no heed to
the demoiselle. The maiden was as much alone as
though she fared to London. The grey palfrey
knew well this ancient narrow way, for many a time
he had trodden it before. The palfrey and the
maiden drew near a hillock within the forest, where
the trees stood so close and thick that no moonlight
fell within the shadow of the branches. The valley
lay deeply below, and from the high road came the
noise of the horses' iron shoes. Of all that company
many slept, and those who were awake talked
together, but none gave a thought to the maiden.
The grey palfrey knew nothing of the high road, so
turning to the right he entered within a little path,
which led directly to the house of Messire William.
But the knight, in whose charge the damsel was
placed had fallen into so heavy a slumber that his
horse stood at his pleasure on the way. Therefore
she was guarded of none—save of God—and drop-
ping the rein upon the palfrey's neck, she let him
have his will. The knights who preceded her rode
a great while before they found that she was not
behind them, and he who came after kept but a
poor watch and ward. Nevertheless she had not
escaped by her choice, for she recked nought of the
path that she followed, nor of the home to which
she would come. The palfrey followed the track
without hesitation, for many a time he had journeyed therein, both winter and summer. The weeping maiden looked this way and that, but could see
neither knight nor baron, and the forest was very

perilous, and all was dark and obscure. Much she marvelled what had become of all her company, and it was no wonder that she felt great fear. None regarded her safety, save God and the grey palfrey, so she commended herself to her Maker, whilst the horse ambled along the road. Nevertheless she had dropped the rein from her fingers, and kept her lips from uttering one single cry, lest she should be heard of her companions. For she chose rather to die in the woodlands than to endure such a marriage as this. The maiden was hid in thought, and the palfrey, in haste to reach his journey's end, and knowing well the path, ambled so swiftly, that soon he came to the borders of the forest. A river ran there both dark and deep, but the horse went directly to the ford, and passed through as quickly as he was able. He had won but little beyond when the maiden heard the sound of a horn, blown from that place where she was carried by the grey palfrey. The warder on his tower blew shrilly on his horn, and the demoiselle felt herself utterly undone, since she knew not where she had come, nor how to ask her way. But the palfrey stayed his steps on a bridge which led over the moat running round the manor. When the watch heard the noise of the palfrey thereon, he ceased his winding, and coming from the tower demanded who it was who rode so hardily on the bridge at such an hour. Then the demoiselle made reply—

"Certes, it is the most unlucky maid of mother born. For the love of God give me leave to enter in your house to await the day, for I know not where to go."

"Demoiselle," answered he, "I dare not let you or any other in this place, save at the bidding of my lord, and he is the most dolorous knight in all the world, for very foully has he been betrayed."

Whilst the watch spoke of the matter he set his

eye to a chink in the postern. He had neither torch
nor lantern, but the moon shone very clear, and he
spied the grey palfrey, which he knew right well.
Much he marvelled whence he came, and long he
gazed upon the fair lady who held the rein, and was
so sweetly clad in her rich new garnishing. Forthwith he sought his lord, who tossed upon his bed
with little delight.

"Sire," said he, "be not wrath with me. A
piteous woman, tender of years and semblance, has
come forth from the woodland, attired right richly.
It seems to me that she is cloaked in a scarlet
mantle, edged with costly fur. This sad and outworn lady is mounted on your own grey palfrey.
Very enticing is her speech; very slim and gracious
is her person. I know not, sire, if I am deceived,
but I believe there is no maiden in all the country
who is so dainty, sweet and fair. Well I deem that
it is some fay whom God sends you, to bear away
the trouble which is spoiling your life. Take now
the gold in place of the silver you have lost."

Messire William hearkened to these words. He
sprang forth from his bed without further speech,
and with nothing but a surcoat on his back hastened
to the door. He caused it to be opened forthwith,
and the demoiselle cried to him pitifully in a loud
voice—

"Woe is me, gentle lord, because of the sorrow I
have endured this night. Sire, for the love of God
turn me not away, but suffer me to enter in your
house. I beg for shelter but a little while. But
much I fear by reason of a company of knights who
are pained greatly, since they have let me from their
hands. Sir Knight, be surety for the maid whom
Fortune has guided to your door, for much am I
sorrowful and perplexed."

When Messire William heard her voice he was
like to swoon with joy. He knew again the palfrey

which was so long his own. He gazed upon the
lady, and knew her in his heart. I tell you truly
that never could man be more happy than was he.
He lifted her from the palfrey and brought her
within his home. There he took her by the right
hand, kissing her more than twenty times; and for
her part the lady let him have his way, because she
had looked upon his face. When the two sought
each other's eyes, very great was the joy that fell
between the twain, and all their sorrow was as if it
had never been. So when the damsel had put aside
her mantle, they seated themselves merrily on silken
cushions, fringed with gold. They crossed their
brows again and yet again, lest they should wake
and find this thing a dream. Then the maiden
told her bachelor this strange adventure, and said—

"Blessed be the hour in which God brought me to
this place, and delivered me from him who sought
to add my marriage chest to his own coffers."

When morning was come Messire William
arrayed himself richly, and led the demoiselle within
the chapel of his own house. Then, without delay,
he called his chaplain to him, and was forthwith
wedded to the fair lady by a rite that it was not
lawful to call in question. So when the Mass was
sung, blithe was the mirth of that household, squire
and maiden and man-at-arms.

Now when that company which so lightly had lost
the maiden came together at the ancient chapel,
they were very weary by having ridden all the
night, and were sore vexed and utterly cast down.
The old Prince demanded his daughter of him who
had proved so untrusty a guardian. Knowing not
what to say, he made answer straightly—

"Sire, because of the strictness of the way I put
the maid before, and I followed after. The forest
was deep and dark, and I know not where she turned
from the path. Moreover I nodded in my saddle

till I was waked by my companions, for I deemed
that she was yet in my company, but she was
altogether gone. I cannot tell what has become
of the damsel, for very basely have we kept our
trust."

The old Prince sought his daughter in every
place, and inquired of her from every person, but he
might not find her whereabouts, nor hear of any
who had seen the maid. Yet all men marvelled at
her loss, for none was able to bring him any news.
The ancient bridegroom, that the demoiselle should
have wed, grieved yet more at the loss of his bride,
but to no purpose did he seek her, for the hind had
left no slot. Now as the two lords were riding with
their company in such fear as this, they saw upon
the road a certain squire making towards them in
all haste. When he was come to them he said—

"Sire, Messire William sends by me assurance
of the great friendship he bears you. He bids me
say that early this morning, at the dawn of day, he
married your daughter, to his great happiness and
content. Sire, he bids you welcome to his house.
He also charged me to say to his uncle, who
betrayed him so shamefully, that he pardons him
the more easily for his treason, since your daughter
has given him herself as a gift."

The old Prince hearkened to this wonder, but said
no word in reply. He called together all his
barons, and when they were assembled in hall, he
took counsel as to whether he should go to the house
of Sir William, and bring with him the lord to whom
his daughter was betrothed. Yet since the marriage
was done, nothing could make the bride again a
maid. So, making the best of a bad bargain, he
got to horse forthwith, and all his barons with him.
When the company came to the manor they were
welcomed with all fair observance, for right pleasing
was this to Messire William, since he had all things

to his own desire. Whether he would, or whether he would not, nought remained to the old Prince but to embrace his son-in-law; whilst as to that greybeard of a bridegroom, he consoled himself with what crumbs of comfort he could discover. Thus, since it was the will of God that these lovers should be wed, it pleased the Lord God also that the marriage should prove lasting.

Messire William, that courteous and chivalrous knight, lost not his hardihood in marriage, but ever sought advancement, so that he was esteemed of the counts and princes of his land. In the third year of his marriage the old Prince (as the tale tells us) died, because his time was come. So all that he died possessed of in wealth and lands and manors, together with the rich garnishing thereof, became the heritage of the knight. After this, Death laid hands upon his uncle, who, too, was very rich. And Sir William, who was not simple, nor grudging of heart, nor little of soul, nor blusterous with his neighbours, inherited all the goods that were his.

So the story which I have told you endeth in this fashion, in accordance with the truth, and to your pleasure.

THE END

LETCHWORTH
THE TEMPLE PRESS
PRINTERS

www.ingramcontent.com/pod-product-compliance
Lightning Source LLC
Chambersburg PA
CBHW050501260626
47157CB00004B/1147